THE UNEXPECTED SALAMI

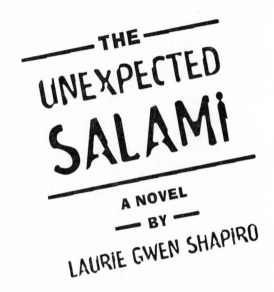

THE UNEXPECTED SALAMI

A NOVEL

BY

LAURIE GWEN SHAPIRO

Algonquin Books of Chapel Hill   1999

Published by
Algonquin Books of Chapel Hill
Post Office Box 2225
Chapel Hill, North Carolina 27515-2225

a division of
Workman Publishing
708 Broadway
New York, New York 10003

For permission to use quotes from copyrighted works, grateful acknowledgment is made to the copyright holders, publishers, or representatives
named on page 298, which constitutes an extension of the copyright page.

This is a work of fiction. While, as in all fiction, the literary perceptions
and insights are based on experience, all names, characters, places, and
incidents are either products of the author's imagination or are used ficti-
tiously. No reference to any real person is intended or should be inferred.

Library of Congress Cataloging-in-Publication Data
Shapiro, Laurie Gwen.
    The unexpected salami : a novel / by Laurie Gwen Shapiro.
        p.   cm.
    ISBN 1-56512-194-5
    I. Title.
    PS3569.H34145U64   1998
    813'.54—dc21   97-36570
                                          CIP

ISBN 1-56512-232-1 paper

10 9 8 7 6 5 4 3 2 1

For my parents,
Jeanette and Julius Shapiro,
who offer wisdom and love at every bend.

וען דאָס מזל קומט ־ שטעל אים אַ שטול.

When luck calls, offer it a seat.
—Yiddish proverb

CONTENTS

Prologue

The assistant director called "Roll it" and Phillip—done up in lime-green makeup and a pointy cap—began slinking toward the camera for the umpteenth time. "I'm bent and distorted," he sang, "Like a gnome I'm contorted, Time beats the soles of my feet, Like the canvas of a drum . . ."

Then we heard the gunfire.

"Did it hit the lens?!" the record label's bottom-line rep screamed. Phillip's ditzy girlfriend, Kerri, vomited. Meanwhile, Doug Lang, the cinematographer and an old friend of Phillip's, kept the camera rolling, catching footage of my insufferable roommate Stuart face down on the floor, blood gushing from his neck and chest, splattered on his dirty jeans and worn-out Nikes. Phillip tore across the street to a milk bar (the Aussie equivalent of a New York bodega) to call the cops. My mouth was frozen in an oval. Colin slipped his arm around me; it took me awhile to grasp that he was talking to me amid the mayhem.

"I said your visa's a year expired, right? Get out of here!"

"What?"

"The police will want to talk to you. Go back to the house! Your visa!" It was Sunday—the next tram might have been an hour away. We heard the sirens coming, and Colin handed me the keys to his panel van. I'm a native New Yorker; I can hardly drive from the left side of a car, let alone the right side of this bizarre vehicle. My heart raced as I merged on to Nepean Highway. The car was a sweatbox from the scorching February sun, but who was going to search for an air-conditioning button when it was hard enough to remember which pedal was the brake and which was the petrol? A lane of cars honked at my lack of road skill.

1

Rachel: FLIGHT

I could have had third-tier fame if I'd stayed in Melbourne—Rachel Ganelli, the Yank band moll who saw it all when the hit went down. When the media started zooming in on our St. Kilda house, I knew on the most instinctive level that leaving Australia was the right thing to do.

Stuart had been pleasant enough when I'd first met him two years earlier. He'd showed me how to make a warm German potato salad, and how the juice from the lemons in our yard could keep an avocado from turning brown. By the time of the filming, however, he was a strung out, fast-talking drummer who had long ago sold his set for cash; Phillip had already replaced Stuart with a new drummer, beer-guzzling Mick-O, who shared a house with his sisters in Spotswood. But then junked-out Stuart still lived with Phillip, Colin, and me in St. Kilda. I'd pleaded with the guys to kick Stuart off the lease before one of his ratbag friends smashed our windows. The original laid-back enchantment of the household, the perfect foil to my overachieving New York circle, was gone. I was bitching day and night about Stuart. Phillip was hostile toward the obvious attraction developing between Colin and me. And I no longer found Phillip's fatuous personality amusing. I was getting the urge to flee again, anywhere, possibly with Colin in my suitcase.

Phillip and Colin were the ones who wanted the fame: what perfect timing for an aging band. How convenient for Stuart to get shot in the middle of the Tall Poppies' video shoot. He'd dropped by the video shoot to bum twenty dollars from Colin. Stuart's habit gave him a funny odor; he smelled off, like old hand lotion. The day of the shooting I could hear him wheedling Colin even from where I stood in the back of the deserted sugar warehouse where they were taping the video.

". . . You don't reckon you could—I need, mate—I need—I need . . ."

"Get off my back, Stuart," Colin said. All week Colin had been tense about the shoot. He was sure that the lighting on the Tall Poppies' last video, *Red Rope Principle,* made his face look fat. "Why did you come here? We're shooting the fucking film clip."

"Come on. Give us a twenty. Just 'til Monday week."

Colin sought refuge in the far corner of the set where Phillip and the director were talking about the next few frames of *Gnome.* Stuart stood in pitiful strung out desperation in the center of the warehouse. Kerri sat cross-legged near the catering table. Her coarse blond hair, that Phillip valued so highly, looked particularly lustrous under the rented lights, like shellacked wood. She was laughing. You knew where Kerri was at every moment; her raucous laugh was the North Star of every Poppies' get-together. I waved but Kerri didn't see me.

• • •

Hours later back on Robe Street, after the cold-blooded mob hit, Phillip burst through our front door. "Rachel, turn the tube on—you can't believe what's happened!" Confirmed. No one had seen me except Colin. I'd momentarily stopped by to give Colin my beige cover stick, to hide the stress-induced circles under his eyes for the video. Who would want to be a material witness?

Burglaries plague Melbourne, but gun crime, not to mention *underworld* crime, is hot copy. None of the locals could recall a death so gorgeously evil. Doug Lang's footage opened the evening news. The day I left, two weeks later, a hastily edited version of *Gnome* played in heavy rotation on Australian MTV.

My mother heard about the murder on a CNN segment, "An Extraordinary Murder Down Under," and recognized the band's name from my scarce letters. Luck has no logic. She treated the situation with downright sagacity. She didn't harp on my lack of judgment in shifting continents to live with sexy guys I had found through the classifieds: three musicians in a house with a rehearsal studio in the garage. The phone fights about my running away and humiliating Will and his family, the deposit on the National Arts Club (a venue we scored through Will's ancient Grandaunt Helen who painted still lifes of wheat and oranges), the flowers, and the booze were, thankfully, history. Mom promised that I could stay in our family apartment for six months free if I immediately came back to New York. She and Dad were willing to move down to their retirement condo in Florida, if that would get me home: "Get on that plane now before things get worse."

The police had no idea that there were any witnesses other than the film crew, the band, and flaky Kerri. Colin had promised to keep his mouth shut. The others still didn't know that I had been in the back of the room. If I slipped away now, I could escape the limelight and keep my dignity. Escape to Manhattan, where no one cares who you are. There, everybody is a walking time bomb; it's part of the city's charm.

"And don't worry about bumping into Will," my mother assured me. "He called us a few months ago to see how Daddy and I were and to let us know he'd moved on. He's okay with it now." Of course he was. Will had been a perfect gentleman even when I blathered some incoherent excuse for my absence from across the equator. In my previous incarnation—science textbook harlot— Will had always insisted that he was "okay" with it, no matter what *it* was. He claimed he wasn't even uncomfortable with my wearing super-sheer black stockings to acquisition meetings with physicists who could pass for my grandfather.

On my flight home from Australia, I watched a love story set in the Brooklyn Hasidic community across the Williamsburg Bridge from my native Manhattan. Generations ago, men from half my bloodline davened, rocked and prayed, in *pais,* traditional ringlets of hair that run along ears.

A neurotic extra from a Woody Allen film, I struggled to open my airline peanuts, trying to divine if I was agnostic or atheist. After the closing credits, a Qantas video informed us that we were over Hawaii and had another nine hours to go.

My nose started to bleed from the dry air. "The perils of travel," I weakly joked to the grandmotherly type next to me as she searched for tissues in her purse. The cute French-Canadian guy on my other side found one in his back pocket. While my blood congealed, grandma told me that she was from Adelaide, the Australian "City of Churches." Her name was Judith; she was an English teacher and a gambler en route to Vegas.

"Are you lucky?" I asked Judith, with a tissue wad in one nostril. "No one I know is very lucky."

"Nonsense," she smiled. "The ultimate win is that from millions of sperm, we have been born at all." Her words had that distinct Australian cadence: the syllables had bumps in unexpected places, like homemade taffy. Non-*sense*. Ul-ti-*mate*.

Judith asked if I had enjoyed the film about the Jews. She wanted to know if I would like to read a newspaper clipping that she'd removed from her carry-on luggage. It was a book review of a top Christ scholar's new tome.

"In ancient Hebrew," the review began, "the word for carpenter was barely demarcated from the word for a learned man."

"A comedy of errors!" Judith said after I handed back her clipping. "Christ never held a hammer in his life. He was a Rabbi."

The steward asked us to close our window shades, and the aisle lighting was shut off. My row of four fell asleep for the night. I woke up in the morning leaning on the shoulder of Francis, the beefy, blue-eyed, black-haired Canadian. He'd earlier told me that, like myself, he'd returned from several nomadic years Down Under. He lived up in Brisbane, working at a pancake restaurant in the Canadian Pavilion of the World Expo, and then picked mangoes on a Queensland orchard.

Francis smiled when he saw me open my eyes. "Bonjour." I removed my drooling chin from his sleeve. I apologized profusely, which he waved off with "Ce n'est rien," it is nothing. There were three hours to go before we would land at LAX. Judith and the bearded man to her left were still asleep, wrapped up in their fuzzy gray airline blankets. Our steward served us breakfast and handed us customs declarations.

"Can you hand one to your girlfriend?" the steward asked, and Francis conspiratorially grinned at me. I felt altitudes above my two immediate pasts.

"And what do you have to declare?" Francis asked. I could smell the mint Chapstick he'd coated on his lips during the night. The scent reminded me of Will, who'd apply Chapstick in the air-conditioned jitney when he dragged me out to our Hamptons' share, his antidote to our East Village studio on Avenue B. "I won't live on the Upper East Side," I'd insisted, although Will could well afford it. "Please, Will! Not where men wear green slickers with whale linings."

I got another good look at my seatmate. I spread marmalade on my roll. "I declare that you are very attractive," I said finally. Francis raised an eyebrow, buttered my nose with his knife, and then wiped the gook off with his thumb. He grabbed my hand, and I let him hold it for ten minutes. He tickled the creases in my palm. It was easier to be horny than to process grief.

"Let's go to the restroom," he whispered in my ear, and we walked to the back of the plane, locking ourselves in the bathroom as inconspicuously as possible. I'd taken my travel-size Scope I had in my tote bag for two years; I took a swig. Francis rinsed, too, while using his other hand to cradle the back of my head. I bit his fingers as he kissed my neck. Francis stuck the tip of his tongue in my mouth, kissing me ferociously, eyes closed. He was probably engrossed in some racy Madonna-whore fantasy. He wasn't playful like Colin, or respectful like Will, but I was immersed in my own illusion: my ready-to-use lover was half Will, half Colin, and we were about to die in a plane crash. Francis and I kissed and fondled until there was a knock at the door; we threw our T-shirts back on.

An Aussie businessman winked at Francis as we emerged from the toilet. "Sorry about that, mate," the man said, "but the other stall stinks to high heaven."

Back in our seats, Francis and I started talking again. When he was twelve, he won a science fair. When I was eleven, I won the class spelling bee. (And the sixth grade science fair, too, but I didn't say that.)

The steward brought a final round of orange juice. I stared down the aisle. There could be a Mafia guy out there who had seen me lurking in the background at the video shoot. But then, Colin had said we weren't the targets. If we weren't gunned down on the spot, we were in the clear. The video camera didn't catch faces, just Stuart lying on the ground after the act. What would the Mafia want with us? Colin had guessed that they would leave us alone. Stuart was the one who had owed them money for drugs. "The mob has their ethics," Colin had said. I am a big Scorcese fan; I knew he was right.

I missed Colin terribly. Had I made a big mistake? We weren't officially boyfriend and girlfriend, but we had spent the last four months in touchy-feely conversation, a trend that culminated in our own session of bathroom erotica. That night we'd had too many African beers at the Ethiopian restaurant on Chapel Street.

"Hot day, one for the record books," Phillip had said, driving us back from the Tukul Eating House, while Colin and I played footsie in the backseat. Phillip went up the road for a packet of Peter Stuyvesants. It was a day between shower curtains. (Phillip had thrown the old one away that morning in a panic; a glob of mold had fallen on his ankle. He promised to pick up a new one the next morning from Dimmeys.) I'd raced to the shower to cool off. Colin walked in for a pee.

"Oh, sorry, Rachel!" he said, and we both started laughing. We'd shared a house for almost two years, but the sexual tension had been unbearable of late, ever since I'd let him use me as a stand-in to show me, exactly, how he held his first girlfriend's hand seconds before their earliest kiss.

"Why don't you join me in the shower?" I asked. We spent all our time together, I adored him, so why not?

In a split second Colin jumped in, clothed. I peeled off his jeans. He rubbed soap over my breasts. "Got to get those really clean!" I reached for the Decoré conditioner and returned the favor. Will who?

We'd barely started a proper kiss when Phillip knocked on the door.

"Hurry up, Colin! I'm going to chuck from that safari food."

"Just a tick," Colin said. To avoid the clucking tongues, he gave me a boost through the bathroom window. In the dark I could easily escape and run naked around the house to my bedroom window. The next morning Colin thought Stuart might be on to us: his window faced the yard. We didn't want to face teasing from our group. That might jeopardize our friendship; what if we realized in a week that it had been only a carnal whim? So we cooled it until we knew what we were doing.

Two days later, I overheard Phillip and Colin talking about how *gorgeous* some girl at a gig was. I'm not Medusa, but I wouldn't call myself gorgeous. Will had admired my sass, my encyclopedic film facts, and my boobs, but mostly he loved that I was the only one who didn't take shit from his WASP-y mother, Amanda. Rarely did she step forward into our studio. The one time she climbed the four flights, wary of the gluey substances that tugged at her heel, she said in front of me that it was a disgrace that he lived like a goddamn "Ellis Island ethnic." They finally tracked me down in Kim's Video, and Amanda begrudgingly apologized to me in front of the horror section. She offered to pay for my video rental and I handed her a case with Linda Blair spitting green vomit. I think that's Will's favorite story about me. But my fiancé never called me beautiful, not once, and that ate at me. As vain as it sounds, I wanted to overhear Colin calling me drop-dead gorgeous like that bimbo at the gig, one person in the world, once please! —And I couldn't see that coming, ever. I started to get particularly neurotic about it, backing off a bit from the romantic path, but I was convinced Colin seemed relieved. Why would he want good old Rachel when he had those saucy nineteen year olds hanging on to him every Thursday night?

And then, with Stuart's sudden death, we never got the chance to have the heart-to-heart we'd been avoiding for a month. I wished we could kiss in a Byzantine way. But our nineties sensibility would never allow it—shtick superballed from our mouths.

It was a darn shame about Colin, I thought, watching the clouds below the plane. What a sweet guy he was: free of the New York paranoia attached to my hometown friends like an exclamation mark. He had laid-back solutions for everything, ingenious really, on how to live. His entire wardrobe was black jeans and black T-shirts so he'd never make a fashion gaffe. And there was that time the manager of Gaslight Records, a schoolmate of Phillip's, offered the Poppies the window display for their first single. The Poppies' label, alas, had run out of promotion money. Colin had calmed a crazed Phillip, xeroxing a publicity still in his friend's office, blowing each portion up on a grid until he had a Chuck Close–style representation that filled the entire window and made it to "The Good Weekend" section of *The Age*.

Although Colin had five years on me, he reminded me of the young reindeer bull that we'd seen on the Australian equivalent of PBS. "Still grazing in velvet: tender, maturing, vulnerable," the narrator had declared. "Rather like you," I'd leaned over to tease Colin, pushing a peroxide-blond strand behind his ear. He blushed when I did that. It was right after the curtainless shower incident, and Stuart was in the back of the living room, changing a CD.

I didn't think much about Stuart's death. In hindsight, it was a sad but apt conclusion for his lifestyle.

But Colin was different. He was my closest friend overseas. Colin looked mighty hurt when I said I was leaving for New York. I tried to imagine the reaction if I had dragged Colin back home to the States. What if I brought him to the Levine Passover Seder or the Ganelli Easter Sunday Dinner? *He's thirty-two, works in a copy shop, and is a fine bass player. We have a lot in common; for example, our flatmate was murdered! And Colin gives an excellent back massage.* Yeah, right. Like we would have lasted a day outside of our Melbourne bubble.

Francis started cradling my hand and I felt a tad sick. I'd forgotten about him.

"Rachel, I will be in Manhattan for a wedding in two months," Francis smiled. "Can I stay with you?"

"Sure, give me a call a couple of weeks before you leave Montreal." I wrote my number, with a digit changed, on a napkin.

"Please adjust your seats back up," the steward said, collecting the last of the juice tumblers.

We began our descent.

Like a moron, I'd forgotten about the reversed seasons. It was thirty-six degrees Celsius when I left Melbourne, a scorcher of a departure day, and nearly as toasty when I poked my head out the sliding doors into the palm-treed LAX grounds during the four-hour wait for my connecting flight. At LaGuardia it was two inches of snow and counting. In my thigh-high cut-off jeans, I dashed down the airport loop to the shuttle bus, and then at Grand Central to a cab destined for my empty family apartment. The building, constructed on an angle, fills and towers over the block's slender pie wedge of Greenwich Village. The lower-floor windows look directly into the stores across the street.

"Your building looks paranoid," the driver said with perfect diction. "That's what they used to do. Buildings were designed to make tenants feel safe." He stopped talking when I handed him a quarter for a tip.

"You're joking," he said.

"I'm sorry. I was living overseas and I'm out of money and I thought I'd have two dollars for you and taxi fares have gone up since I left." I quickly closed the door in shame.

My parents, true to their word, had left two days earlier for their Florida condo. There were messages blinking on the answering machine.

"Sylvia? Virginia. I want to wish you and Joe a safe trip to Miami. I'll check in on my niece, don't you worry." "Mom, it's Frank—when is she coming? I think I'm not going to be able to meet her." "Welcome back, baby—sorry the house is a sty—we'll need you to ship the rest of the boxes UPS when you're settled. Call me." "Hi, Mrs. Ganelli—it's Janet. Frieda told me that when she called Rachel a few days ago, Rachel said she was coming home—is this true? Could you call me at the Mayor's Office for Film? 555-4641. They'll page me. Thanks." "Hiya Rachel, it's Mom. Calling again to see if you're back. Give us a call!"

The family apartment reminded me of the cluttered Peabody Museum I'd visited in grade school as part of an overnight field trip to Boston. Mom and Dad had papers stacked on magazines stacked on mystery boxes—an abode where only a lifelong curator could have found a particular item in less than a day. The last time the apartment was my permanent address was when I was seventeen, ten years earlier.

After staring out my parents' sixth-floor kitchen window onto King Street, I entered the old room that I'd shared with my brother. When Frank's voice started to change, the room had been cleaved down the middle by a metal room divider. My parents apparently had the divider removed while I was in Australia. It disoriented me to see that room opened up once more. I could see fragments of the masking tape we were never able to scrape off, browning on the floor. Until my mother found out about it, Frank charged me ten cents for each crossing over his tape line, even though the door was on his side of this first unofficial room divider.

I started to pull boxes out of the closet and discovered a cache of comics remarkably well preserved in Zip-loc bags, each treasure documented on an enclosed index card. Frank had been brutal about what was drivel and what wasn't. He spent his entire weekly five-dollar allowance on issues of *Fantastic Four,* Jack Kirby's *Forever People, Conan the Barbarian, Powerman,* and *Marvel Team-ups.* "In Zip-locs, they'll age better," he'd said. With my three-dollar allowance, I bought *Archie* and *Richie Rich* comics, despite Frank's moans of disbelief, and what's more, stored them in an old pink doll box, sans Zip-loc. True to Frank's prediction, they had yellowed in cruel air.

An envelope taped to the back of the closet wall read, "Do not open until the year 2000." The envelope glue was barely sticking; I extracted a slip of paper dated January 1, 1974. "I bet $10,000 that Frank Evan Ganelli will not shave his head bald on New Year's, 2000." I tried to recall the sincerity of an eight-year-old girl and her ten-year-old big brother. I put the envelope back in its sacred site with fresh Scotch tape. There were another eight years to forget about it.

I rummaged a bit through the master bedroom, a not small thrill. I couldn't recall a previous occasion affording such unchecked nosiness. Opening my parents' file cabinet, I examined my birth certificate and my grandparents' death certificates. I was really born and they were really dead. I fished out a manila envelope from the deepest recess of the cabinet, stuffed with Marilyn Monroe articles and the very first *Playboy,* with Marilyn Monroe on the cover. I tried to imagine my famously reserved father harboring a celebrity crush, fantasizing about the ultimate Other.

I clicked on *Geraldo.* The change in accent shocked me. Americans seemed earnest and loud.

Frank, who'd traveled throughout Europe after college, had warned me against condemning the United States when I returned. "Everyone," he'd said, "goes through that stage, and it's boring." Still, there were no crass confession shows in privacy-conscious Australia, where the government doesn't even release census records to genealogists.

I didn't feel like calling my parents yet. Jet-lagged, I succumbed to the couch in the living room.

My mother woke me up around six P.M. "Rachel! Ah, baby, now I can sleep. Why didn't you call? You're home, away from that rock murder mishegoss. I've never heard of anything that crazy!"

"Hi, Mom."

"Kiddo, we love you so much. You're too smart a girl to get caught up with that scary element. Tell me about your flight."

2

Colin: HOUSESHARE

The more a guitar gets played the better it sounds. I don't know the scientific reasons for this. The sound gets in the wood. Say you had a hundred new Fords from a factory. After ten years, each would have its problems—some in the boot, some on the axle. Same with a guitar. Every time the string vibrates, the wood vibrates. But the beauty of a guitar is that over the years it develops a warmth to it that a new guitar doesn't have. Andy Summers always used a '63 Telecaster, even when he was at the height of his career with the Police. I saw a photo of it in *Musician*. The paint's chipped off, but he said in the interview that it sounds better every day. The only trouble is that you have to keep getting it fixed.

It took two years to sink in that Rachel and I had a wild rapport going, a perfect timbre that comes with time. After I had spent months hanging out with her, the girls I met at gigs and parties seemed like space cadets. If I even shot the breeze with one of those tarts, Rachel would rail into me about my lack of self-respect. I knew she was jealous though, and it made me feel good.

• • •

I'd been away for the weekend; my Uncle Jack had remarried up in Swan Hill. By the time I returned, Phillip and Stuart had already selected Rachel for Simon's old room. Phillip ran an over-the-top houseshare ad with the word *abutting* in it. I'd had to laugh. He wrote it with a thesaurus, the way he wrote his song lyrics. Rachel called it a Mary Poppins ad, which she said meant that its oddity was a magnet. It's still in my black organizer:

Financially sound, artistically and musically attuned f. 22–30 wanted to share with 3 m. musos in an only slightly dilapidated house. St. Kilda. 60pw. Working fireplace in bedroom, abutting trams, groovy shops. No New Agers. Phillip/Colin/Stuart 510.1070.

I'd written the ad the time before, and we'd gotten Simon, who never took a shower. So I kept my mouth shut when I saw Phillip wanted a girl. Like he didn't have enough girls from the shows. The "abutting" ad attracted sixty responses. We'd gotten three inquiries when I wrote mine—Simon, and two astrology nuts.

When I rang from Swan Hill to check on the response, Phillip explained his decision not to wait until I returned to fill the room. He didn't want to lose her.

"She used to work at a New York radio station. Who knows who she knows? You'll like her, Colin. She tells stupid stories like you."

"What does Stuart think?"

"That he likes her smile. He's not getting *any* these days. Probably wants to dip his wick."

The night I returned, Rachel had moved in only hours earlier.

I went into the living room to say hello. This quirky, leggy Yank with a black ponytail was splayed out on the sofa like she owned the place. She looked so American in her jeans and T-shirt. Her eyes were deep brown and followed you everywhere, like Stuart's. I had never met an American before, except for the odd tourist asking for street directions, and a wanker with a square American jaw who once needed blueprints "by yesterday" at the print shop. I couldn't believe that she was going to live with us. She could have been a movie star the way I felt. Though I didn't act that way of course.

"G'day," I said, "I hear you're my new flatmate."

"Hi. I'm Rachel."

"Colin. Love your accent."

"You're the one with the accent," she teased. "That's a movie line, I think. I can't remember which one."

I thought of an anecdote that might sound half intellectual: when I was little, I'd believed the American accent was the TV accent (or the telly accent, as my family called it then), and that shows were made in in Australia. Hollywood, where they made the cowboy movies, would be up North maybe, near Brisbane and the Coral Reef. But one day when my family was watching a cop show, a news presenter had interrupted with word that Robert Kennedy had been assassinated, like his brother. Robert Kennedy was running for President of the United States of America. A diagram of Kennedy's head was shown as was footage of him collapsed on the ground with blood streaming out of his ear. The news presenter had been handed an update: "Robert Kennedy, I'm told, won't live." My parents' reactions and the tears of the people on the screen amazed me; Mum mistook my staring for terror. "Don't worry Colin, it's far away. It's in America. It's happening on another continent." It was the first time I'd heard the word *continent*. I began to realize that *Australian* meant distance from power and for the most part, from cold-blooded violence.

"How long have you been in Australia?" I said instead.

"About three weeks. I stayed at a hostel for a week, and then I moved in with someone I met waitressing while I found a place."

That amazed me. I could never do that. Shift countries, get a job, get someone to let me use their house as a crash pad.

"What are you reading?"

"Some stories by T. Coraghessan Boyle. He's pretty hilarious, ever read him?"

T what? I hoped she didn't see me redden. "No."

"I'll lend you the book when I'm done."

"Great. Want to join me for tea?"

"Sure."

"I'll fix us some then."

"Thanks."

I went to cook the chops I'd just bought, and the mint peas in the freezer. It was odd that she didn't even offer to help. So comfortable on her first day in a new house. An alien being. I brought out a plate for her.

"Here's your tea, dig in."

"Oh, thanks," she said, looking baffled, "but weren't you making tea? I ate dinner before with Phillip."

Tea is the Aussie word for dinner. I explained that to her. I felt like I was from the sticks or something. There she was from New

York, and here I was offering her chops and mint peas when all she wanted was fucking Earl Grey. She offered to eat the meal, but I said don't be silly and knocked on Stuart's door to give it to him. Again, this was before he had a habit.

In less than a year Stuart began seeing that tart Melissa Rizziola, a dancer and a junkie who frequented the Greyhound Pub. Melissa got him hooked up with a shady, drug-abusing crowd whose personal hygiene was more than a bit on the nose. The few times I met any of them over at our house, I disinfected the couch after they left. Not like the band scene is a hall of saints, but shit, we'd put out a bona fide album. We worked hard to have the little slice of the musical Melbourne pie we had. And the one unbreakable band rule was *no drugs*, with the exception of a little pot now and then. We weren't Christian maniacs, but being in a band is a *job*.

But it was a normal thing to do in the early days of knowing Stuart, giving him the leftover chops. He basically kept to himself outside of rehearsal. Stuart was someone I didn't think about much.

I read this exotic American's T. Coraghessan Boyle book that next weekend—a funny writer but he's a bit too much of a smart-arse for me—a couple of good stories. But I kept that to myself.

"Tell me about your childhood," she said later that week during a commercial. I didn't think she *really* wanted to know anything as boring as that. "Where did you grow up?"

"Seaford. It's down the Peninsula."

"Is it a nice place?"

"Not really," I said. Phillip interrupted with a funny story about the captain of the ambulance corps who had a drinking problem. She left me alone.

Not long after Robert Kennedy's death we moved out to Seaford, a few kilometers from Frankston. Close to Melbourne, Frankston was a rough, small city, chockablock with working-class poms, English immigrants. Seaford was small, too, but a distinct step up to lower middle class. It was quieter and less developed, almost a country town. My mother's big selling point to my father was the nearby beach. Aunty Grace and Uncle Patrick, parents of my cousins Liam and Anna, had moved to this outermost edge of suburbia when Uncle Patrick was offered a job managing one of the resort hotels further down the Mornington Peninsula. The local development was so recent that cows grazed in the field past the public golf course.

Aunty Grace said she liked it, and furthermore the affordable house next door was up for sale. Mum convinced Dad to move from our flat in Richmond, even though he would now have to commute an hour to the clothing shop he managed in Melbourne. Dad had thought moving next door to Aunty Grace was rabbit warren-ish, and at times our part of the block did feel like one big house. This really good kid, Cormac Kennedy, and his mum and dad lived on the other side of us—far flung from the American breakout achievers of their family tree. Cormac was five when I moved to Seaford. He watched me from a go-cart his dad had built for him. There were a good three years before he would begin dying of leukemia, when he would give me his beloved Cadbury wrapper collection. Mr. Kennedy often claimed that he had the same great-great-grandfather as John Fitzgerald.

Rachel grew up in the most exciting city on the planet. Why would she want to hear anything about my ho-hum childhood? I maybe even worshipped her that first month, especially her brains. Every now and then I identified another glitch in her personality, but it was inevitably minor, like the way she skimmed books she didn't have the patience for. That really gave me the shits. The house was a five minute walk from the St. Kilda library. Rachel was always reading, or at least checking books out. She flipped through masterpieces like my mum did with those romance novels she bought in the supermarket. But with her in the house, I did read more than I ever had with Simon in that room, for what that's worth. Rachel checked out *Crime and Punishment* during one of her "I'm slipping behind" fits. "A guilt literature moment," she owned up a day later. "It's too subtle for me, you'll get more out of it." She was right. She had the attention span of a teenager. If she couldn't finish a book in one or two sittings, she wouldn't read it. She'd give it to me, The Snail. I'm no bloody Einstein but if I'm going to bother to read a book, it's going to be a meaty one and I'm going to savor it like good wine. It took me forever to read *Crime and Punishment*, but I remember everything. Nothing happens for the first million pages, according to Rachel. But in my opinion it's the lingering details that make it great. Raskolnikov is the main character, and Porfiry is the inspector who knows that Raskolnikov has committed a double murder. But Porfiry doesn't have enough proof to dob him in. Porfiry uses reverse psychology, slowly closing in. He warns Raskolnikov that he knows he is guilty as fuck and tells him that he will surrender one day. His steadfastness drives Raskolnikov fucking crazy.

The reason Rachel and I grew closer was that we had shopping and toilet duty together. Stuart had the rubbish and the sweeping, and Phillip washed the dishes and organized the rent. I thought for sure that Phillip and Rachel were getting it on. That first month, Phillip had her sipping the green tea his yoga teacher sold him and rubbing his pressure points, like the back of his ear and the two cavities in his neck. He once moaned so hard that his new girlfriend, Kerri, just through the door, thought they were having sex.

Phillip and Rachel had both gone to uni to study film, and could trade annoying references. But when we were rolling the cart down the pasta aisle it came out that she didn't think Phillip was all that bright. I was secretly relieved, although I also couldn't believe that I had a daily relationship with a guy who wrote such bullshit lyrics. I enjoyed Phillip, but there's no denying his lyrics were dated and rang hollow. I put my foot down once or twice, like when he used a rhyming dictionary to pair platypus with Oedipus. Even the band name was straight out of the eighties: the Tall Poppies. Everyone around this time had one-word names like Nirvana. Or over-the-top names like My Friend the Chocolate Cake.

Rachel liked Phillip well enough even if she didn't like his words. No skin off her back if she lived with a handsome bad lyricist. After a year, enough time with Phillip to pale anyone's view of him, Rachel had a repertoire of hilarious comments about his sickly sweet breath, the jar of peanut butter in the medicine cabinet which, he said, let him get a closer shave, and the overpowering patchouli he dabbed on instead of cologne—he'd bought ten vials at an Indian spice shop. But she never went for blood. Phillip amused Rachel. He was a cartoon character for her. He was a hack, but he wasn't lazy. Phillip was our Captain Kirk, a kind idiot we could make fun of, who kept life easy for us by making the decisions, such as which day we had to write out the rent checks. By then, Rachel's venom was reserved for Stuart.

"Why can't we kick Stuart out?" Rachel was forever whining.

Rachel could laugh Phillip Harvey off. But as band members you're married to each other. I could hardly justify to myself why I joined, let alone stayed, in this bubble-gum band in the first place. My taste runs a little harder, pop with a sprinkle of dissonance.

A customer had needed a gig poster printed. I filled out his order form. Phillip Harvey. Robe Street, St. Kilda. Phillip had flat ears you couldn't see when he stood directly in front of you. His body was disproportionate—his legs, muscular like a huge frog's legs, were too big for his frame. But girls never saw that. Girls liked his red lips and violet eyes and big shiny smile. He smiled with confidence, a good-looking man.

"I'm a muso, too," I'd said, casually. "You know anyone who needs a guitarist?"

"No, but hey, you know anyone good on bass? My bass player and keyboardist are moving to Sydney next month."

"I play bass, too," I said a bit grudgingly. Playing bass or drums is the only way to join an established band. Everyone wants to be up front with the guitar or singing.

"Yeah? Bass? Where have you gigged?"

"I was in Ursa Major, towards the end of the band." (A bit of a stretch. I played with them for one week before they broke up, for one show, two years after they had their number one Australian hit.)

"Yeah? I'll try you out. I got a new drummer three weeks ago. Stuart. He's an insane drummer—learned everything in a day. I'm thinking of reforming the Poppies as a three piece."

"Worked for the Police."

"You want to jam?" Phillip asked.

"Better than playing in my bedroom with the door locked."

A whole swag of friends was over at his house. It was Bourke Street in his living room. He'd even converted the garage into a soundproofed rehearsal studio. Phillip's offer was a tidy little package: a whole new house and social set if I joined his band. And I needed to break from my houseshare; my flatmates at that time hadn't spoken to each other in a month, ever since Nigel had a threesome with Helen and Justine. Justine had gone down on Helen, not part of their arrangement. I'd heard Helen screaming at Justine about her indiscretion, and Nigel had happily clued me in on his sexual adventures at the pub. The household tension back at Imperial Avenue was hard to stomach, plus how come I wasn't invited?

This mysterious singer Phillip could make his mob laugh. He had stacks of old Warner Brothers cartoons on tape. He did spot-on impressions of Foghorn Leghorn and Daffy Duck.

That very first day I came around his house to jam, Phillip left the room for a minute to get some firewood from out back. I asked his new drummer, Stuart, who seemed like a quiet, watchful type like me, what he did. Phillip had said that Stuart had moved into the Robe Street house two weeks earlier.

"Me?" Stuart looked startled that I'd asked him. "I do construction out by Preston."

"You go up on scaffolding?" I said. "I'm afraid of heights."

"It's nothing once you puke the first time," Stuart said, almost red. He seemed like an okay bloke.

"You pay the rent yet, Stuart?" Phillip said, resting down an armful of logs.

"I'm getting my check tomorrow," Stuart said defensively, unsure why he was the sudden center of attention.

"Thath no exthcuth. I'm thick—I'm thick and tired of your exthcuthes."

Stuart laughed. He didn't have money trouble then. He saw now that Phillip was only going for the Daffy joke. Everyone was having such a good time. I moved in.

Four years later I'm on stage with Phillip Harvey, options severely limited, and I'm still his flatmate. What the hell else was I going to do? In Melbourne, the chance of landing a major label deal is slim unless one of your band members is a uni student. Crowd is everything to the A&R reps, not to mention the club owners. If you're older, you're not about to pull in twenty-four beer-guzzling classmates with girlfriends to an unheated Richmond pub in the middle of the winter. Two good things I'll say about Phillip. He had enough people coming to our gigs. There were always heaps of nurses from the ambulance corps; he was like Hawkeye with the nurses, which never sat well with Kerri.

And Phillip did get us a record contract, although with Shock, not Mushroom or EMI. In Australia, though, you don't get jackshit for mid-size representation. Crowd-pulling was too depressing for me. I left the people stuff to him. I felt like the Poppies' gun-for-hire, sleeping in the house, showing up for rehearsal twice a week with the bloody bass.

Then came that summer day, the day after New Year's 1992, when managing the print shop and strumming four strings for the dedicated local crowd didn't do it for me anymore.

Rachel had her shift at the Dog's Bar, and Phillip had his ambulance video job. I'd added days to my New Year's holiday because it was use-it-or-lose-it time. I heard noise in Stuart's room. I figured either he was rooting some bush pig, his horrible term for his pick-ups from the pub, or outside his window there was a possum in the tree warming up for a full-blown screech.

His door was near the kitchen, and on the way back from fixing bread and jam, curiosity got the best of me. I opened the door, and Stuart let out a yelp.

"Don't kill me! I'm going to pay you back!"

I got raspberry jam on the sleeve of the *Money Talks, Bullshit Walks* T-shirt I'd somewhat adopted from Rachel; her brother had sent it over from the States wrapped around a gift salami.

"Mate—what the hell is going on?" Recently, Stuart had been acting weird, the few times he bothered to come home. Phillip was even thinking of giving in to Rachel and kicking him out. He thought Stuart's habit was getting too deep to turn the other cheek anymore.

"You scared the shit out of me, Colin," Stuart whimpered from atop his homemade loft. I could see his stringy brown hair sticking out from his sheet. He had a cricket bat in his hands. The room stank of cigarettes. Our big fat cat, Hector (Phillip's really, but Hector loved Stuart), was in his usual state, curled up under the loft on a dirty old jumper. One of Stuart's skinny legs hung over his loft's edge, vibrating in fear.

"Stuart, what's happening? Calm down and tell me." I was always the one Stuart trusted—lovely honor that was. Turns out he thought I was sent to kill him. Jesus. Said he owed money to "people." I kept trying to assure him it wasn't that bad. But he was strung out. I tried calming him down, but he kept saying it was the end, that if he had a way of getting away he would. It saddened me; he was never the most articulate guy in the world, but he was, as Phillip had promised, a terrific drummer. In all honesty, he was a better musician than Phillip and me combined. Stuart was part of a group, not trying to steal the show with ridiculous overplaying, the way his replacement, Mick-O, did sometimes. He understood that rhythm should be seamless, like a Möbius strip.

But Stuart wanted to hang out with Melissa, sniff or shoot whatever she had, forget rehearsals. We decided to boot him out of the band. He was a low-key guy, but even so, particularly passive about his dismissal from the Poppies. Was it his cry for help? It was so strange that I told Phillip that we should let him live with us as long as he kicked in for the rent. Why kick him when he was already down? He had it hard enough as it was; he was from a common-as-dirt housing estate out near Airport West. And Rachel told me Stuart had bragged that his father was killed in Vietnam, picking up a baby stuffed with a grenade. We both felt sorry for him, that he was reduced to a lie like that.

"You can just tell he's trying to compensate for his lower-class childhood," Rachel had said, doing a lax job attacking the mildew in between the shower tiles.

"His father's probably a boozer on the dole," I'd said, taking over the brush and showing her how to really scrub.

Those last few months it had surprised me that Stuart always made his rent. He'd been fired from his construction job for not showing up. I didn't dare ask how he got the money, though my mate Gary (who was a cabbie that year) swore he'd spotted him hanging around Fitzroy Gardens hustling swishy old men. I didn't want to hear it.

"Get some sleep, Stuart. You'll feel better. I'll give you some Panadeine." I gave him four tablets. Panadeine is Panadol with added codeine—I get shocking migraines. (Rachel always bummed two Panadeine off me for her period cramps. She couldn't believe the stuff was over-the-counter.) Four's enough to knock you out for hours.

Since Rachel and Phillip were at work and Stuart was zonked out in misery in his room, I retrieved my locked metal box from my closet. That's where I kept the tapes that I was too embarrassed to play when anyone else was around. I also stashed important papers in it: my birth certificate, my Swinburne diploma, and the Cadbury wrapper collection Cormac Kennedy had given me the month before he died. Cormac had been ridiculous about keeping those wrappers; they attracted bugs for the first few months I'd had them. But they meant so much to him that I never threw them away. He said that he had twelve of the twenty-two different kinds. *Caramello, Energy, Cadbury Dark*. There was a little painting of the inside of each wrapper on the front so Cormac could see beforehand if he would get a cherry filling or an almond one. I was about thirteen when he died. It was pouring, and the spouting was full of gum leaves. My father, wearing a purple Speedo and a shower cap, had climbed the roof to dislodge the mess. My parents were laughing at Dad's absurd outfit, and I was angry because, well, he looked ridiculous, and the way your dad looks matters when you're thirteen. Anyone could have seen him half naked up there. And then we heard a wail, and Dad climbed off the roof to see what had happened. But we knew. Cormac Kennedy had died. And my mother rang the ambulance as Cormac's father sobbed in my Speedo-clad father's arms. Fuck. He was around eight. I'd promised to finish off the collection for him, but I only got around to adding a *Fruit and Nut* wrapper a few years later.

There were no more noises from Stuart's room. From the locked box, I took out my Peggy Lee tape that I'd almost worn out. I put on a bit of Peg. My life was at a standstill. I was blue as I'd ever been. I recently found out that Peggy Lee is still alive, in a wheelchair. But I used to tell Mum back in Form Two—around the time Cormac died—that if I was on the scene, Peg would never have committed suicide. Listening to her every word, I was sure that she'd offed herself. And I knew that I could have loved Peg right. I had Peg's life figured out. She'd needed someone to indulge her, to make her laugh at her self-obsession. The day is long, I'd have told her, but you've got such a voice. "Let go, Peg," I would mouth as I came into my hand.

We were going to shoot *Gnome* in three weeks. I knew that Phillip would take charge. He even had his mate Doug Lang doing camera work. A Phillip number, like the time he'd offered to video-tape Mick-O's British grandfather at the old man's nursing home talking about the World War, and spent fifty minutes confusing the ninety-one-year-old bastard with questions about the wrong war.

The gnome outfit Phillip wanted to hire for the film clip worried me. Another doubtful decision. And where was that going to get us? I put on my headphones so I wouldn't wake Stuart.

"Is that all there is to a fire?" Peggy sang.

3

Rachel: THE UNEXPECTED SALAMI

I was back in New York just over two months. I'd convinced myself that the shooting was behind me: a fantastic memory, like having been elected student union president in a far away time. Temping at a fire extinguisher company, I was miserable, and no one, not even Frieda or Janet, was helping. "Welcome back to the vortex of depression," Janet would say, ad nauseam. Frieda had a slight variation: "The nineties are a collective nervous breakdown."

The living room was a constant mess of newspapers and photo albums I never returned to their shelves. More than a few nights, I fell asleep on the couch in my clothes, once even breaking one of Mom's good European water goblets. My reaction? Hmm, I'll get to it later. Later, like everything else: morals, goals, and a haircut.

I felt I should be in better touch with Colin. I made a list on the back of my overdue telephone bill of why I liked him better than Will. For one, Colin was less concerned with what the cultured world thought. He openly despised chamber music, my secret bane. (Will also adored Light Opera and once ruined my imminent orgasm by crying out "I am the Captain of the Pinafore!")

I underlined that Colin's eyes were powdery blue and kind, the eyes of a good listener, while Will's were a grave and steady blue, a genetic gift from some colonial silversmith forefather.

I'd sent Colin an any-more-drama-going-down note early on. I wrote him another postcard.

Dear Colin,
Yesterday I heard on the local news that the latest craze Down Under is walking on fire coals.(?) And they're descended from convicts, the other anchor said. Please safeguard your feet. (I'm lonely.) Scratch Hector behind the ears, he must miss Stuart. Do you? Love, Rachel

My apathy was in full force. I never did mail that one.

I started to hang out solo in coffee shops; particularly one near my apartment called, oh so post-modernly, Coffee Bar. I didn't want to alienate anyone with my funk. Could I honestly not care that Stuart was dead? At the time I thought so; he had been a consistent heel for most of the time that I'd known him. I only felt sorry for his family, although Colin had written that no one had come forward as kin since I left.

I lacked a belief system. Hebrew School Saturdays and Catechism Sundays had long ago canceled each other out. Everything else seemed forced. Atheism, or whatever this was, was damn depressing.

Finally home after an endless Friday at FireQuenchers sorting through invoices and typing white labels for Penderflex tabs, I threw my scattered clothes into my parents' washer. The machine sputtered after the first cycle, and, cursing, I fished out the culprit: a hanger cleverly concealed by a towel. Stashed under the kitchen sink (with my father's nuclear-holocaust supply of extra toilet paper) was a stack of plastic shopping bags. I loaded up two, one from the MoMA giftshop and one from Bernie's House of Prime Beef, and schlepped them to the laundromat a few blocks away. I packed in my soused clothes tighter than the posted rules allowed.

I opened a thick letter from Colin, chock full of the latest "good news" from the murder fallout; the Poppies had been offered a global contract with EMI Records. When I looked up at the folding table, a seventy-ish man seemingly afflicted with Parkinson's was having enormous difficulty gathering and creasing the legs of his plaid pants. Will, had I still been with him, would have said that the old guy should be lauded for self-sufficiency, not pitied. But the loneliness I sensed in this shaking man put me over the edge. I watched from my sixties-era, pastel-yellow plastic seat, digging into my 501s for a few more quarters for a diet root beer from the soda machine. I imagined that the folding-man's wife had died and he couldn't afford a nurse; that he was once as cool as Dean Martin; that he would fight back tears if his dead spouse could see him now in a grungy Village laundromat, taking ten minutes to fold a pair of pants, surrounded by a half dozen arty types in cookie-cutter black, the two by the bulletin board no doubt on a particularly high dosage of unlawful substances. Pulling out my load, I realized the spin cycle of the Maytag was no match for my over-wet belongings. Over the sink, I got the dry heaves.

The next morning, I emptied an instant oatmeal packet into a bowl of hot water. It was a crisp weekend day. I grabbed a jacket and walked downtown toward Battery Park, waving sadly as the Circle Line passed by. Once, that was enough to keep me happy for a whole day. A half dozen people waved to me from the boat; Wyoming and London mothers perhaps, telling their daughters to wave, too. *See, honey, New Yorkers are friendly.* My own mother had taught me to wave to the ships passing through New York Harbor. "It is your duty as an ambassador of the city to do so," she would say with a straight face. I would wave, proud as a new private breaking in a uniform. She'd nudge Frank, who'd roll his eyes, but ultimately move his arm up and down. He couldn't help a small grin when the far-away tourists responded.

I'm twenty-seven, I thought, which suddenly seemed not so far from fifty. The water under the docks shimmered in a way that made me feel biblical. I walked back to the Village via Broadway. I drew a hot bath, which I eagerly awaited. In the house in St. Kilda, the hot water always ran out. I eased in, onto the red antislip rubber mat with suckers on the bottom. I let my decayed rubber duck float past my belly. My dad had bought it for me when I was five. He enjoyed having it on the edge of the tub, a rare display of sentimentality. Dad is all for the new. "Science is the new religion," he likes to say. I lowered my neck down the white enamel, letting water clog my ears.

That night I must have been gnawing at my hair again; when I went to pee at around eight in the morning, I felt a wet and frayed clump against my cheek. My mother called.

"How are you?"

"Okay." I opened the fridge, removing Kraft American slices and milk.

"Where are you working today?"

"Still at the fire extinguisher joint."

"Keep your chin up. We won the Gulf War. The economy picks up after a war."

"It was a week-long war, Mom."

"You watch. How's Frieda? Wasn't she having a party?"

"Yes, and she's fine—"

"Were the other girls there?"

"Janet, but Veemah was in India. She flew in on Monday."

Veemah had asked me about the party at brunch, as she ordered a Western omelet.

"You're back from a month in India and you're worried about Frieda's party?" I'd said.

"What do you think I do in Agra? Ride a tiger in the yard?" Veemah had said. "My grandmother spent my entire visit telling me that if I don't stop dating white boys and wearing jeans I'm going to be labeled a whore. I'll be worse than an untouchable."

"Are the girls happy to have you back in New York?" Mom said.

"Probably."

"Did Frank tell you that Noreen had the baby?"

Noreen is my unbelievably dull cousin. "No?"

"Yes. Lydia Sue. Seven pounds, two ounces. You should give Noreen a call."

"Okay." I picked up the pack of processed cheese from the Formica kitchen table and started scanning the ingredients. When I had interned at an adult-contemporary radio station the summer after my sophomore year of college, a DJ I'd had a clandestine something with would play the "ingredient game" to pass time on his shift. He wasn't sharp enough to spout acerbic commentary on the day's events. He'd read the label of an everyday product with heaps of twentieth-century additives and have listeners call to guess what they thought the mystery product was for a prize of concert tickets. I thought the game was bullshit. I was supposed to take the ninety-seventh caller, but I'd wait a few minutes and pick up the phone. He kissed great though.

"I see you're as talkative as usual," my mother said.

"Mom—don't start—"

"Start what? You never finish a sentence with me. Have you heard more about the murder case?"

"No, I got rid of the cable. I can't afford it." Would she offer to pay for it?

Nope. "Well, I haven't seen anything more either." My mother sighed. "You seem too blasé about that murder, Rachel. My God. A *roommate* of yours was murdered! And you were there! Help me. I'm feeling a generation gap."

I deflected the scrutiny. "You still sweeping those frogs out the condo door?"

"No, we hardly see them anymore."

There was an excruciatingly long pause. "So how are you?" I asked. This was extortion.

"You finally asked!" My mom meant it lovingly, but still it annoyed me.

Back to Coffee Bar again: my new center of gravity. The man across from me at my long "antichic" linoleum table

looked interesting, though a bit seedy, grinding numerous cigarettes into the ashtray as he sipped from his herbal tea. He had a
zigzagging scar over his eyebrow; gray sideburns. I caught him
ogling the two seventeen-ish girls in baby-doll dresses, braided
pigtails, and patent leather shoes, particularly the girl with the
D-cup chest. He saw me staring and probably thought I was coming on to him. He flashed his rotting teeth.

I'd learned about rotting teeth from Stuart. I'd had it to here
with him and had wanted the guys to show him the door. But they
said that it wasn't fair, he was paying his share: mateship bullshit
going strong. I'm not saying all Aussie men wear slouched hats and
burp their days away, but even the most sensitive Melbourne University philosophy major partakes in testosterone bonding; for a
white male Australian to go against the two hundred-year strong
societal grain is as inconceivable as a Savannah gent not opening
a car door for a woman. My silver drop earrings went missing.
Then my zoom-lens camera, my biggest purchase of the previous five years. I'd wanted the fucker out, but Colin and Phillip
had tried to calm me down, suggesting that we try locking our
individual doors. Then Stuart couldn't steal money or sell our
valuables.

Ironically, I had to ask Stuart to pick my lock two weeks
later when I dropped my keys on the St. Kilda pier, right into Port
Phillip Bay. I couldn't afford a locksmith and Stuart was most oblig-
ing, completing the job in ten seconds. I offered him a chunk of the
Katz's salami in the fridge as a thank you; my brother had sent the
salami to me from the famous New York deli, subverting strict

Aussie customs regulations by filling in "Restaurant Souvenir" on the official green form taped to the box.

Our sibling mega-joke, *the unexpected salami*. I'd wrapped one up in a Saks Fifth Avenue box for Frank's graduation from the Rhode Island School of Design. Tit for tat, he'd managed to have room service deliver a half pound one to me while I attended a vacuum physics conference in Chicago, the week after Will and I announced our engagement.

Stuart had eaten half the salami while I was at the pier. I could tell by his breath and the missing meat. But since he'd opened my door, I pretended I didn't notice and made him salami and eggs the way my Uncle Barry had shown me years ago. "The Jewish bachelor's caviar," Uncle Barry always said. Stuart and I got to talking, and he acknowledged his heroin addiction indirectly, commenting on a funky street-type who was being interviewed about the Australian recession on the news.

Stuart looking straight at me: "He's skint 'cause he's been shooting up for a year I'd say. My teeth looked liked that a year ago. You can tell by the teeth." That's how I came to learn that rotting teeth on a person dressed in cool-as-shit black is almost certainly a sign of heroin.

Traveling for two years had wised me up a bit, though not in the way the Ganellis and the Levines viewed growth: i.e., a masters degree, professional job, good solid man, things to have nachus over, bragging rights, as Grandma Chaika would have said. And it wasn't just heroin teeth. I knew tons of new stuff I couldn't put on a résumé, tidbits like the names of three men at the helm of the

Australian Government who routinely received blow jobs at an up-scale Melbourne brothel called The Planet. My former neighbor was their whore: a transplanted Perth blueblood who studied Japanese at Melbourne University. A simple act, like catching a glimpse of a man across the table of a coffee bar with brown teeth, brought out fractal memories that at some future time could be pieced together authoritatively, like a geometry proof.

I ignored the sleazy Coffee Bar patron, instead burying myself behind a literary 'zine from a neighboring table. On the back cover, some hapless soul had started listing the states: "Alab. Ariz., Dela., Calif." I searched my blue Danish schoolbag for a pencil and started to finish them. At least this I could do. I had memorized the states when I was seven and recited them to my eight-year-old cousin, Tony, at the Ganelli Easter Sunday Dinner. Aunt Virginia took me aside and whispered, "No one likes a show-off, Rachel." In Coffee Bar, a few centuries later, clenching my pencil, I wrote them fast, but only managed forty-seven. It didn't matter of course, not being able to complete what had once been child's play. But I wanted to finish my list. My mind canvassed about: I tried to imagine the states as jigsaw pieces, and I remembered the boxing glove, Michigan, and even caught myself smiling a bit.

The tooth guy kept looking at my paper. "New Hampshire," he said.

"I would've gotten that." I said, trying to remember the last one.

"Are you afraid of me?"

"I'm in a solo kind of mood, you know?"

"Look, I noticed your body language—you seem in need of

company." The weirdo offered me a cigarette. I shook my head no. In another time I'd have been sane and moved away. But for some reason—okay loneliness—I gave in. I half smiled.

"You down?" he asked, swinging his chair around to my side of the table.

"It's not the heat, it's the humidity," I said. The acid New York reply to everything, even when it's thirty-five degrees outside.

"Want coffee and a slice of blueberry pie? On me. My life story sold today for $20,000."

"And so who are you?" I asked, more than somewhat obnoxiously, as the sleazoid flagged the waitress and ordered.

"A fading icon." He dragged a new cigarette. "You might not've even heard of me."

"Oh c'mon, don't taunt like that. Who are you?"

"Who are you?"

"A woman at a coffee shop asking you a question—"

"Danny Death," the man said. Danny Death? One of the founding fathers of punk rock. Danny Death, damn. We got our food and got to talking.

"I read that article about you in the seventies-nostalgia issue of *Rolling Stone*. The reporter didn't like you much." Nastiness is my adorable side effect to nervousness. I couldn't believe I said that.

"You're a sweetheart," Danny said with exaggerated anger, forking his pie.

"I don't know what to say to you—that I once carved a line from one of your songs into my desk during algebra? Sounds too much like fawning."

"Which line?"

"'Man is in transit between brute and God.'"

"Stole that from Norman Mailer. *The Naked and the Dead.*"

"Oh. Well, you stole it well." I couldn't look him in the face. I didn't want him to gather how pathetic I was, sitting there stuck in a depressed late-twenties state, like caught fabric.

"Why don't you tell me what has you in your obvious rut?" he asked.

"Long or the short version?"

"Short will do. I'm a famous guy."

"A celebrity might be pushing it," I said, with an unsuccessful straight face.

"Fuck you." I knew by Danny's steady glare that he actually wanted to know.

"Let's see. I fled my boring job and my oh-so-perfect fiancé to live in Australia. While there I lived with three musicians, one of whom got killed by the mob during my new quasi-boyfriend's video shoot. My mother, with whom I have poor communication, lured me back to my family apartment with the bait that my parents would move permanently to their condo in Florida. Now I'm back on the road to nowhere—instead of having a plethora of middle management editing jobs in the offering, I've returned to a job market where the only ads are for situations wanted—I can only temp. I desperately miss my quasi-boyfriend, Colin, who's fifteen thousand miles away working in a copy shop, and I hate myself and my friends, although they think I'm as adorably sardonic and top-of-the-world as always. My mother thinks I'm a freak for not having an ounce of concern for the murder of my roommate, which by the way, I witnessed. He was a pig though.

A fucked-up pig heroin addict thief asshole. And I'm at a loss about where I can go. I'm fucking around again with every Joe, Dick, or Harry I meet on a plane or at a party—I can't make a decision about grad school, let alone what to do to make hours go faster—"

"I see," Danny said, signaling for our check.

"That's it? That's what you say after devouring my miserable life story? You pump it out of me and then that's it?"

"Whoa!" the legendary Danny Death said, looking like he didn't have time for whiners. "You need to get some fucking perspective. Decisions don't mean shit. Once you've made one, ride it for its dimensions. So you've cut your first tooth. Why should I feel sorry for you? You speak well, you have great tits, you've had high adventure. You're able to live in another country for two years without mention of a serious job—"

"I had savings from my New York editing job, plus I waitressed—that's not fair."

"But you knew you could wire home to Mommy and Daddy if you needed to. True?"

"True." Fuck him, the bastard.

"So, you had a place to come home to, and it wasn't a hicktown hell in West Virginia. And as for the murder, it sounds like you got a kick out of it. If the guy was an asshole, he deserved it."

"Fuck *you*," I squeaked, my eyes steady on the table's yellow polka-dotted contact paper that would make a homemaker scream in horror if she'd bought an old house and opened her cabinets. "What right do you have to say that to me?" Sometimes it takes a nihilist to really shape you up.

• • •

My life wasn't blueberry pie, but over the next week, I felt more grounded. I called my mother to say hi, and she sounded delighted at this unforced cheer. I even managed a trip to the Forty-second Street library's map room to look at the newest acquisitions.

"Haven't seen you in years," Jorge, the map librarian, said. On a shelf behind his desk was a bumper sticker that said *Happiness is knowing how to read a road map.* "Rachel, right? I have great scarves to show you. Soldiers secured them around their necks in World War Two. The scarves had maps on them in case they got lost in the jungle."

I spread out the silky samples he brought me on the table and entered their space. I imagined myself as a pilot lost in the jungles of the Philippines with only a map of Luzon to guide me. Colin had known what I meant by my map space: he'd said that as a child he'd gone with his cousin to the beach, and as each boat passed, they'd enter a fantasy of journey.

The librarian came over to retrieve the scarves. I asked him to bring out an 1890s map of Melbourne the way one would order an after-dinner sherry. Nepean Highway, the expressway where I drove Colin's panel van on the day Stuart was shot, was marked Nepean Road. The hallmarks of the gentrified inner suburbs were lifetimes away—Fitzroy's artist cafés and tapas bars, St. Kilda's pastel art deco homes, and the outdoor Sunday thrift market at Camberwell, where Colin scooped up a ketchup-stained cookbook for me. (It was inscribed "the kitchen of Mrs. Newton-John"; a chocolate walnut cake was marked "Olivia's favorite" in red pencil.)

An afternoon of geographical escape and pleasure; I was in a bona fide good mood. I left the library and started to walk home down Fifth Avenue, admiring, as an incalculable number of people had before me, the beauty of the Flatiron Building in sunset. Finally, a day in which I didn't mind that I was part of a continuum. Saved in the nick of time by Danny Death.

On Fifth Avenue and Twenty-second Street, Eisenberg's Sandwich Shop beckoned me inside. The Eisenberg tuna sandwich (Bumble Bee fancy white albacore moistened by just the right amount of Hellmann's mayo, a pickle, and a sprig of parsley) would be a perfect cap to the day—a treat I'd missed while in Australia.

Aunt Virginia had taken Frank and me to Eisenberg's whenever my parents went on their "romantic getaway" weekend bus trips to places like Cape May, New Jersey, or Brandywine Valley, Delaware. Aunt Virginia was, and is, a no-nonsense woman. Everything about Eisenberg's suited her "just fine"—the Old New York narrow room with the faux-marble counter, zero-pretense red vinyl stools, and water served in promotional cups bought in bulk—in recent times, last summer's Disney tie-in.

"Your Grandpa Ganelli ate soup here," she'd remind us if we lobbied for McDonald's (at the time, the early seventies, the golden arches had but one outlet on East Twenty-third Street, a destination as exotic and inviting as the only intimate café in drive-in suburbia).

I smiled in relief as I took my stool. Some things are constants. Three hand-painted wooden signs were tacked onto the walls, plaques from opening day in 1929:

SALAMI	BACON & TOMATO	PEANUT BUTTER
ROAST BEEF	BACON & EGG	SWISS CHEESE
BOLOGNA	TUNA FISH	HAM & CHEESE
LIVERWURST	HAM & EGG	COTTAGE CHEESE
HOT PASTRAMI	SALAMI & EGG	
SLICED HAM	CHICKEN SALAD	
CORNED BEEF		

And a plastic fourth menu from the fifties over to the side:

STEWED PEACHES
JELL-O
PINEAPPLE
GRAPEFRUIT JUICE
TOMATO JUICE
FRUIT SALAD

I greedily accepted my tuna fish sandwich and savored each bite. I imagined Grandpa Ganelli, who I hardly remember, eating sliced meatloaf on a roll, perhaps crossing paths with Mom's socialist father, Murray Levine, who was probably the first in his five-thousand-year-old line to abandon kosher laws to the temptation of a yummy BLT.

I daydreamed about enrolling in Columbia's film school, persuading Frieda and Janet to get me into their production assistant circle. Mom had those great PR contacts she was always offering to call. If I borrowed her old Rolodex I could set up some interviews for steady, non–fire extinguisher money. I had a pulse again.

The guy at the far end of the counter wanted to pay his bill. "I had a tuna salad sandwich, mate," he said, in a distinct Aussie accent.

I knew that voice. I leaned in close to pinpoint who it was. One of my Dog's Bar customers?

I dropped a sandwich half in my lap. I went over to the end of the room to get a better look. It couldn't be. I've been told by my friends and family that I amplify my details, but that moment I almost had a seizure of glacial proportions. At the very least, I could feel hot color blitzing my cheeks.

Stuart looked like he was the one seeing a ghost. "Shit, Rachel!"

"My God, Stuart!" I spit a large chunk of tuna onto his shirt. "What the fuck is fucking going on here?"

He stared at me, frightened.

"What the fuck?" My hand quivered. "I saw you dead. They pronounced you dead on arrival—there was blood—you were dead!"

"I thought you'd be cozy in Oz with Colin," he said shakily. He had a bit of lettuce on his lower lip.

"What is going on?"

"You have a light?"

"WHY AREN'T YOU FUCKING ANSWERING ME?"

"Some things you are better off not knowing about. I don't think you should go telling anyone you saw me."

"Like fucking hell."

One of the two women at the far side of the counter called for her check, and the waiter reluctantly left our part of the counter space. Stuart leaned over; he smelled of pickle and drugs. "Let's say

I needed to be dead fast. And I reckon Colin and Phillip needed the fame. Simple as that. You got a place for me to stay? I just got here from Buffalo. Fucking oath, I came to this coffee shop because I'd heard you telling Phillip and Colin about it."

"The guys *needed* to be famous? What does that have to do with this?" My voice had gone from loud to shrill.

"You know, my family is gone, except for me mother's cousin in Buffalo, New York. I'm the end of the Gibbs line." I barely listened. I wanted to rip his slimy guts out. "I reckon you want me to lay it all out like on Batman."

I knew right then. Stuart had run afoul of his shady circle and wanted out. Phillip—thirty-four, an aging hunky rocker with a we'll-give-you-one-last-shot recording contract. He'd do anything to prove the naysayers wrong about his being too old to put money into the band. Phillip made films for the Victorian Ambulance Corps. He could have faked a death on film with his medical cronies or his old film-school buddy Doug Lang. And his roommate who got married and was always dropping by the house, the video documentarian, worked for the Melbourne police; *he* could have helped carry it off. My mind was racing. Who did they know at the morgue? I couldn't figure out how Phillip could have gotten Stuart a passport, but I was sure I'd find out soon enough. I had been an utter idiot. And whatever the cockamamie plan had been, it had worked.

"Did Phillip mastermind this or did you?"

"It was Colin's idea, Chickie." At first I thought Stuart was laughing at me, but then I realized he was embarrassed for me.

Colin? My Colin? I was shattered.

I opened the floodgates: Stuart slept in my parents' bed that night. That lying parasite had forty-five cents in his pocket and planned on sleeping in Central Park. He'd get killed for real, or get arrested for vagrancy. Then perhaps Colin and Phillip would get arrested, when I could have prevented that. Stuart Gibbs, the unexpected salami to end all salamis. I'd sort out my emotions in the morning.

Around one in the morning, I woke up and peeked in the extra bedroom to check on things. Stuart had wrapped a tie around his arm. Dad's dinosaur tie, a forgotten Father's Day gift from the American Museum of Natural History.

"Not in my house," I said, defeated. "This is my house." Stuart was naked except for his socks. I tried not to look at his penis, flaccid and uncircumcised; it was about the least erotic thing I'd ever seen. He shivered. I was far too late.

"You've got to get off the goddamn treadmill," I said softly. I had never seen the "strap" before. Even though I knew Stuart was at it all along in St. Kilda, I never chose to explore what went on behind his door. Like the majority of Manhattan residents who live below Fourteenth Street, at least those that read the downtown press, I was obliged to be a fan of Lou Reed, John Coltrane, and Charlie Parker; I'd read plenty about heroin abuse. But there was the fabled strap, in a dinosaur-tie incarnation, bulging the vein of a foreigner lying on my mother's Bloomies' white sale Ivan Stanbury flannel sheets in my family apartment, the last bastion of nothing-ever-happens. I sat there in stunned silence for several minutes. Stuart's eyes were closed.

"If you had relatives in Buffalo," I then asked out loud, "why did you come to New York?" I didn't think he heard me.

"You told me anyone could get lost here," he said.

Frieda rang my buzzer. "Hi," I said through the intercom, "I don't think it's a good time."

"Sorry to butt in on you, but do you mind if I crash in your extra bedroom? I left my keys at the office, and the front door there is locked."

"Frieda, I have a guy here."

"Oh, God, I'm sorry. Who is it?"

"Look, I have to go. Call Janet—she left a message that she was staying home to read. Call me if she's not there."

"Okay. But first tell me who it is."

"A friend from Australia—he's sleeping."

Stuart's thin frame was in a fetal curl on my parents' comforter. Without Australian sunlight, his angular face, softened only by round eyes, was now the color of uncooked macaroni. Near the bed was our auxiliary bookcase full of secondary books my family didn't think should be shelved on the living room bookcase with Virginia Woolf and Mark Twain. *The Consumer's Guide to Electronics. The Inner Game of Tennis. The Book of Lists.* Under the computer table were Mom's detective novels.

"You have so many books," Stuart said in a dozy narcotic tone. "How can you afford so many books?" He picked up a tattered maroon paperback of *The Catcher in the Rye*. Frank and I'd both done book reports on it. "What's this one about? Tell me what the story is."

"C'mon, Stuart, you're high. You must have read *The Catcher in the Rye*."

"I don't know how to read."

If this particular moment was a cartoon, Danny Death's words would have been above me in a thought balloon: you need to get some fucking perspective.

Stuart's eye contact alone terrified. It is scary to be needed by someone you hate. Stuart didn't have a home left, let alone money.

"How did you know where to go for heroin?"

"I knew the people to look for. I asked them where to go."

"Great skill you have," I said under my breath.

"Help me, Rachel? I want to read . . ." He zoned out again.

Another thought balloon: oh fuck, I could jump to the next goodness plateau. "You ask enough favors for someone who's legally dead," I said, holding Stuart's hand, his blackened, shaking thumbnail pushed into my palm.

4

Colin: CATALYST

It was the morning after I gave Stuart the Panadeine to calm him down that the ridiculous thought of "killing" Stuart started to gel. ("It came from a part of my brain I had never used before," Dad said when he'd discovered that he could knit better than Mum.) I had an old mate, Peter, from my graphics course at Swinburne. He could help me do up a fake ID. Peter could do anything. Paste and scissors is an art form lost in the computer era, now that they have those little icons that you click on to move things around. It's not the same. Peter once redid a comic book for one of our Swinburne classmate's twenty-first. He photocopied our faces from photos and pasted them onto the superhero backdrop. All of us fuckwits were characters, even the car-park attendant. Fucking brilliant.

I rang Peter, who didn't want to know what the ID was for. He'd always been that way. He'd make a great spy. He said it was easy as anything to pull together an ID, and I sent him old band slicks of Stuart when he was still our drummer. (Later on, with the massive news attention, I saw Peter at a pub and he winked at me. He's that kind of mate.)

That same day when everyone was out of the house, I nervously sat down with Phillip on two crates in his room. He was wearing a brand-new green shirt. Everything in the room was green. His wardrobe, his amplifier cabinet, his Stratocaster. If that wasn't eccentric enough, Phillip kept his things in green spray-painted milk crates, from books and socks to bars of Toblerone. His bedframe was made out of crates. Staring around, I felt more strongly than ever that we needed a major miracle—like Stuart's death—to push us out of the almost-but-no-cigar category. A fun nutcake bandleader wasn't going to get me where I wanted to be.

"You're out of your bloody mind!" Phillip said, staggered at my plan. This kind of scheme was up his alley, not mine. He kept fiddling with the new edition of *Beat*, flipping the pages and bending the corners up. But when the day was done, he was in it. I appealed to the actor, the lead singer in him.

We got it down. Stuart would die. Phillip wanted Rachel in on it, to juice her brain. But Jesus, I did not want her involved. I had other plans for Rachel. I knew that she liked me; we'd had a horny night in the toilet the previous month. But I wanted to ask her to move out with me into our own place. Maybe the scam would get me the money. I would present my new fame as part of the reason she should go out with me, that she'd mistakenly pigeonholed me as stalled. I wasn't going to be a plush toy for her to squeeze when she needed companionship. From now on, I was going to take hold of the reins.

Looking back at the moment of birth of this lunatic plan, I can't chart the bullshit that flowed through my mind. I'd turned thirty-two a month earlier; I was desperate. We got Doug Lang in on it. His career was also going nowhere; he'd been reduced to helping Phillip film accident prevention clips for the Ambulance Corps. Doug was always harking back to his lost career; he'd done filmwork in the seventies for Countdown and even Paul Hogan's TV show before "Hogues" hit it big with Crap-odile Dundee.

The Sunday week, Rachel left to go to one of her Dog's Bar friend's poetry readings. Stuart was watching his soap. Phillip sat on the couch watching it, too. This was the only time he ever spent in the same room with Stuart, so it didn't seem abnormal. I made like I was going to compile a mixed tape, piling my CDs in a stack and staring a minute or two at the back of each one. Then Phillip asked Stuart if he wanted to join us for fish and chips down on Acland Street. His shout: he'd found a twenty-dollar bill that morning in the toilet and didn't know whose it was, Rachel said it wasn't hers. My arsehole clenched at this transparent maneuver; Phillip wouldn't be seen with Stuart these days, and twenty dollars in the toilet? Stuart looked a bit suss over the toilet money story, even though he was still strung out. But he knew that we knew he was hungry. He'd eaten the two bagels Rachel had bought the day before, one of his many selfish habits that was sure to get her screaming at him. She was one to talk; her room could have been condemned.

"That'd be good." He headed for my panel van. I felt bigger than him, but Stuart was about two inches taller than me, six one or six two (Australia turned metric when I was a kid, but I still think of height in feet.) He was skittish as hell, eyes darting around for whomever he owed money to. His fear was fine by us; it would make our pitch that much easier. We bought some flake, scallops, and potato cakes, and drove the few blocks to Port Melbourne pier.

The wind whipped our skin. There wasn't anyone around. Phillip said bullshit like "We're worried for you, mate." Phillip, in his own way, felt awful. You could see it in his mouth, which never wavered from a straight line.

Cormac couldn't be saved, I rationalized to myself, but I could ship Stuart away from Melissa, away from the streets where he'd spent his childhood in poverty.

Stuart still looked jittery, but he wasn't saying anything like "Why don't you two go fuck yourselves?" I gave him an envelope with the fake ID, which had Stuart's new name, Ian MacKenzie, and the passport we'd gotten through a Vietnamese bakery. Peter had heard the bakery could get you anything for the right price, which in our case was $300.

Stuart looked over the documents and didn't say a word. Then Phillip took out $500 and said we'd give him another $1500 to get him off to an okay start. We told him what we wanted out of his death, how he would have to play dead for Phillip's ambulance mates. He kept my gaze. I imagined him thinking that I was the true prick in the end—the wrong one to have trusted those past few years. But he had money in an arm's reach. He was a dog who'd do anything for a chunk of stew. "All right," he said finally.

The last thing I said before we went back to the flat was "Don't say a word to Rachel." Stuart had the money in his hands and stared at me. I saw that he was going to do it, for the $1500 more than anything else, and that he hated us for it, too.

The Victorian Ambulance Corp staff we clued in were Robert and William, twin emergency techies. They were identical down to their bushy gray moustaches. "The only way anyone can tell them apart is by personality," Phillip had said. "William's the big talker, and Robert nods at everything he says. William told me in seven ways over ten pints of VB that he loved the mateship of the plan."

The twin techies loved Phillip. He was the Elvis of the Corps, amusing them for hours on end about the girls he fucked behind Kerri's back. What a beaut idea—help a small-label band get off the ground! William and Robert were going to say Stuart was wounded, not dead, but critically ill. Stuart would have to be whisked away towards the hospital, but they would say he died en route, and subsequently direct the corpse to the Victoria Forensic Science Centre in Macleod. William had a brother-in-law who was a big-shot over at the Forensic Centre. He scheduled himself to be senior staff on duty so when the body was brought in by the twins from the criminal investigation site for analysis he was going to "ask for the case." He told us to schedule the video shoot for Sunday, when he could see the body alone. William's brother-in-law would say it was clearly what it appeared to be—gunshot wounds to the cheek and chest—and arrange for a prompt burial. No one would ever be suspicious enough to take another look at the body. In a midnight brainstorm session in Phillip's Ambulance Corp video suite, more suggestions dovetailed from the existing plan. The twins' younger brother, Tim, a failed actor, had a blue Nissan we would paint white. Tim would play the role of mobster.

"It'll be the biggest role I've had yet," Tim had laughed. "I'm not exactly flat out with work." Five men besides Phillip and myself were in on my demented, Peggy Lee–inspired plot. Would they keep their mouths shut? But these were five Australian men. *Members of the we-have-a-dick-and-we-stick-together club*, Rachel might have said. After five beers, the idea seemed possible, even exhilarating. Magic. And it worked. William's brother-in-law announced publicly that he'd arranged for a simple burial when no relatives came forward.

Melissa wasn't even at the funeral. She came over to the house with another junkie who she was obviously bonking, a week after Stuart's death. They wanted his things. How fucking transparent that she and her smelly friend were planning to score off Stuart's effects.

"He sold anything of value months ago, thanks to your lot," Phillip said. He was a beautiful liar. "We gave the clothes to the Salvation Army."

"You had no right, he was my boyfriend!" Melissa yelled right near my eardrum.

"Give her some money for his things, you cunts," her new boyfriend said.

"You can have his sideboard," I said, and that shut them up.

There were holes we'd left open in our enthusiasm—like which cemetery? But no one realized it was an elaborate scam. I didn't have journos around shoving recorders in my face. It wasn't a pressing whodunit. The general consensus was that the Mafia made good on their promise to settle the score with anyone who didn't pay them back a loan. It fucking worked! Only much later did I feel like Raskolnikov.

After we honored the bastard Bendigo Institute of Technology gig, our new manager Angus decided that now that we were his boys we wouldn't be playing any more country-town shows. He wanted us to save up the gigs, not spread ourselves thin playing every bullshit venue in the sticks and outer suburb big-hair pub in Melbourne. "From now on," Angus said, "the Poppies will play snob gigs every three months. With the amount of publicity you've had, you have to watch out for overexposure. You'll play Lounge or Prince of Wales in Melbourne, or the Phoenician Club in Sydney. Fuck Brisbane and Adelaide, no one lives there."

Phillip thought Angus didn't have a clue. "How long could the fame from 'Gnome' last?' Phillip wanted to milk all the money he could from the song and set up a recording studio like Greg Ham, the sax player from Men At Work, did. I tried to point out to him that Men At Work had *the number one album in America* for a fucking year, but as far as Phillip was concerned, Men At Work were one-hit wonders. Flash-in-the-pan definition differences aside, he was willing to accept asterisk fate, if he got enough dollars from it. There was a three-piece suit underneath those green seventies polyester shirts and tapered black jeans he'd bought in the secondhand shops on Greville Street. If Phillip was a Beatle he'd be Paul fucking McCartney.

During the band direction meeting, Phillip kept bringing up that guy Joe, who owns a mod clothing store on Brunswick Street with his wife. Years ago Joe wrote "Shaddup You Face," the novelty song of the century. It was even a surprise smash in the States: "Whatsa matter you, Gotta no respect, Whatya thinkya do, Why you looka so sad, Itsa notso bad, Itsa nicea place, Ah shaddup you face."

"Joe's fucking laughing," Phillip said to me after Angus left the room. "He's got a great house off those residuals."

Unfuckinbelievable. Phillip knew how to piss me off saying things like that. I wasn't a *Eurovision* or *New Faces* contestant; I was a serious rock musician and I wanted to have some impact. I was hell bent on letting our fucking manager fucking manage. We risked jail for our fame. Why did Phillip have to cut us down now? I mean the Beatles had arse luck right? No one goes around citing "Love Me Do" as poetry. They ran with their success. They matured because of the limelight. If we were ever going to be consequential musicians, this was the time to go the elite route. And things were going fine. Stuart, that canny bastard, had kept to his word. As far as everyone knew, he was dead; there wasn't a hint of his not being dead. Even our drummer Mick-O thought that the murder had happened. And the ultimate test: bullshit-radar Rachel was fooled, though I felt rotten about that.

But Phillip came to his senses with that EMI Records contract. It took us all by surprise, even Angus. The CNN bit was wild, but it didn't truly astonish me, that's the kind of coverage we were going for. But EMI, fuck, that's the label the Beatles signed to. I thought if all went to plan, we might get signed to Mushroom, the major Aussie label. This was getting bigger than a kick-in-the-arse catalyst. If I wasn't already shitting myself, I began getting really nervous—like a bandit on the lam. Where the hell *had* Stuart gone? He had told us he was going to Buffalo. He'd promised to send a postcard from "Aunt Sally" once he got there. I was pretty sure Buffalo's a city in Canada.

That Friday we were offered a three-album global contract with EMI Records. The extent of our deceit began to hit me full force. I wanted someone to lampoon Phillip's lack of business sense with me. Rachel would have had me in stitches.

I'd planned on telling her about the whole scheme a few days after the film clip (and Stuart) was shot, but her mother had gotten her panicky about the publicity and couriered her that ticket to the States. After that, the time never seemed right. Rachel wasn't the first person I would think of when envisioning a partner, though she was a decent looker. I had always pictured a docile sweetheart who wasn't going to care about my life compromises. Like my mum and aunties who put up with the slack men in their lives. But after that kiss in the toilet, the month before Rachel flew home to New York, I'd first likened our connection to the relationship I have with my guitar. I didn't tell her this because she would have spat "misogynist" at me; she has no idea how much a muso can love his guitar. I played bass for the Tall Poppies, but it was my guitar I chose to spend free time with. She was moody and her room was an obstacle course, but I did seem to want to spend every minute with her. And no one else ever thought I could do more with my life. For some mysterious reason, Rachel thought I could.

I had it pretty good for Australia. Not many people go to uni, I read something like five percent. Rachel had once claimed that in the States, anyone with money gets a spot. In Oz, it's a privilege. I had a degree, the first in my family—not from Melbourne Uni or Monash, but Swinburne wasn't anything to sneeze at. And graphics wasn't rocket science, but it was a full three-year course. I was going okay with the graphics; a few years out I was the art director of a small card company. Then came the big switch to computer graphics, and it was out-with-the-old time. I could have retrained; the company wasn't so hard-boiled that they'd leave us out in the cold. They offered to pay half of the training course. But I wasn't interested. Graphics was always tactile for me. I liked selecting the colored Textas and positioning the paper on the waxer, the way I like feeling the strings on my guitar. Most of the others in the firm adapted and learned Quark and Pagemaker, but I got an easy job running a printing and architectural blueprint shop. It was a rut I didn't know how to get out of. No one ever seemed to question what I was made of. Except Rachel.

I wrote Rachel about the new recording contract, but I never heard back from her. I had planned to ring her with the full story, but I was afraid there was an outside chance that the police might tap the line. They were centering their investigation on pinning down the mob connection.

Mum was calling a lot to see how I was. Aunty Grace got it in her head that I might be caught up with heroin, too.

Mum and Aunty Grace were lifelong best friends. Aunty Grace wanted me and Liam, who was a month older than me, to share the same type of relationship as she had with my mother. I was sad to leave my St. Kilda schoolmates behind—terrified was more like it—but much to everyone's delight, Liam and I became super close. There was a reason Aunty Grace wanted us to become best friends, Liam confided. He had been caught sticking an exploratory finger up the "private place" of Tina, his last best friend, a classmate who lived in the neighboring town of Carrum Down. Tina's thumb was missing. She'd told Liam that she might have been born that way because of a "nuclear stream." She and three other Carrum Down kids talked to a judge in a big powdered wig about their missing body parts.

Angus and I eventually convinced Phillip to shut up about more suburban gigs. We played to a full house at Lounge in Melbourne, and this gorgeous redhead named Hannah started talking to me afterward. A potter ("a ceramist," she corrected me)—before the murder we'd get okay-looking banktellers, or a travel agent at best. Hannah had a brain, and shit she was beautiful. And since Rachel was not writing back, after four letters!, I figured she'd shacked up with a New York surgeon or someone of that breeding. Hannah suggested that we go to the Valhalla to see a new print of *Pandora's Box*, a classic silent movie. Jen, a friend of hers, had been commissioned to do a live violin accompaniment that weekend. I was impressed as hell. I didn't have friends who played the violin.

Hannah and I started going out. Phillip and I didn't talk much about the plan that had served us so well. It was creepy the way the bad points disappeared.

5

Rachel: BATHOS

The next morning, for the briefest moment, I considered tracking down Will. He'd always kept a clear head, even when I'd pulled the plug on us from a distant land. I hadn't spoken to Will since that dreaded phone call from Melbourne. Calling him now to steer me through the reverberations of my original wormy sin would be more than vulgar.

My parents were planning a thirtieth-anniversary trip. They'd talked about it since I got back; they'd never been to Europe together. "Not with you two in college, we never had the money for a proper trip to Paris." They didn't need this mess. Sylvia and Joseph Ganelli were hip enough for sixty-somethings, in an updated sitcom way. They recycled. They sporadically used terms like *cyberspace* or *alternative rock*. But aiding a heroin addict?

And I did not want to get my girlfriends mixed up in Stuart's salvation. Then I'd have to spill the story, and I couldn't chance that. Frieda knew a Brooklyn-based Aussie filmmaker, and Veemah the Jetsetter—oh boy. Veemah was the warlord of us gossips. We'd spent many an entertaining afternoon together tearing some bitch to shreds. Loose lips sink ships. I imagined a knock on the door from Interpol.

Janet, a Mayflower descendant, was an outside possibility; she was bred to keep her mouth clamped.

Other relatives? They'd go straight to my folks. Lord help me if Aunt Virginia got a whiff of this. She'd hail a taxi and a priest to sprinkle holy water over him.

Weren't methadone clinics impossible to get into in New York? What was methadone? Did I want this approximately 150-pound weight around my ankle? I didn't have savings.

After three morning coffees, I settled on my trustworthy childhood plan of action: whenever I'd been terrified by a creepy-crawler, I'd called big brother.

"Frank?" I said to his machine, after his beloved soundtrack snippet of Charlton Heston's soliloquy as the sole functioning post-Apocalyptic survivor in *Omega Man.* "You there? Frank?" I was going to dial his second number, used mostly for his modem, when he picked up.

"Hey. Can you drop it a few decibels?"

"I need your advice."

"Shoot."

"Tell me everything you know about heroin."

"What kind of request is that for ten A.M.? You better not be telling me you're getting fucked up with that shit?"

"Not me. A friend of mine is in trouble."

" 'A friend of mine'? What, one of your super-achiever friends dropped out of corporate America? Doubt it. What did they try, grass? Flash bulletin—pot ain't heroin. She's not going to die."

"Please. Listen! I need to know about heroin."

"Are you insinuating that I know these things? I'm offended."

"You know more than me." Frank knows that much more than me about everything, except supernovas and PMS. "My friend's in trouble."

"Read *Basketball Diaries*. Or *Junky*. Carroll and Burroughs sinned for our entertainment."

"I've read them already—"

"Then you know what I know."

It is difficult for Frank and me to talk without ironic phrases. Even at Uncle Barry's funeral, we bantered our way through grief.

"This is real. Now. I want real advice."

"What do you want to know? It's all about the Man—energy revolves around the Man. Jones is the craving. It's about the ritual as much as it's about the drug. You have a jones, you find the Man."

"How much does it cost to feed a habit?"

"I don't know—ten dollars a bag? Rachel. Lesson over. I'm not a junkie. If you're so keen to know, snort a tiny bit. You're not going to get addicted off a tiny bit. Someone who's got the habit really wants to numb a life. I think you have to try it fifty times before you start to form a habit."

"Remind me not to let you baby-sit my kids. Get serious. What do you know about withdrawal?"

"Stand outside a methadone clinic on East Broadway and watch people."

"Ask a junkie nodding off, foaming at the mouth, Yeah so what happens next? What do *you* know about it?"

"You sweat and puke and scream. What else is there to know? Where's your friend living? Seriously, maybe you should call her parents and get her into a treatment center."

"*He* has no money. He has no parents."

"Who's he?"

"Stuart Gibbs, the guy who got shot."

"Come again? This isn't another sniper on Fifth Avenue yarn—"

"He's resurfaced. The roommate I saw dead in Australia." I started to sniffle. Jesus, hurry up, Frank. Tell me what to do. A few seconds to internal combustion.

"You trying to bug me out? Get the fuck out of here."

And into outright bawling.

"Rachel? You okay? Take a breath. What the fuck is going on? What can I do?"

"Can you come over?" I impaled out of my mouth. "Maybe we can have him go cold turkey here."

"Oh shit, you can't do that there. Are you crazy? I'll come over but—"

"I'm in over my head. Stuart was given money to pretend he was dead."

"This is the craziest thing I've—"

"He has no money and he's strung out on Mom and Dad's bed and he needs to get off of it or everyone I know is going to be thrown in jail."

"He's in Mom and Dad's bed? Are you out of your fucking mind? You know what you're getting into? Addiction is vile—this shit's nasty. Brice went through this hell with his cousin Tim. Quitting cold is a nice concept, on paper. Tim tried shooting up anything he could get his hands on. Coffee. Laundry detergent—"

"Laundry detergent?"

"Christ, Rachel, I'm in the middle of stretching canvas—okay, here's my RX—take everything out of the apartment, install a drain in the center of Mom and Dad's room, taper the walls, throw meat in, lock the door, and hose the fucker down every two days."

I didn't respond. Frank hates that even more than my high emergency pitch. In our Jewish-Italian family, silence is the ultimate SOS.

"Oh, fuck, fine, I'll bike over. You shouldn't be alone with him. Give me time to shit and shave. I'll be there in forty minutes."

I brightened a tad. I wasn't going this alone.

"If nothing else, I'll get my comics out of there. I don't want your resurrected smack addict selling off my *Fantastic Four* number forty-eight, the first appearance of the Silver Surfer."

"Frank, please, we have to get him sober—" In times of true duress, I am known to outright squeak.

"Don't make that sound. The guy sounds like a loser—he's already dicked you around. And this isn't about getting sober, Rachel. He's an addict. He could hurt you. Keep him calm. Offer him milk or something."

Just about the second I clicked the receiver, Stuart rolled into the kitchen with a rank odor and a three-day stubble. He'd put his greasy jeans back on and a red T-shirt I knew from Melbourne. Christ. This was real. "There's Raisin Bran and *milk*, if you want it."

"Raisin Bran? You mean Sultana Bran?"

"Americans eat Raisin Bran." I stared at him like Elliot the morning after he found ET. I passed him the box, the milk, a bowl, and a teaspoon. He didn't touch anything.

"I'm skint. Could I bot a twenty off you 'til I see you next? I'll be out of your sight this afternoon."

Why did I care one iota about saving this cretin's soul? Where was his fabled relative in Buffalo? Goddamn. "You're not going to live on twenty dollars. You need help. Remember last night, you asked me for help?"

"You were good to put me up here, but I'm leaving."

"You're in no position to leave for anywhere. Where are you going to go? My brother's coming over to help us sort this through—"

"You talked about this?"

"Listen to me will you? Frank's cool. He's an artist. His best friend's cousin went through an addiction—"

But Stuart was already in the living room, packing his army surplus knapsack.

I yelled from the kitchen: "I'm going to help you, Stuart! Don't you see I need to help you?" I stood there, pulling my fingers as far back as I could. When I came out to take a look, Stuart was riding my Dad's rusting exercise bike at about five miles per hour, staring out the window onto Avenue of the Americas.

The phone rang. Divine intervention? "Glad I got you, Rachel," Selena from Temp Solution said. "I have another job for you. I think it should last about two weeks. It's not glamorous, but the pay is seventeen dollars an hour because they're in such a bind."

"What is it?" I said, breathing hard, one eye on the door. I wanted to be sure that Stuart wasn't going to bolt.

"At a nice private school, Friends Seminary on Sixteenth Street

—the lunch staff's on strike. They need someone to serve hot food to the students."

"Selena, that was the school I went to for eight years, I don't think I could do that."

"You shouldn't be proud. That's loads of money for moving some spoons around. We're in a recession. Everyone needs the money."

"Look, I'm not proud, but I won't cross a picket line." Bullshit, Rachel, you'd die before being seen in a hair net by one of your old teachers. "But Stuart, a friend of mine who's visiting New York, he'd take it." I heard the bike noise stop.

"From out-of-town? Is he American?"

"No, but—"

"Working papers?"

"No—"

"Sorry, we couldn't help him. You don't want the job?"

"Yeah. Please call me though with other work."

"Okay, but I have to tell you that the people who accept every job get called more often." She hung up. Cow. Stuart was sitting on the couch now. I put on a game show, and we sat there in silence.

Eventually, I heard the lock turning. Frank propped his bike up in the hallway.

"Is he still here?"

"On the couch."

"So, you going to introduce me to the French Connection?"

"Shh!"

Frank poked his head into the living room. I have a proud feeling when anyone meets my brother. He's actually very average looking, five nine, brown eyes, a slightly pointy nose. But even when he had his retainer, cats ran to his lap. Sideburns hadn't come back into style yet. (They'd be in the next year.) But Frank had them now, long black rectangles.

"Stuart, isn't it? Frank—Rachel's brother."

"Yeah."

"So how's it going?"

Stuart shrugged his shoulders.

"I hear you're a drug addict."

Stuart looked to me to protect him from this strange creature with no mercy. No way, Problem Child. Frank is Easy Street compared to other fates I could have thrown your way.

"First trip to New York, right?"

"Yeah—" What do heroin addicts think of between injections? Stuart was so expressionless I thought his head might be empty except for where to get his next purchase. A mindless loop. See worm. Catch worm. Raise wings. Fly. See worm.

"Rachel tell you I'm an artist? I'm picking up some comics I have in my old desk. I want to be inspired when I start my new piece. Lichtenstein made a million bucks off his comic book collection, right?"

No response from our mute. Anesthetized existence, no Art 101 under his belt, downright intimidation, all three.

"Talkative, huh? I was going to take Rachel out for lunch, to calm her down. She's freaked out over your arrival—and you don't want her going off the rails, yeah? Want to join us?"

"I can't afford any restaurants, ta."

"Ta? What's *ta*?"

Stuart looked confused. He was in no shape to comprehend that lower-class Australian is as much a dialect to Americans as Northern Territory pidgin is to Melbournians.

"*Ta* is 'thanks' in Australian," I said quietly, the UN translator.

"Ta? Yeah, well, it's my treat. Why don't you? I'm not a priest, man. No jive from me." Frank's street talk was embarrassing, but as always, somehow he carried it off to great effect.

"You're paying? Yeah, sure."

"Throw something else on, man—it's fucking cold out there for April. Let me pick up my comics from the back. I should be able to dig up something warm for you from the closet. My mother never let us throw out anything. Depression-survivor mentality."

Stuart slipped on Frank's old double-layered RISD sweatshirt. My brother carried his precious cargo with him—The Silver Surfer was safe. The three of us went out for lunch at the local Greek coffee shop.

"So let me get this straight," Frank said, taking a sip of ice water. "The head of the morgue pretended you were dead?"

"Yeah," Stuart said, grabbing a roll.

"This guy Colin has goddamn chutzpah."

"New York for audacity," I translated.

"What's audacity?" Stuart asked.

"Fucking nerve," I tried again. That got a small smile from Mr. Gibbs. "What do you want, Stuart?" Frank said when the waitress came over.

Stuart looked nervous again. His eyes were watery. "Your call."

Oh, right. He couldn't read the menu. At home, he could have faked it by ordering a basic Australian standby, like a hamburger topped with a fried egg. "You can get a great cheeseburger here," I said, a shield for further embarrassment.

"Nah," Frank said. "I know. We'll have three *cold turkey* sandwiches."

Stuart again raised the slightest corner of his mouth, John Lennon–style. Frank was breaking through, talking to Stuart like a regular Australian mate, ignoring the sheila, the woman, *me*, at the table.

"Man, that was some crap you pulled on my sister."

"Rachel wasn't part of it."

"How can you say that? You see how out of whack she is. The way I see it, bro, she's an accomplice if she doesn't turn you in. I think my sister's pretty fucking nice offering to help you out—"

"Yeah, well—"

"Pity you're splitting town. We could've saved your ass. My best friend's cousin went cold turkey last year. I know how it's done."

Frank had pulled the one-armed bandit and come up with three cherries. Stuart took the bait. "Where's your friend's cousin now?"

"It was rough. But he's off the shit. Started his life over. Think he even has a job now. At a magazine. Rachel, what's that magazine Tim's at?"

I never even met Tim. "*Life*."

"He works for *Life*?"

"Yeah," Frank said, with a frown that said I should have picked a more reasonable life jump, like *Guitar World*.

Gold at the end of the strung out rainbow. Why were we feeding him this? We wanted this so badly?

"We could use my place for you to chill," Frank offered.

Suddenly Frank was caught up in my plan. I wished I knew what it was. I felt like we were side characters in a *Mod Squad* episode, Frank's favorite show when we were kids. He even had the metal lunchbox. Frank looked at my hands. I was torturing my knuckles again, pulling fingers back until they almost broke off. He gave me a "stop that" head motion. "Rachel, is there anyone else you trust? We would need to take shifts. I'd have Brice help us, but he's back in London."

"There's Janet. She's discreet."

"I don't know about a chick watching me eat meself up." Stuart tapped out a hesitant rhythm on the counter.

Frank ribbed me under the table. He was reeling the fish in. Lucky us. "You'll like Janet," Frank said. "Unlike Rachel's other friends, she's not a motormouth."

"I don't know."

"Great ass," Frank said. "Janet's ni-iicce."

"Right, send her over." Stuart leaned over toward him. "I'm going to need your help, man." Aussies don't say man, they say mate; that stereotype holds true. This male bonding was obscene.

When Stuart went to the bathroom, I leaned over to Frank. "Do you have to bring yourself down to his level?"

"It worked, right? I know how men think."

When Stuart returned, the three of us agreed that we would get the Ganelli detox unit rolling in two days. Frank promised Stuart that he would take him down to Clinton Street to secure last-hurrah smack for the evening. My job was to prevail upon Janet to join our Florence Nightingale junkie crusade.

"Hi, bit of banana in my mouth, sorry," Janet said.

"Yo, dig the fruit-in-cheek greeting," I said, and I meant it; answering the phone like that was out of character for her.

"Hey, where've you been? I thought you were dead—"

"Sorry about not returning your calls. I've been in hiding. I forgot how brutal this city is."

"The vortex of depression. You okay now?"

"Uh, somewhat. Do you think I could come over for a bit?"

"The place is a pigsty." Janet's idea of a pigsty was a sweater arm hanging out of an armoire. (We had lasted three seconds as college roommates. Veemah had fared better with the Queen of Neat; I was the one forced out of the freshmen triple for being a slob.)

"Not likely," I said.

"I guess I could vacuum. How long are you going to be?"

"Half an hour?"

"Don't forget those photos of Australia. It's been two months and I haven't seen what your roommates looked like."

How about dinner with the dead one who washed up in a bottle? "There's maybe one roll. I wasn't on vacation in Australia. I was—"

"Running away?"

"Look, whatever. I have bizarre shit to throw your way, so be prepared."

"You're going to leave me hanging on tenterhooks, aren't you? I hate when you do that. You can't tell me now?"

"I'd rather not." This mess needed the exact psychological moment.

• • •

I looked at the clock. I planned on leaving for Janet's house in twenty minutes. Her parents had bought her the top floor of an 1880s Eleventh Street brownstone when she graduated. Her folks lived back in Montecito, an old-money suburb of posh-to-begin-with Santa Barbara. Janet's relatives back East had relayed the suitable block for her to live on in the Big Apple.

When I visited their home sophomore Thanksgiving break, Janet's father told me that he encouraged his daughter to go to a school back East so she could explore her genteel heritage. The Alexanders had an ancestor from Casanovia, New York, the one proper suburb in the blue-collar city of Syracuse. On this thread of history, Janet accepted a spot at the family Alma Mater Syracuse University, now "known" for a preponderance of spoiled girls from Long Island. Regardless of ethnicity, the prominent faction of girls there were uniformed in big banana hairclips, Champion sweatshirts over leggings, and Timberland boots. They were derided as JAPs, Jewish American Princesses. Girls who studied food science (cooking), or retail management (shopping).

I used *JAP* several times during a university break, and my mother was shaken. "You're half Jewish and worse than an anti-Semite!" I couldn't believe how flipped out she got. My father joined her: "It's a degrading word, Rachel. Plenty of Italians and WASPs and Irish kids are spoiled rotten, too. And you're no innocent. Look where you're going to school. After Columbia offered you that generous physics scholarship."

I continued to sit in the kitchen, preparing myself to go tell Janet that the sky had fallen. I had indeed been a brat. My City

College–educated parents wanted me to go Ivy, my college counselor wanted me to go Ivy, but I wanted to go to Syracuse. There
was a strong film and television program there, a discipline too
garish for the Ivies. I made my point something fierce, even though
Columbia offered a free ride if I was willing to live at home. "Syracuse is willing to give me a fifty-percent scholarship if I dual major
in physics. They need more women in science journalism," I said,
a blatant attempt to win over my father, who maintained that commercial TV was crass. "I could become a science ambassador, like
Carl Sagan."

I was frozen in a meditative stare at one of Frank's high school
paintings, an abstract canvas that won him his RISD graphics
scholarship—three amorphous bodies in reggae-bright oils. Frank
had pointed out the figures when he hung it up: my red wailing father cradling my purple dead grandmother's head, my orange
mother staring toward the viewer's perspective. Frank told my
folks that it was called *Family Portrait*.

I'd realized that senior year of high school that after years of
private schooling for my brother and me, even half-off expenses
would be tough going for my family. We were the last of a dying
breed in dichotomous rich-poor Manhattan. An outsider might
think that we enjoyed a cushy upper-crust existence. But to a New
Yorker in the know, a different story was evident. The civil servants
and labor-leader middle class in our building bought their apartments eons ago, before the eighties boom. Give up a New York
apartment? Not my neighbors. Any new faces were subletters, and
they were almost always a neighbor's niece or a friend's son.

Middle-class families like ours sent their kids to private school only after giving up on a P.S., a public school, maelstroms of black versus white tension in the late sixties and early seventies.

In real time, I was crushing Domino Dots with the handle of a steak knife.

Mom had cried when she and Dad pulled Frank and me out of our public grade school; we were the only white children left and racial tension was getting out of hand. "If the Democrats don't have hope," she said, "this city is screwed."

I put my denim jacket back on, getting ready to go to Janet's. Why did Frank know about Clinton Street? I would think that you could get heroin in Washington Square Park, where men in black caps whisper "sens, sens," short for sensilmillia, a potent kind of pot. But then Frank always knew the crevices of Manhattan. The Sunday I got back from Australia, the magazine section of *The New York Times* ran a puff piece on The Best Slice in New York. Frank told me about a five-star pizza joint that the author failed to ferret out, one adjacent to a blini store out in Brighton Beach. "In the City," he said, "there's always a better slice if you do the legwork." I looked at the clock. Ten of. Time to go.

The well-heeled brownstone rentals from University Place across to Seventh Avenue and from Eighth Street up to Thirteenth Street are for the most part leased to ex–Ivy leaguers and Seven Sisterites who brand themselves hip. I'd never pinpointed this until I'd started dating Will. I would go to a party thrown by one of Will's buddies from Dartmouth, or one his buddies' Vassar alumna girlfriends, and inevitably the address would fall within this five block radius—only blocks away from my mammoth brick building teeming with fifty-ish Italian women in big curlers throwing Hefty bags down the incinerator chute. New York is like that. One street can divide whole classes.

In the elevator ride down, I remembered that three years prior—while rinsing out the Epcot mug I'd received from my shared secretary in the Bell Press kitchen sink—I'd fancied myself the anthropologist. I'd spent my whole life trying to be like those people, I thought: upper crust. But their apartments all had the same cloying details. An exotic mask from a primitive tribe like the Asmat of New Guinea, the last Stone Age people discovered, who now fly commuter planes in Adidas shorts with bones in their noses. The women who lived on those social registrar–approved streets installed imposing books as interior decoration—*Seven Plays* by Henrik Ibsen, perhaps, propped up against a vase of lavender pruned from Mom and Dad's weekend estate. The men used nice stationery from Italy, or box sets of Navajo-blanket greeting cards they bought at the Met. Men with nice stationery irritate me.

With another four-and-a-half excruciating hours to the end of the work day, I had lost myself in my "fieldwork"—christening the district the Ivy Ghetto. I doodled a map of the Ivy Ghetto over a report on likely suspects to contribute a chapter for Bell's particle accelerator journal. Why did I hate them so much? I'd lived twenty-five years of a life of enormous privilege. Not ski trips to the Alps, maybe, but private schools, trips to Yosemite.

While walking the few blocks that separated Janet and me, I decided that in retrospect, none of the highbrow crowd was that terrible. Some members were scholarship kids who had worked hard as hell to get where they were. I'd been covetous, if I had to name the exact word—despite my early private schooling, my acceptance to Columbia, and my continued ticket to peripheral blue-chip existence via engagement to Will. I was jealous, but at my core I never wanted any of it.

Janet answered the door in a pastel-yellow polo and madras shorts, her straight strawberry blond hair in a ballet-school chignon. "So what's so urgent? Do you want a nosh?"

Janet didn't mean nosh like a Borscht Belt comedian ordering a bagel with a smear. She was employing it in its English usage. She'd spent her first summer after college abroad in a centuries-old cottage rented by her parents, and ever since had peppered her sentences with Anglish-isms. Bangers instead of sausage. Porridge instead of oatmeal. And then there was her precise language. Spearmint, never simply mint. Or a hint of camphor or cedar; nothing ever smelled "nice" to Janet. A study in contradictions—that's why I liked her. A proper girl who in her quiet way was as much a tawdry film nut as me.

"I'll take a soda if you have it."

"Sprite?"

"Sure." I popped back the tab and poured a few inches into the glass. She swooped up my can like a bird of prey. Yes. This was the confidante Frank and I needed. There wasn't a speck of mess anywhere. Janet would put my slipshod life in order. "I'm in a bind, Jay. I need you to hang out with one of my roommates visiting from Australia."

"Did Frieda put you up to this? I told her to stop trying to fix me up. I may be dateless, but I'm not desperate."

"No, I wish that's what I'm asking—no, I'm going to need you—"

"I've never heard you ask me for anything. This must be big stuff."

"It's complicated. I'm trusting you won't tell anyone anything—especially not Frieda and Veemah."

"You know me better—what could you need me for anyway?" I waited as Janet nervously retrieved her hamster Harry from his habitat, scratching his ears and under his chin. His little rodent face was in ecstasy.

"Well, the reason I came home was—well my Aunt Lillian wasn't ill—I left because I witnessed a murder—"

"Get out—"

"One of my roommates was killed by the mob." I had never phrased it this way before, even to Frank; it sounded ludicrous. I meant to cry but I broke into a peculiar half-smile.

"Stop, Rachel, you're a terrible liar. This is like your shameless story, the one where your boss offers you a stick of gum while a loony is shooting at your office."

"Listen. I'm not going to argue that one anymore. I was telling you my roommate got shot by the mob."

"Uh-huh."

"It wasn't a murder after all. I was duped. So was half of Australia. Two of my roommates made a satanic pact with the third one, who got shot. A complete set-up. He gets dead, and they get the murder on tape during the filming of their video. Instant fame." My voice cracked by the end of the full histrionic explanation.

After a few still moments, Janet had convinced herself that I wasn't shitting her. She was out of tissues and opened a drawer in the coffee table, and handed me a roll of Charmin. "Wow."

"No kidding."

"What do you need my help for then? I'm scared to ask."

"Look, Frank or I would be with you always. Remember that Otto Preminger flick in Sy Cooper's class—*The Man with the Golden Arm*? Everyone kind of sat guard—"

"You want me to be *there* with you?"

"Uh, yeah," I said. "Frank's going to be doing the ugly stuff." I wished I knew what I meant by that sentence.

"Frank's in charge?" She widened her eyes in contemplation. Janet had always had a bit of a crush on Frank, but then so did Veemah and Frieda. Frank was flirtatious with everyone, even Mom. Before he moved to Minnesota, where Ingrid had him locked away from his many fans, any combination of my gaggle of friends might run into him in the park while he was shooting some hoops. His adventurous spirit was infectious; he might have treated "his girls" to "out-of-this-world wheat noodles only a ferry ride away" in Staten Island. "I ask you, Ladies, which would you prefer for three bucks—a greasy Big Mac in midtown, or a scenic boat ride and a tasty platter of Malaysian food?"

Janet has that unfortunate Anglo-thin skin that tears like mica. Her cat, trying to get at the hamster, scratched her lightly; blood dripped from Janet's arm. She hit the cat rather hard on its cheek, which made me wince.

"Whatever you need me to do," Janet said. Was she angry or scared? "I'm on vacation this week."

Janet and I were surrounded by pink, tan, and black dildos of ridiculous lengths and widths. We were waiting near the counter at the Pink Pussycat, an erotic gift shop favored by the weekend bridge-and-tunnel crowd. Stuart had had the noble idea of handcuffing himself to one of Frank's wooden bedposts. "Then I won't kill one of you in a no-dope frenzy," he'd said. Captain Frank thought it would be a good idea to have Stuart help shape his own withdrawal program, like a dieter developing his own 1200-calorie menus.

The middle-age saleswoman with a studded dog collar was serving a biker who was buying Edible Undies.

"Such bathos this afternoon," Janet whispered. *Bathos* was one of Janet's distinctive words; she'd picked it up from her granduncle, who'd been a Princeton authority on Lewis Carroll. Janet always thought that I was a magnet for bathos. (The first time she said it, I thought she was implying that I was pathetic. I took great offense.)

"A nice addition," the saleswoman suggested, "might be Emotion Lotion. Rub it in, blow on it—it makes your partner's skin hot and tingly." The biker put a drop on his inner arm and blew.

"Great," he agreed, choosing a lime rickey flavor. She added it to his bill.

"And what can I do for you girls?" the saleswoman asked.

"We'd like handcuffs," I said.

"We have a selection over in the counter. The more expensive ones are stronger."

"We'll need strong ones," I said. She slid open the counter

glass and pulled out a red metal pair. She reached for my wrists and locked me in, passing Janet the key to undo me. "Fine. How much?"

"Those are $39.99."

"Okay, we'll take them." Janet wasn't saying a word, she was fidgeting with a lipstick molded to resemble a penis tip.

"Would you like anything else?"

"No."

"You girls might like a strap-on. The Boss is on sale."

"No, thank you," I said.

"Very well. Enjoy yourselves, girls."

"A strap-on?" Janet said a few minutes later, on the corner of Seventh Avenue South.

"A cock on a belt."

"Why would you want that?"

I laughed and licked her ear puppy-style. Through college, I'd liked to shock her with my bravado—she'd been an easy target to unnerve. The passing mailman didn't even flinch. "She thought we were dykes."

Janet grimaced as she wiped her ear with her finger, but she started smirking about a block later.

"What?" I asked.

"You'd be on top, you know."

"Duh—like that's why she was asking me about the Boss," I said, in perfect Valley Girlese. We snickered most un-PC-ly until we got to the corner and I extracted the handcuffs from the pull-string bag.

"He's going to lock himself in?" Janet asked to the ground. "And then what happens?"

That sobered us up.

After Frank had secured Stuart's left arm to the bed-post, I handed over the universal remote. Stuart decided on the *Young and the Restless*. Not a mystery there: Phillip and Stuart had been out-and-out *Y & R* addicts back in Australia. Australian episodes were four years behind. (It would have spoiled the fun for them if I'd revealed the fate of a villain, so I'd kept quiet.) Stuart's eyes were glued to the Olympic-spaced time warp as we locked him in. "Wait? Lauren's kidnapped? Bloody hell."

Frank spread out the Scrabble board on the far side of the loft. The two of us set up behind an old pale-blue sheet with blood stains from my first eighth-grade bungled tampon/Vaseline experiment. (I'd soaked that sucker for two hours, but it had been ruined and was used as a last resort back-up linen, never for company.) Frank had taken it from the back of the linen closet over at my folks' place and thumbtacked it to his ceiling so Stuart could have a bit of privacy.

"That sheet has stains, Frank. It's gross. Why don't you drape something else up?"

"This isn't the time to fret about interior decorating, Bozo."

"Fine," I snapped. "Let me keep score."

Playing Scrabble without Aunt Virginia for competition felt odd. It was a pastime Frank and I had shared with her since the days when she'd picked us up from Sunday school. Frank treated the game as an extension of Dada: never mind the rules. Aunt Virginia, however, was a consistent true match. For a God-fearing Catholic, she was a board-game mercenary, having memorized every two- and three-letter word in the dictionary like *ai*, a three-toed sloth, and *ich*, the fish disease. I liked to win and had no problem putting down a mundane word if it gave me maximum points. The three of us played numerous matches the year before I left for Australia. (My Dad was in the hospital for a week with chest pain that later turned out to be gas. Every once in a while Will joined the game, but mostly he found the aunt/niece rivalry ugly. But Aunt Virginia and I valued the distraction of combat. Every clan has its rites, no matter how trivial.)

For the previous seven years I almost always put down JEW for my first word. Even Aunt Virginia would laugh at this mysterious coincidence. If anything was ever going to get me back into a house of worship, it was my deific draws. It was as if fate had a trusty yellow highlighter and continuously underlined our family's sore point.

With Stuart chained to his post on the far side of the sheet, I looked over my current letters: W T O O O E J. I gasped. I lay JEW down across the middle pink star.

"Get out of here! Again?"

I wrote down "26" on the pad. Frank shook his head. "I'm calling fucking Ripley's. Anyhow, isn't *Jew* proper?"

"I've told you ten times, Frank. You can use it as a verb—jew down. It's in my regulation Scrabble dictionary."

"That's awful. Mom would have you fucking re-bat-mitzvahed if she knew you use *jew* as a verb."

I checked on Stuart for a second while Frank contemplated his next draw. With his left arm raised and fastened to the headboard, Stuart looked the lost cause, nodding to the last traces of junk.

"They've got to kill Michelle," Stuart said. Kill Michelle? The withdrawal was no doubt kicking in, making deranged words flow out of his mouth—like the New Orleans junker without his H in the William Burroughs book Frank had facetiously suggested I reread. But then it struck me that Stuart was still in TV land. I left him alone.

Janet rang the bell, dressed in a revealing black T-shirt and black leggings. I didn't know "Muffy" owned anything black other than a proper little cocktail dress.

"How is he?" she asked.

"Right now," Frank conceded, "he's surprisingly okay."

"Oh, well, I brought some chocolate pâté," Janet said, removing a small mason jar from her public television tote bag.

Chocolate pâté?

"Sounds delicious," Frank said. "Is that the new Milan Kundera book?"

She brought a book?

"It's a wonderful read."

"You read such interesting things, Janet. Let me get a pen, you might as well write down a few titles for me while we have the time."

Frank spooned out pâté for each of us. I gave her that fucking book. And before that, Frank had given it to me, when I first got back from Melbourne. My territory problem was flaring up again. "I think we're forgetting our mission, guys."

"Of course. Can I meet him?"

Frank handed me a scoop; I let it melt on my tongue as I pushed past the sheet to the bedside of our very own Elephant Man. "Stuart, you want to meet Janet?"

He smelled my breath. "I think I'm going to sleep until the craving hits. Can I have some of that chocolate?"

I went to get him a spoonful of Janet's pâté. "He's not too bad, really, he wants to sleep though. I'm going to give him some chocolate."

"Is that okay to give him?"

"Let him have anything he wants," Frank said. "Though I thought you can't sleep when you're going off heroin."

I went back to hand him the pâté, which he ate in a drowsy state. I quietly left the room. Frank had resumed our game, with Janet as scoremaster, and vertically laid down E-S-S for JEWESS.

"Excellent, Frank," Janet said.

"That's such a waste of your esses," I jeered.

"But it's a cool word. It *looks* good," Frank said.

"It's proper anyway," I said. Frank removed the letters and put down SKID.

When the game was over, I went to check on the patient, who had finally fallen asleep. *Live at Five* was on, the gossipy news with Sue Simmons. Jimmy Stewart was promoting a book of poems, and Sue had allergies.

"Gazun-tight," Jimmy Stewart said after his introduction.

I sat down for a moment in a chair splattered with dried blue paint drips. I twirled the handcuff key ring like a top. I wasn't sure what was coming next. Why wasn't anything climatic happening?

Wasn't Stuart supposed to twist and moan and attempt to scrape his eyes out?

I heard the phone ring. "Oh hi, Virginia." Frank calls my aunts by their first names only. He finds the word *aunt* embarrassing.

"No, Rachel went away to her friend's weekend house. No, don't worry—she's fine—a little blue, she's looking for a job. I'll tell her you asked after her."

"Anything new in there?" Frank called.

"Not yet."

Frank insisted that Janet should stay. I went back to the smackhead-saver part of the loft again and could tell in a glance that Janet was pleased with Frank's extra attention. Take a number, girl.

After an hour, Janet offered to check up on Stuart—we hadn't heard a sound. "Oh shit!" she screamed from the other side of the blood-stained sheet.

6

Rachel: LOW

The first month after I had joined Bell Press, Gordon Christopher, the President, called me to his office and handed me airline tickets for a conference in Pittsburgh. I was expected to convince Benno Heilbronn, a Nobel-laureate physics pioneer, to put his name atop the masthead of an embryonic academic journal. Gordon didn't wanted Heilbronn to edit *Particle Accelerator Quarterly*, he only wanted Heilbronn's name there and was willing to pay $10,000 a year for it. The journal was going to a handful of universities—because this was rare and knotty technical knowledge, my company had felt it was fair for a four-issue subscription to cost $15,000. It cost a few thousand dollars to print and mail the issues, so Bell was aiming to make $75,000 a year on only five subscriptions. They had almost 200 journals set up with those kinds of ridiculous subscription rates. *The Journal of Vacuum Physics* —eighty-five libraries at $8,000 per year; *The Journal of Neuralphysical Electrodynamics*—thirteen subscriptions at $11,000 a pop. These journals paid the bills for the book division. And the science-center librarians fell in line; the campus research teams knew they would be up shit creek if they missed scholastic developments. If that meant the slashed-budget library had to forgo a new copier or three work-study students, so be it. And Bell annually increased the rate by ten percent; we had them all by the balls. Keisha, my lunchmate from accounting who had secretively lined up another job, gave me the lowdown when I bitched to her about Will's considering a major PR job offer at a tobacco company. Even so, I failed to ride off into the sunset on my high horse: I kept my mouth shut and didn't leave Hades on Third Avenue for two more years. Will never took the cigarette job, God bless his sanctified soul.

"It would be an honor to have you listed," I'd said to Heilbronn. "You're the inspiration to so many young physicists." I followed that up with more sticky-sweet praise.

He kept switching topics from my flattery to physic theories. He was amazed that I double-majored in physics and film/television.

"But you really know the theories?" he pressed, ignoring the contract still unsigned by the water glass. While I wasn't ever going to get a medal draped around my neck in Stockholm, I could hold my own with sound bites.

To hawk the new journal, I had worn a low-cut dress to lunch —which Heilbronn wasn't ignoring as he ascertained how much I knew about alternative universes. (My boss had confided in a barely-shy-of-a-sexual-harassment voice that the seventy-five-year-old physics star was a notorious chest man.) Heilbronn was a firm believer in what is called the Many Worlds Interpretation, an idea first put forth in the 1950s. In every situation, the choices you face offer roads into infinite universes. Every universe that can exist, the theory goes, does exist.

"Perhaps," Heilbronn said, "in a distant era, mankind will laugh at theories like isolating alternative universes and harnessing cosmic strings for time travel—like we scoff at chariots holding up the world." I copied his poetic words in my confidence-prop notebook. Heilbronn turned his head ninety degrees to read his words on the page, and smiled at me.

"In another universe, Rachel, I'd sign that contract and not worry about screwing over the libraries. Listen, sweetheart, I'm a righteous old man with arthritis and a bit of fame, and I'm not going to sign that paper. I have to wake up every morning as a righteous old man with arthritis and a bit of fame. But that's the world I accept to be true. I get up, look in the mirror, and seem to think I was there before."

I thought Heilbronn remarkable. But when I had told this story to Colin, early on in our friendship, before we ever rubbed toiletries on each other's body parts, he'd said, "Yeah, but how come the righteous bastard didn't tell you not to waste your humiliating pitch before lunch? I'd say he wanted a longer peek at those New York knockers." At that, he'd leaned over the Safeway shopping cart to leer down my shirt, and I retaliated with a grab at his crotch.

That night I dreamed Alternate Universe #87239: I'd carelessly left the handcuff key ring near the floor by the chair. Stuart eyed it when he woke up, and released himself. He'd filched Frank's wallet out of a pocket of my brother's bad-ass seventies-style quilted leather jacket draped over a chair. We attempted to track Stuart down through the seediest streets of New York, with an obligatory stop at Clinton Street, the area where Frank had taken Stuart for his final score. No one remembered Stuart crawling back to the site, but one of the dealers asked Frank if he wanted his regular nose candy, and it now made sense how he knew to take Stuart down there in the first place. The dealer's question would taint my respect for Frank for many years to come. But Stuart the drug addict, that fuck of a puck, had disappeared into the night. Over time my whole foray to Australia was erased, like a stray mark on a sheet of Corrasable typing paper, and with it my memories of a far-off mysterious place brimming with glorious horrors and marvels. Like Alice and Dorothy, I moved on. I married an architect and lived by the sea.

But in the universe I accepted to be real (because the next day I knew I was there before), the reason Frank knew about the methadone clinic on East Broadway, and Clinton Street's menu of goodies, is because he was and always will be the self-appointed King of Things I Know That You Don't Know. And Stuart was still an illiterate heroin addict chained to the King's bed. I'd left the key ring on the floor, but Stuart didn't see anyone or anything when he'd woken up except Lucifer and his horned buddies. There's a gun under the mattress, quick—rewind and shoot the bored girl waiting for something to happen.

When Frank and I raced to see why Janet had screamed, we saw behind the sheet a feverish, shivering, terrified young man, gnawing his cheeks, choking on chocolate pâté vomit. My one comfort as I think back to that horrifying afternoon, is that Sy Cooper, my *Cinema in the Age of Television* professor, would have loved this universe. Sy would have had his other class (Frieda's

Tuesday video-production seminar) re-create it with the slow 360-degree pan. Instead of callow mafioso dons-in-training, however, the filmgoer would see three cocky kids of privilege, the sort of kids who studied Film Noir's and Cinema Verite's shadows and angles, shocked out of their cocooned, referenced existence.

Janet had crouched on the floor; the two of us were paralyzed, deer in headlights. Frank's olive complexion, from the Ganelli side of the family, looked greener. He recovered quickest (of course) and found rubber gloves by the sink with which to clear Stuart's face and throat of his possibly HIV-infected, fudge-colored vomit. I cleaned the floor near the bed with a squeegee mop and rinsed it out by the shower stall. The mop was propped up in a bucket of dirty water for a month afterward, a cat-o'-nine stalk emerging from the millpond.

"You're going to pull through this, man," Frank said. He didn't look so sure. Stuart was oblivious with withdrawal. Janet looked like she wanted to go home. She asked Frank if he thought it was okay to unchain Stuart. Frank nodded. We knew he wasn't going anywhere, and he was in enough pain.

I answered the ringing phone. Was it the Chinese food delivery guy, lost? It was my mother. Shit!

"Rachel? Didn't I call Frank? I'm getting ditzy these days. Better start looking into those nursing homes—"

"Not yet Mom, you did dial Frank. I'm hanging out with him this afternoon." Mom called over to Dad. "He's eating an orange on the porch. I have to send you and Frank a box. The honeybells from Spike's Grove are beautiful this year—here he comes—I have your daughter on the phone—can you believe it, Joe? The kids are 'hanging out.'" She got back on the phone. "That's great, honey. You two have had such rotten years. Family is important. But it's funny, Frank and Brice used to torture you, remember? Sticking bits of Slim Jim beef jerky in your after-school doughnuts. Those two were quite the brats. But you used to get your revenge. You'd bite your arm and say Frank did it."

"You knew?" I forced a little laugh, acknowledging with a tilt of my head the note Frank had slipped under my nose: "Don't Tell Her."

"I'm a woman. We have to stick together sometimes. Men are fucks."

"Thanks, belatedly."

"Anytime," she said, lowering her voice. "Do me a favor and don't tell Daddy that I sent you that extra $200. You're okay for money, right?"

"Yeah," I lied.

"Good." Her normal speaking voice resumed. "You're still sending your résumé out? Why don't you swallow your pride and call Bell Press?"

"I really don't want to work there again, Mom."

"Well you should be able to get a meaningful job when you put your mind to it. You always have. You're going to have to start paying the maintenance soon, kiddo. I'd be a bad mother if I didn't cut off the charity before you get lazy. Three more months, right?"

"Yep. A deal's a deal."

"Let's talk before Daddy and I leave for France. I'm letting

Frank know which bank has the safe deposit box—in case anything bad happens—you'd forget."

"Don't talk like that." In the background, Stuart was spewing
again.

"Better to be safe. When you're a mom you'll understand. Can
you put Frank on? Daddy and I haven't heard from him for ages."

Six hours later, Frank made us pancakes from an all-
in-one mix, while Janet held Stuart's hand. Janet had led him to the
bathroom; he had peed in the shower, the toilet too small a target.
He looked a millishade better, but in no condition to be left alone.
Frank had been right after all; we had to take turns working and
sleeping, like Grandpa Ganelli and the men of his immigrant met-
tle had.

"To earn money to send for their wives," Aunt Virginia once
explained, "three men would sign one lease and sleep in eight hour
shifts." The previous time she'd babysat for me and Frank, she'd
told us about the buckets of tomato skins Grandpa had fed hogs
back in Italy.

I stared at Frank's cutlery as he ate his stack of Aunt Jemimas.
His fork and knife had once been part of our everyday dinner set.
There were black bas-relief circles on their stems, a stainless design
to accompany our childhood 1970s orange-and-tan wallpaper.
When Frank was done eating, he put on the radio, pricking three
holes at a time into the empty blue Styrofoam plate with his fork.
The weak-signaled, cutting-edge station WFMU in East Orange,
New Jersey, was static hell to listen to; Frank's loft was less than a
mile from the World Trade Center's master antenna. I tuned the

radio to ninety-seven, which I knew would come in loud and clear. The only reason either one of us listened to mainstream radio was for its nonthreatening distraction from crisis. The New York market is too big for the alternative music we otherwise craved.

"In New York, it's more lucrative to be number four in the baby-boom market than number one for the post–Baby Boomers," a station sales executive had explained to me during my summer internship interview. Tony Fedele, the program director, wanted me to meet the whole staff; he was excited to have attracted such an overqualified candidate, the current president of a major university's school union, to fetch sandwiches for DJs. I even got to meet the infamous shock jock Howard Stern at the sister station across the hall, and he commented on-air that the new intern by the other elevator bank looked like Valerie Bertinelli, but with better bazoombies, and Gary his sidekick hummed the theme song from her old sitcom, *One Day at a Time.* The Adult Contemporary station had a clear-as-a-bell signal. It was owned by one of the Big Three networks, who probably acquired the license soon after Marconi put in his patent. The chief engineer said the two mega-stations could reach Florida under the right weather conditions.

I listened in the loft as Frank and Janet compared their assessments of Stuart's condition. The station played the same Mommas and Poppas song that had been in rotation the night I bid adieu to my internship and DJ-lover.

Stuart shat on the sheets. He'd been constipated since the night after I met him at Eisenberg's Sandwich Shop. Janet and

I rolled him over to change his linen. She put on the rubber gloves and wiped his ass with a dishrag.

"I'll do that, Janet," I said. "You're going a hell of a ways beyond the call of duty."

"It's not a problem." I loved her and her loyalty so much that I wanted to kill her. Janet had to go home to feed her pets, and I hugged her.

"I'll never judge you again."

"Rachel, you'll be judging me until you die. But it's okay. I know I pass muster." I had to hand it to her for that comment. She was getting down the New York stance.

I hated this all-in-one-pancake-mix world and told it so under my breath. Frank had passed out on a pile of pillows near his stereo. I took one of Frank's travel books from the bookcase that he carried off the street with a friend—*The Lonely Planet Guide to Chile*. I ran my finger down the string bean-y map in the front. Frieda once told me about a cultural story she'd been commissioned to produce for a Latino TV show, a freelance video assignment she'd gotten via her Argentinean step-aunt.

In Santiago a folksinger's arm was cut off during the 1974 military coup, in the middle of a stadium of his fans. The legend goes that he defiantly went back on stage after the soldiers did that, and played guitar with one arm. Then the fuckers shot him.

Frank had been to Chile once, and I went to see if he had a tape or CD by that guy on his rack. Victor something. Of course he did: Victor Jara. I listened to a song called "El Niño Yuntero," which the notes said means "child of the yoke." It was eerie and soothing.

Was Stuart catching my eye? No, he was grimacing into space. The two of us were exhausted.

I sunk into Frank's ten-dollar Salvation Army beanbag thinking about Sy Cooper, the month he learned he was going to be fired, the month he told me and Janet to harden our souls. Sy Cooper's favorite director was Mike Leigh who wasn't so well known then. It was hard for Leigh to attract a widespread audience for his relentless films about the underbelly of the U.K. While his characters are always no-hopers, Leigh never condemns them or puts them on a pedestal. There are bastards in the lower classes, and there are near saints. The hilarious scumbags are more interesting though. Sy revered Leigh, although not as much as he worshiped Scorcese. Sy was a minor ex-Beat who sold a few of his experimental eight-millimeter films of Jack Kerouac and Allen Ginsberg to the Museum of Modern Art. He was also an alcoholic.

After Sy Cooper was turned down for tenure, he decided to inflict a mini–Mike Leigh fest on my poor sucker of a class—three films sated with unsympathetic characters: *Nuts in May*, *Death*, and *Hard Labour*. To top off his ad hoc half-semester-long examination of Leigh's oeuvre of misery, Sy coupled *The Man with the Golden Arm*, the don't-use-heroin Frank Sinatra movie, with John Huston's *Fat City*, a dirge of a film about a boxer who's the toy of bad fortune. But for the last class, his piece-de-resistance: he screened *Shoah*, the harrowing nine-hour subtitled French documentary on the Holocaust, which we were required to sit through.

Janet and I sat next to each other during the film. Janet hunched over the desk in her Henri Grethel sweater, ready to puke at the next mention of a skeletal child. I touched her knee under my desk. "I'm going down with you," I wrote on the corner of my spiral notebook.

"You're not going to believe this, one of my grandparents was a Nazi, isn't that terrible?" Janet scribbled back in tight letters. I blinked theatrically. Was the all-American blood diluted?

"Were either of your Italian grandparents Fascists?" she whispered hopefully.

"In Brooklyn? Probably about the Dodgers," I said, not quite truthfully and loud enough for Sy to hear. The biggest family scandal had happened at my parents' wedding when my tipsy Grandma Chaika called Grandma Rosa's visiting cousin, Sergio, a murderer. According to my mother, my grandmas didn't speak to each other for five years.

I swear I saw a glint in Sy's eye when he sat down next to us in one of the many dropped-out student's seats and said, "Toughen up now, girls, or you'll be eaten alive." He was fired that summer for not adhering to the departmentally approved class outline. The establishment might say he wasn't teaching his students, but Janet and I knew that semester that we were witnessing his swan song.

I needed to toughen up. My ex-flatmate was a long way from recovery, but I had to go to work. I had twenty dollars left.

When Frank woke up, he took over as watchdog. I went downstairs to the corner of Bowery and Grand in search of cheap eats. I bought one-dollar bags of food from Chinese street stalls: broccoli, skinny purple eggplants, six hard-tofu slices, and a fish, species unknown.

I walked home to the apartment to water Mom's succulents, an emotional break from the loft drama. There were bills for the phone and my student loan payments, and a no-more-excuses jury notice with which I had to contend with in two weeks time. Thank God my parents were picking up the maintenance for another few months.

I played the one message: "Hi, girl, it's Veemah. I'm back again. I had to sit in on a new show in London."

Veemah and I had been the only two incoming freshman girls out of five thousand who'd checked both Physics and Media on our college roommate compatibility forms. I was envious of her vision; from the time she was fifteen she knew that she wanted to develop new planetarium shows. "I hear from Miss Frieda that you have a sexy houseguest from Australia. We're going to smoke you out if you don't call soon to fill us in."

I left a message. I knew she wouldn't be home. "Hi, Veemah, it's Frieda. I have a big mouth, and I don't know what I'm talking about. Call me."

I had to be back at the loft in an hour. I ate humble pie and called Temp Solution again.

"Rachel Ganelli? —Oh sure—you're still available for temping? I was sure by now you would have secured a full-time job with all that professional experience. Well, I have one job for thirteen an hour, there's no word-processing involved, but if you didn't want that school job—"

Okay, bitch, let's move this along. "Oh no, Selena. I'll take what you have. I'm in a bind for money. What does it entail?"

"Well, we don't send many people over there. You have to be ready to deal with it."

I didn't care what the job was. Broke is broke.

"It's a publishing group, but they have, well, pornographic magazines." When I didn't say anything she proceeded as if each word was being strung on jewelry wire. "They need a receptionist. The work isn't hard, but the last person we sent thought that the job was so demeaning that she walked by lunchtime. We haven't felt that there was someone adequately hardskinned to send over. I wouldn't have them as a client if I had a choice, but the owner's our vice president's cousin, and well, the work is yours for the asking."

"Is this *Playboy*?"

"You should be so lucky," Selena said almost sweetly.

Porno pics I can deal with—as long as I didn't have to venture out in that cafeteria hairnet.

I was supposed to work at Taitler Inc. for a week, until their receptionist returned from vacation. I made sure I wore the closest thing I had to a potato sack. The office was in a regular midtown glass tower on Madison Avenue, a leftover thousand feet of office space that the law firm on the floor hadn't yet gobbled up. There was no sign on the door that said TITS INSIDE. Just a plain brown plaque. I was told to ask for Greta, who turned out to be the office manager. A coiffed woman I'd mistake on a bus for a Park Avenue trophy wife.

"Have you been informed by your agency of the type of operation we are in?" Greta asked. She didn't want a repeat of the suffragette scene from the previous week.

"Yes, don't worry." I tried to look nonchalant. "I'm a regular sex shop customer," I said, which, considering my recent purchase with Janet, was mildly true. Greta looked at me for a second like I was a flasher. She showed me the key for the restroom in the desk drawer, demonstrated the straightforward phone system, and gave me a list of the employees and the fake names they used on the job. Harry Dershowitz was "Moe Turner." Sherri Ng was "Wendy Hurtz."

"You might get heavy-breathing calls," Greta warned, "but don't worry, it's horny teenagers who think there must be a naked woman on the other end of our subscription line." She handed me an assortment of Taitler Inc.'s magazines—in case adult book-stores called with orders. I looked them over while waiting for the aroused teen brigade to ring. The publications were, in a word, smut. A mag for every special interest perversion, a concept not unlike Bell Press's extremely specialized science journals.

For men obsessed with big butts, there was a periodical called *Cr-ASS*; women were still giving the standard blow-jobs and getting laid, but each photo was set up so that their behinds took up half the page. There was *Black Lesbo Pussy*, and *Shaved Pussy*. I gasped when I saw *Incest World*. One spread featured a bald middle-age man, with a nose discolored by either skin cancer or alcohol consumption, licking out a young girl's vagina. I swear I saw him in the office heading toward the water fountain, a forty-ish penny-loafered man who later introduced himself as the owner of the company.

"You're doing a great job," he said. "You'd be surprised how many girls can fuck up reception." I'd gone low before, but this was touching the core of the earth.

Instead of calling the FBI Child Porn taskforce, I calculated thirteen by thirty-five hours, thirty-seven point five if I took a half-hour lunch for the week, and grit my teeth. The money wasn't great, but I had Stuart to support for at least a little while. It wasn't fair to ask Frank to lay out money.

An assistant art director I recognized from Bell Press (a dim and tan-in-February bull who had once asked me if Ganelli was a Swedish name) appeared in the late afternoon to drop off freelance mechanicals. We pretended not to know each other.

Nine hours had elapsed back at the ranch; when I returned Stuart was sitting up. "Well, hi," I said, surprised. He had showered, too. I had interrupted Stuart and Frank in an instructional game of two-up, an Australian coin-tossing game that World War I soldiers, the diggers, had played to pass time. I guess Stuart thought an American quarter was an okay substitution. Frank had ordered another pizza.

"Hi," Stuart said, embarrassed. He was scratching himself on the arm.

I rested my butt near where they were sitting. Stuart still smelled metallic from withdrawal, with an extra whiff of apple pectin shampoo. "I didn't expect to see you up yet. What have you been talking about?"

"I told Frank about me dog Sylvester."

Stuart had a dog named Sylvester? In our two years as flat-mates, he told me three intimate facts: an almost boastful claim that his father was killed in Vietnam picking up a dead baby stuffed with a grenade (which I didn't believe); his heroin-teeth acknowledgment; and that he'd do anything for Melissa, the girl-friend who'd started him on the downward spiral. It wasn't the time for jealousy again, but did everyone always have to fall in love with Frank's charm?

"I was about to tell Stu about your turtle," Frank said, flipping the quarter—obviously not a good flip since Stuart took a hand-ful of Frank's jelly bean pile.

I tried to mimic Frank's easy style. It sounded forced. "Frank convinced me that turtles like merry-go-rounds and got me to leave Mertle on our turntable for hours. He died of dizziness, I think. My mother found my dead turtle spinning round and round."

Mom had made Frank explain to me that he had done a bad thing and that he was trying to fool me. She tried to follow the Quaker discipline model at our school—no corporal punishment, unlike Colin's Catholic school with its ruler-wielding nuns.

("They hit you for anything," he'd once said, tying up the kitchen garbage—Stuart had long abandoned his job responsibil-ities. "Sister Patricia once slapped my wrist for my tic acting up.")

When my Grandma Rosa insisted I go to Sunday school if I was going to go to Hebrew School, Mom made sure she found a class taught by a retired divinity professor who was too riddled with arthritis to hit us. Quakers want to be sure that their kids un-derstand what they did wrong; Frank and I learned early on a good bullshit story could get us out of anything.

"I loved that turtle," I said, and Stuart offered a sympathetic smile.

"But not as much as Brice loved Cookie," Frank added.

"Cookie?" Stuart asked.

"A fuzzy yellow chick my friend Brice took home from school when I was nine."

I hadn't thought of this in years.

"Cookie was hatched in our classroom incubator," Frank continued. "Everyone got to take a chick home for a few days, but Brice refused to bring his bird back. His divorced mother indulged him, and let Cookie grow into a chicken in their apartment. Cookie shit on everything and pecked holes in their couch until one of Brice's aunts made his mom send it away to a farm upstate."

"Did Brice see Cookie again?" Stuart asked, a three year old distracted from a bleeding knee.

"I don't think so. Anyway, chickens make lousy pets," Frank finished. "There's a reason you break their necks and fry them."

Stuart laughed out loud. His whole face lit up; he could have been a cousin from Odessa, who emigrated the previous week into our kooky, capitalist family. Frank and I knew this story cold, even though years had passed since one of us had retold it. Stuart came from a childhood without narrative. He was taking sanctuary in ours.

"So, hey," Frank said, "how's the new temp job?"

"Okay. It's a magazine company." I sat down on the mattress. I smiled at Stuart. Maybe he wasn't such a sore on humanity. "You can come back to my apartment tomorrow, and I'll help you look for work. We'll put our brains together, okay?"

"Jesus, Rachel," Frank said, "Stu's barely back from the dead. Getting over the need for the Man is hard shit."

A need for the Man? Stu? Please. "I'm saying it's okay if you want to move back into the apartment. I took a job this week. You don't have to worry about money for a week or so. You can watch TV or something. And Frank has a shower stall, I have a bath."

"Whatever," Stuart said. I gave Stuart an uncomfortable "you survived" hug and left them alone for a few minutes while I chilled out by the radio.

No one had moved the dial since Frank last turned it on. It was the top of the hour. Richard, the ingredient-reading DJ I'd bonked during my internship summer, played the station ID audio cart. He announced the time and the weather. Then he popped in the contest cart from the promotions department. Oh, sloppy, Richard. I could hear him putting in the cart.

The promo featured Richard's voice over an old INXS hit, "What You Need."

"Give us watcha need, watcha need," cooed lead singer Michael Hutchence.

"I know watcha need," Richard said, "two tickets to Madison Square Garden for the June sixteenth Foster's Down Under Tour featuring INXS. Opening act is the Tall Poppies, who'll perform their hot new hit 'Gnome.' Listen for your chance to win." A second of Phillip's chorus kicked in, "Like a Gnome I'm contorted. I'm a Gnome"—, and then the climax of the promo, a final "watcha need!"

I clenched the armrest of my chair in disbelief.

Richard went back live to the mic. "On your mark, listeners, the ninety-seventh caller gets a stuffed koala from the Steiff Toys World Heritage animal collection, and a chance to enter our grand prize drawing. Five grand prize winners and their guests will be driven to the INXS concert in a stretch limo, and escorted to their front row seats. Up next is Gary Puckett and the Union Gap, with one of my favorites, 'Young Girl.'"

I heard Frank asking Stuart about the best pizza slice in Melbourne. They had not heard a word of the promo. I kept my mouth shut about this sudden development, a new concept for a Ganelli. I shut off the radio and put up the kettle. I looked for the bible Aunt Virginia gave me for Communion but settled on Frank's new copy of *Halliwell's Film Guide*. I put my finger on *Citizen Kane*. Let the wild Indians storm the cabin; I had strength in my heart. Frank moved past turtles and chicks, and was on to describing his first two-wheeler to Stuart. I was not having fun.

7

Colin: TRAVEL

Phillip's crazy call came the night Hannah started converting her cats to vegetarianism. She was propped up on a neckroll and pillows, poring over recipes from a vegetarian pet cookbook. I couldn't believe it. I told her that animals shouldn't be subject to human morality, and she insisted that I was forcing *my* steak-and-eggs Australian morality on them. "It's okay to determine what kids eat," she'd said, "so why not cats, as long as it's good for them?"

"One of my old schoolmates back in Seaford was so attached to his dog that he'd share turns having licks on an ice-cream cone. They both came down with the flu."

"Your story has nothing to do with our argument."

I think it did, but in any case, you can't tell me it's right to make a cat eat tofu.

There was another reason I was sulking. We hadn't had sex since the week we'd met after the gig at Lounge. I didn't want to be a brute, like her last boyfriend, the conductor, who she claimed forced sex on her. But I lay there, lusting for her great cheekbones and her unbelievable spine that flowed through her petite body. Not to mention those perky white norgs.

Hannah had on peach satin underwear from Georges, one of a whole drawerful of horny, not-too-revealing underwear. Hannah never put it all out there; that's what got me barred up the second she got undressed. Lately, she limited my advances to letting me feel her groin through her panties with my feet, which she thought were beautiful and graceful. (I secretly think my feet are pretty great, too. They're among the few parts of my body I don't have complaints about. Even the little toes are in perfect proportion. I could be a male foot model.) Hannah's eyes were a glassy gray; they set off her red hair. A frigid stunner who I wanted to fuck about every five seconds.

Lying there with nothing to do but watch her read, scrape my heel on her body, or otherwise mark time, I started comparing her to Rachel. I hadn't thought about not hearing from New York in a while.

Rachel's eyes were more startling than beautiful, those deep-set brown circles that chased you everywhere. And she was much taller than Hannah, five eight or so; the crown of her head came up to my forehead. Despite her model height, she was not what you'd call a graceful girl. She knocked over our standing lamp near the TV at least once a week, or her black tights often had a ladder that ran down to her calf. And despite the fact that she was urban-gothic white, as she called it, even in the summer, Rachel insisted on wearing black basketball runners everywhere; high-tops, she called them. She could have bowled everyone over with her knockout legs if she wore silk stockings and European high heels like Hannah, but she didn't give a shit. "It's a look sure, but high-tops without socks doesn't look good on your pale skin," I'd say.

"Dress yourself," she'd say.

"As your closest friend in the Southern Hemisphere," I once said, "I'm telling you that you could tone it down more." She was headed out the door for her shift, in her purple American bowling shirt embroidered with the name *Susie*, tucked into her bright red miniskirt. And those fucking high-tops.

"Will you chill out? Is there a law against color? The world is drab enough." Rachel had a name and an answer for everything.

Phillip once said it best: "She's great, but sometimes I wish she'd shut the fuck up." I didn't know how Rachel was in bed; I imagined full-on sex with her would be fun, but wordy.

A sound like feet trudging through mud came from the corner. Marjoram and Smudgeface were devouring their Happy Cat liver and bacon. Poor suckers had no idea of the meatless fate that awaited them. I was bored. Hannah had a book by Rilke on her Art Deco dresser.

"My old flatmate Rachel read Rilke. But she thought his writing was 'pompous male poet sentimental mush, like Rimbaud's and Verlaine's.'" Rachel was always going off into tirades like that, even when she didn't mean it; she made me write down those two writers' names to force me to check them out of the library and see if what she said was true. I have to confess I never did. I could tell that once again she was thinking midair. Like that time I drew a caricature of her from a bad angle and she acted like I was her executioner for fifteen minutes, and I felt like utter shit for it, like a boar, and then a second later she asked if there was milk left in the fridge.

"Rachel is not a delicate woman," Hannah sniffed, "Rilke is sublime." I tried to kiss Hannah's sublime little breast, but she said,

"I'm reading now, Colin. Why don't we do that stuff when we're in Mount Buller?" Her sister had a share at Mount Buller for the ski season.

So, we were lying there, frustrated bastard and bombshell Kelvinator on the coldest setting, when Phillip rang with the news. "Can you get that, honey?" she asked, without looking up from her cookbook.

"Leser residence, Colin speaking," I said, like Hannah had told me to—she didn't approve of my standard "Yeah?"

"Mate!" Phillip said, "Wait until you hear this! Angus rang the house. That Aboriginal pop band Yothu Yindi, you know them?"

"Of course—"

"Well, the lead singer's developed nodes on his vocal chords from having one too many global gigs during the official United Nations' Year of the Indigenous People—"

"And you're excited by this?" I asked.

"Hold on. They're in the middle of a tour with INXS, and the promoters needed another opening Australian band since it was a Foster's tour, and guess who that band is? I'll give you a hint: you're right, Angus is one cluey bastard of a manager."

"You're shitting me."

"He had Deirdre from the Sydney EMI office ring their American office to remind them about our Yank-friendly press hook with the murder. And the tour's promoters rang Angus, who brilliantly told them we'd perform for a third of Yothu Yindi's fee. EMI's and Atlantic's American offices struck a deal—they're gonna tie our song to the new INXS ballad—if a station doesn't play "Gnome," it won't get the new INXS single first in their market."

"Brilliant," I agreed.

"We're gonna replace Yothu Yindi on their last three shows in America. Buffalo, Syracuse, and the finale in a New York City arena!"

"Jesus!" I almost screamed—his words were sinking in. Hannah looked up from her feline deprivation recipe for a second. "Jesus!" I pulled the phone cord out of her room and lowered my voice to a whisper: "But wait, shit, Phillip, Buffalo's in America? Isn't that where *Aunt Sally* is?"

"Relax, Colin, America is shorthand for North America. Stuart's not going to show up at the Canadian gig anyway."

"But what if Aunt Sally's relis see the press, or someone else she knows?"

"Stuart is not a bloke who'd make many friends these days. Anyhow, they're not going to run the murder victim's face in the newspaper, they'll print that it happened over in Australia, and that there was pandemonium when it happened—"

"What if Angus gets them Doug Lang's clip?"

"Mate, you're gonna have to ease up if we're going to pull this off. I'll talk to Doug to remind him that Stuart's in Canada."

"Yeah, good."

"We're meeting Angus at Mario's, in the back booths—ten A.M. sharp. I'll ring Mick-O as soon as I'm off with you. Angus already booked us a flight. Do you have a passport?"

"No."

"Bring your driver's license and birth certificate then. Angus can get an emergency passport and visa for you through Ausmusic—they have an arrangement with the U.S. Consulate. We've got to get photos taken right after brekkie, 'cause we're eligible for something called cultural ambassador status."

I hung up the receiver. I had Hannah's attention. "What was that about? Why are you looking like that—Colin?" I blew on the antique glasses she bought in a shop in Armadale, which she used for reading books in bed, books like *Italian Pottery, A Field Guide to Roses*, or *A Treasury of Romantic Poems*.

"Oh, stop! You're breathing like a dog!" But she was smiling. She knew something good was up.

"We've been asked to play an arena in New York City. In New York City! Jesus Fucking Christ."

"You're kidding! That's amazing."

"We're replacing Yothu Yindi—"

"The Aboriginal band?"

"Long story—the lead singer has nodes on his vocal chords and—"

"Who's Aunt Sally?"

Phillip was right. I'd let my cool slip. Everything was going great. "Aunt Sally's a Canadian aunt of Phillip's who's a Born Again. She hates the fact he's a rock singer, calls it devil's work."

"Oh."

I sat naked on the corner of Hannah's bed, my tic starting up from the excitement. Should I ring Rachel to say we were coming over, go ahead and roll out the red carpet? Hannah startled me by caressing my back and neck. She gently bit me on my nipple, and we made love for the second time in the month.

• • •

My seat was next to Angus, who was telling me about how I should talk to the American media. The plane headed down the runway for liftoff. I wanted him to shut up. I had never been on a plane before and was nervous as hell. Angus had been overseas to America and Europe more times than he'd ever dreamed. "New Orleans's good," he said. "Europe, okay. Seen one castle, seen them all."

I passed air as the plane lifted, because of the hemorrhoid air-pump fiasco. Hannah had done this crazy thing that night we finally had sex: the last few minutes before I had been about to come, she'd slid her finger right up my arse. I mean *right* up in, prodding around with her long sharp index fingernail. Fucking weird. It felt like she was fishing with barbed wire in there, but I didn't say anything. She must know what she was doing—a *Kama Sutra* thing perhaps, since she had that on her shelf. But the next morning I bled out my arse. I was afraid Hannah had done some damage. My flight was in twenty-four hours. I enlisted my mother for help getting an emergency spot with Dr. Leach, her doctor.

Mum paused on the phone when I told her what area needing examining. "What exactly happened here, Colin?"

"I wasn't thinking. I was trying to clean an itchy bit out of my bottom with a screwdriver."

"Oh, Colin!" Mum burst out laughing.

"Don't make me tell you anymore, please Mum, please—"

"Can I tell your father? He looks so bored."

"Mum, please no."

"I'll ring Dr. Leach for you if you promise to buy me a bottle of Smoke. That's a fragrance my new neighbor Caroline is going on and on about. You can't buy it yet in Georges or David Jones yet. Will you write that down?"

"Hold on a sec, okay."

"Smoke, by Ivan Stanbury, the American designer. Caroline picked it up in a department store called Bloomingdale's, if that's any help."

"Deal. But ring right away."

"I'm so proud of you, Colin. You always said fame would happen and it did. My little rock star."

Dr. Leach was on a golf holiday up on the Gold Coast, but Mum got me an appointment with Dr. Leach's intern.

"Just fix me," I said to him. The intern hooked me up to an air pump mechanism. He left the machine unattended while he took a call from his girlfriend or wife. After a while I felt like a blimp was up my arse, and I called out to him, but he assured me that it's normal to feel pain. I screamed after another few seconds—that made him take a look—the gauge was at fucking maximum. The jerk apologized in a fluster, no doubt afraid I was going to sue.

I told him not to worry, but I fumed like hell while he wrote out an ointment prescription for the plane. The side effect was that I passed air nonstop since my appointment; not smells, just air.

"What's that noise?" Angus said.

"Sorry, I had a crazy meal last night in celebration," I said, trying to mask my terror at leaving the ground at a forty-five degree angle.

"You're a legend, Colin," he said.

When the plane evened out a bit, the stewardess by the curtain let a pretty girl from the economy seats up front so the girl could ask Phillip for his autograph. His fan looked like she was minutes away from her puberty burst. Phillip tried to look like he didn't care, that it happened all the time, but I knew it was his second autograph, even with the national publicity we had. Australia isn't a nation for celebrity worship. I could see it on his face: Phillip hoped America was all that and more.

Mick-O was asleep, his head propped up against Phillip's shoulder. Phillip and Kerri were having a bit of a row over the autograph request and the fact that Kerri was on the plane at all. She somehow managed to get a visa at the last second and Phillip was mad as hell as he envisioned himself with a swarm of New York nymphomaniacs.

Hannah had a ceramics seminar she had to give at Daylesford. She didn't even try booking a flight. I was supposed to be back in Australia in a month, and Hannah said she could use the solo time to read. I was disappointed that she couldn't come. I wanted to have someone who mattered watching me on stage, someone I could talk to afterwards, and if I'm honest here, someone I could show off to INXS. Hannah turned heads.

Angus nudged me awake for our dinner; he'd put down my tray, and the food was waiting for me.

"Thanks, mate."

"Not a problem."

There was a piece of paper accompanying the meal:

To celebrate our new, improved business class to the South Pacific and the United Nations' Year of the Indigenous People, this month, for business and first class only, Continental Airlines has added special items to our menu for flights between America, Australia, and New Zealand. Some of these items may be incorporated into your meals. From North America: turkey, cranberry sauce, wild rice stuffing, blue corn chips. From New Zealand: mussels appetizer, Hangi-style pork. From Australia: barramundi, mock emu stew, wattleseed ice cream. We hope you enjoy your unusual meal and take time out to consider how important it is to preserve indigenous culture.

I heard Phillip say to Mick-O, "For Godsake use a fucking fork." Our flight got the barramundi, which tasted suspiciously like the everyday flake you get at a fish and chips shop. For a bonus dessert in addition to the wattleseed ice cream, there was a chocolate chip "cookie" made in Sydney. I hated the way everyone, especially Dale and Geoff, my second cousins from Dad's side, let American words replace those I grew up with. My cousins said sneakers instead of runners, cookies instead of bikkies. Geoff, who was fourteen, wore a Chicago Bulls sweatshirt instead of a footy guernsey.

"Would you like something to drink with your dinner?" the black American stewardess asked. She sounded like Rachel taking a drink order, like the job was beneath her.

"A Coke would be great."

"Are you excited about your tour, Mr. Dunforton?"

"How do you know I'm on tour?"

"Flight attendants know everything," she smiled. She had adult braces like Liam's wife. "We even know which customers in first class used coupons to get there."

"Well, in that case, I better tell the truth. Yeah, I'm pretty excited. I've never been further than Brisbane."

"Am I the first American you've met, too?"

"No, but I only know one Yank well. You sound a bit like her." I stopped myself from saying that she was the first black person I'd met. Even though I hadn't been overseas before, I knew that it wouldn't be a good thing to say. I had one of Oprah's shows running in my head—"Dialogue between the Races," the one Phillip and I imitated for a week—this black girl with tight rows of plaits said straight into the camera, "No, don't ask me if you can touch them, I'm not going to touch your awful perm, you hear me?"

"Is your friend from Baltimore, too?"

"New York City."

"People from Baltimore sound nothing like people from New York City. But you'll find that out soon enough, that's what travel is for."

The old stick on the aisle turned out to be an eighty-four-year-old amateur scientist who was touring the world, at his own expense, to convince skeptics to change the week from seven to eleven days. "Son, we made a terrible calculation 'round about the Roman times."

"You think so?"

"I know so."

Fortunately, just then one of the stewardesses gave us customs forms to fill out. Welcome to the United States of America, are you carrying fruit?—that sort of thing. Angus, who had awful breath from the flight, leaned over. "Tick no for everything."

"Angus, do we fill out this form even though we're flying on to Canada?"

"What?"

"Aren't we going to Canada first for the Buffalo gig? The plane at two o'clock—"

"Buffalo's in the States, Colin, in New York State." He was looking at me like I was a dunce. "Remember, you only got a visa for the States?"

"Sorry, I'm talking crap," I said, trying to suppress a class-A heart attack. "I thought it was right near Toronto, that one visa is good for North America, and—"

"Well, Buffalo's right up there on the Canadian border, but mate, you better not say idiotic things like that to the press."

I tapped Phillip on the shoulder and motioned for him to walk to the back of the cabin with me, past the curtain to the economy toilets. I pretended to be stretching my legs as I poured water into a paper cone. "Buffalo's in the States—Angus told me—the top of New York State. Our flight from LA goes to Buffalo, New York State, not Buffalo, Canada."

"I was sure Buffalo was in Canada," Phillip said nervously. "Maybe there's a Buffalo in Canada, too, like Perth in Scotland and Australia."

"Maybe."

"Look, when you and Peter made up that Ian MacKenzie ID

for Stuart, did you get Stuart a visa for Canada or the States? Did the plane ticket say Canada or the States?"

"Fuck, Phillip, I don't notice things like plane codes. We didn't even look at ours, right? I told Peter that 'Ian MacKenzie' needed a visa for Buffalo, and he gave it to me with the other papers. What country was it for?—*you* saw it, too."

"I can't remember," he said. "Christ. Let's calm down though. What's the big deal if he's in New York State? He's not about to come to our shows—"

"What if he thinks of blackmailing us for more drug money?"

"He's not going to do that. He's not that smart—Mick-O told me he thinks Stuart can't even read. He never signed his name to anything; he x-ed the paper. He tried to tell Mick-O that he heard Danny Death used to do that for autographs. This is a bloke who thought the mob was after him. Nah, it's going to be fine. We're driving ourselves crazy. Let's go back and get on with becoming mega-stars, right?"

"Yeah," I said. We walked back to our seats.

"That must have been some dinner," Angus cringed after another whammy of air-pump-fiasco air came out when I sat down.

After clearing customs, we raced across the street to catch our connecting flight. Everything in that mad rush between terminals seemed different: the big palm trees, the cars, the air, even the metal looked sturdier to me.

We landed at Greater Buffalo International Airport five hours later. Angus handed us each $500 in mixed American bills. Then Kerri made us wait while she changed some of her money. American money all looked identical to me—who's the idiot that decided to make every denomination the same green? I used a fifty-dollar bill for a cigarette packet at the airport newsstand. I wouldn't have taken the change if the cashier didn't come running after me.

A limousine that EMI ordered was waiting to take us to our suites at the Hyatt Regency Buffalo. Even Angus looked surprised, like it was sinking in that we were really in the big swim, that this was a huge gig even for a hot-shot manager. The highway was backed up due to a collision; our driver took his chances on side streets. Buffalo houses lacked the front lawns Melbourne houses have. Most of them were double-storied with a chimney, houses an Australian kid reared on American picture books would draw. Several homes had an American flag hanging from the front. If an Australian family was so shamelessly patriotic, they'd be laughed out of town.

At the check-in desk, I offered to share a room with Mick-O. Angus wanted to spend more time prepping Phillip, his 'lead attorney' for the interviews the New York EMI office had arranged. On the writing table was a basket filled with grapes, bananas, apples, two small boxes of American cereal, and two red kazoos. "G'day Tall Poppies!" the note attached read. "On behalf of the Hyatt Regency staff, welcome to Erie County, home of Niagara Falls, the Buffalo Bills, and the birthplace of Cheerios and the kazoo. Break a leg!"

Phillip munched on a red apple with little knobs on the bottom. It looked like the ones in the Time-Life books we used for references in my illustration class. My class partner, true-blue Peter who doctored Stuart's papers, had smiled when I said the apple didn't look right, that it hadn't developed fully yet. Peter had spent a month in San Francisco and knew they were U. S. apples, *delicious* apples. I had a song in my head I'd plugged into on one of the legs of our flight, by the Cowsills. I hadn't heard it in years: "The Rain, the Park, and Other Things." The Skychannel host had said the Cowsills were the band they based the Partridge Family on, which I had to be sure to tell Rachel on the odd chance she didn't know that already. I sang out the backing vocals. "And I knew (I knew, I knew, I knew, I knew) / She could make me happy (happy, happy)."

"Are you listening?"

"Huh?" I said, looking up at Phillip's face, which needed a wash. "Sorry, I had a song in my head."

"You always have a song in your head, Colin."

"Mate, you still got sleep in your right eye."

"Me and Angus are going to work on my delivery," he said, shutting one lid and flicking something crusty towards me. "Then I'm going to go over to Kerri's for a bit." Kerri was staying a few blocks away at the Best Western. After she'd surprised Phillip on the plane, Angus had insisted that during the tour she had to stay, at her expense, in a separate hotel. "A coupled man is a liability when you're trying to build a fan base," Angus had determined. A bastard thing to do, considering Kerri was on an aerobics instructor's wage.

Mick-O was alive and kicking, no small wonder after sleeping for most of twenty-five hours. I wasn't as hyper as him, but I agreed to go down to the lobby to have a look around.

Mick-O ordered two Foster's and brought them back to our

table. I gave him a quizzical look. Back home he despised Foster's, he was a Toohey Red man.

"They're our sponsor," he said, "did you forget? Our meal ticket."

The Foster's tasted like piss. Rachel once told me that there was a much lower legal alcohol limit in the States, even for imported beer.

Behind the lobby was an actual pub, with a piano man noodling around on the keys. Mick-O talked me into going inside. I was reluctant because I was still passing air, and there were women inside. Over by the windows, there was a table of five girls with big hair and awful make-up—giggling in our direction.

"American girls look like they're from bloody Broadmeadows," Mick-O said, referring to a suburb of Melbourne not known for its fashion sense. But he wanted to go over. A man without standards.

"Nah," I said, "I'll pass." But he went over anyway and asked the prettiest of the lot for a light.

"Are you with the INXS tour?" I heard the girl ask in a loud whiny voice. Mick-O floored the table when he said yes. He bought the girls a round with one of the bills Angus had given him. He waved me over.

"Are your parents convicts?" one of the girls said.

"No, but I'm a relative of Dame Nellie Melba," Mick-O replied.

"Is she royalty?"

"Nah. The greatest opera singer in the world. She has a perfectly curved palate. My whole family does. That's why I can sing perfect pitch, right, Colin?"

So perfect we stuck him back in the drum section, where all great opera singers thrive. Nellie Melba died when? World War II?

"You girls want tickets for tomorrow's show?"

They squealed. Angus was going to kill him for this. He went to the bar to get matches, and I followed.

"Aren't you ready to call it a night yet?"

"Colin, I'm kicking goals here. We have our pick."

"Happy choosing. I'm going upstairs."

I practically collapsed from exhaustion.

Moans and groans from the other bed woke me up. I peeked at the alarm clock: four A.M. I saw Mick-O sucking on a breast. I pretended I was still asleep.

We had to perform three days in Buffalo instead of one. Originally it was going to be at Rich Stadium, which held 80,000, and not Memorial Auditorium, capacity 16,000. Kenny Rogers and Dolly Parton were rained out the week before. Since they were still touring in New York, the mayor of Buffalo, their devoted fan, had personally promised Kenny the date verbally committed by the city's cultural commissioner to INXS.

The tour promoter's representative went ballistic at every stadium and city official he could keep within earshot. "There are thousands of refunds! Even with three days we lose that revenue. INXS is exhausted. It's the tail end of the tour—they have *one* day to rest for Syracuse."

The Mayor's official of business development was apologetic. "We goofed," he said.

"Your *goof*," the tour representative said, "is fucking costing millions of dollars. We're going to sue this ugly fucking smelly city's ass off."

Angus and INXS's manager joined in on the screaming. Off on the side, Mick-O, Phillip, and I were quietly relieved. To go from 500 people at Lounge to 16,000 was enough of a jump. Syracuse's Carrier Dome was next with 90,000 people reported to have bought tickets! The extra performances in Buffalo would give me time to get used to that gut-wrenching notion. Eventually, after hours more of King Kong chest beating, the promoter's rep gave in to the city's take-it-or-leave-it offer of three concerts or no concert. He agreed to let us do the gigs at Memorial.

From nine to eleven, the three of us did an interview with a newspaper arts section and two local rock stations. Mick-O was so jet-lagged and/or sexed out that he fell asleep on one of the station couches. Phillip was animated, I'll give him that. Angus said maybe we should rethink strategy and have Phillip do the interviews solo —with me as the backup for college stations. This didn't worry me. Phillip loved being the center of attention, and Angus was probably right. Mick-O's punctuality was not to be trusted, and I do have a somewhat monotone voice.

Our first soundcheck at Memorial would be ready at four o'clock; we had five hours to kill. To get us out of his hair, Angus arranged for a limo to take us over to Niagara Falls while he sorted everything through. "Don't go to the Canadian side of the Falls. I'm not sure about your visa situation."

We waited in the Hyatt lobby. Mick-O copped a stare from the doorman because he was blasting "You Are the Sunshine of My Life" on the gift-basket kazoo. An old-time driver with a gray face, like a dying fish, held up a sign for Phillip Harvey. Mick-O hopped in the front, like he was in a taxi in Melbourne. Ted, the driver, talked mostly to Mick-O, but his words boomed off corners and hit you in the face.

"What do you think of Buffalo, Mr. Mick-O? She's a pretty Victorian city, don't you think?"

Mick-O made the mistake of telling Ted that Melbourne's in the State of Victoria, and Windbag was off on a new topic.

"That's right, it is, too. Been to Sydney. I had a pretty fair night there when I was on leave. They make the girls *big* there. Couple of hookers I couldn't get my arms around." He had a husky cigarette laugh like my Uncle Jack.

"Could be the sun or the Vegemite," Mick-O said. "That'll make 'em grow."

"You think Prince or Springsteen would press a button to shut them out?" Phillip leaned over and whispered.

"Yeah," I grinned. "But we can't. Not yet."

As we neared the Falls, I asked Ted which section has the best view.

"Pity I can't drive you to the Canuck side. Orders from my boss. It's nicer. I'll tell you though, right here in the U.S. of A. there's a perfect spot which is practically under the Falls."

"Bewdy," Mick-O said.

You could hear the water roar as soon as we got out of the car. At the edge, my balls ached from the sheer drop.

Aunty Grace used to call an open drain near my house Niagara Falls. She didn't want me and Liam playing near it because she'd heard it was contaminated. She thought we might drink from it. When it was dark, Aunty Grace would call us inside for tea, make us swear on our grandmother's bible we hadn't disobeyed her. Aunty Grace knew I loved her meatloaf, which she made with a hard-boiled egg in the middle. Mum's specialties were veal and mushrooms, and chicken grilled with orange rind. Occasionally, Mum made rabbit stew, which was my Dad's favorite. Aunty Grace, the two families agreed, made the better afters—homemade vanilla ice cream from Carnation milk, to be served with hot baked apricot slices. Most more-ish of all were Aunty Grace's lamingtons—chocolate and raspberry layers with coconut topping.

Phillip hated our sidetrip. He felt like a school kid sent out for recess. He wanted to go back and rehearse in his room. But Mick-O insisted that we buy tickets for the boat ride. Before boarding the Maid of the Mist, a tour girl showed the passengers how to snap on our "pond-chose."

As the boat ride began, Mick-O blew his kazoo again. You couldn't hear a thing, but Phillip took advantage of this vulnerable moment to snatch it and throw it into the water.

"Hey!" Mick-O said.

"March 29, 1848," the loudspeaker said, "was the one night the town of Niagara was strangely silent. Ice had formed a dam, leaving the Falls dry. Two days later the dam broke."

8

Rachel: THE HUMP

After the final reel of *Shoah*, Sy Cooper had decided to drive me and the other five surviving students of his "Cinema in the Age of Television" class off-campus for drinks. The gesture was against the rules, the university's academic guidelines as well as state law. That year, 1986, the drinking age in New York was raised from eighteen to twenty-one. Unfortunately for my classmates, all of whom had tasted the splendor of a legal beer, a grandfather clause didn't exist in New York. Lester's, the well-off-campus bar Sy Cooper drove us to, was seedy and depressed, a place the novelist William Kennedy might have immortalized for his readers if he wasn't so fascinated by hometown Albany two hours southeast. A vintage Budweiser sign, a barmaid with a tooth missing— Lester's was the kind of drinking establishment that location scouts immediately beep their producers about.

The six of us stood out like a brownie troop at a Hell's Angels' rally—a fifty-year-old professor, four mod underage film buffs, and one preppy underage buff, Janet, in her cardigan and brown and black houndstooth jumpsuit. Sy ordered a scotch, straight, Janet asked for a vodka tonic, and I got myself a Harvey Wall-banger, a drink I liked because overly dramatic film stars ordered it in vintage flicks. The barmaid said "Hiya, Sy" and didn't ask us for IDs.

Holding court over the weathered wooden table near the radiator, Sy gave his final instruction: "It's imperative to reinvent your origins." He removed his black wire-rimmed glasses to further emphasize his point: "The great actors and filmmakers did. The Kennedys did."

In careful analysis afterward, seven years afterward, as Janet and I waited for Stuart to finish a convalescent bowl of oatmeal, I guessed that this had been our lovable alcoholic professor's way of admitting to his reluctant disciples that he was less than a minor Beat. He was in fact a pop-culture asterisk, like Colin used to call Australian bands that topped their careers with a number thirty-two single on the local charts.

"Asterisk, that's good used like that," Janet said, picking the sausage off her pizza slice. We used newspaper for plates because the sink was full of dirty dishes.

"Colin's word, actually." I was sad at the memory of what had become, and my voice cracked a bit.

"It's terrible that Colin turned out to be such a conniver."

"Yeah," I agreed. "Hey! I'll eat that." I leaned over to salvage the meat from the cardboard box.

Stuart let go of a long, mucousy shocker of a cough. Janet thought it was disturbing enough that we should check for blood.

"Stuart? It's Janet. Let me take that bowl from you." He'd fallen backward when we weren't looking; a tablespoon of chalk-colored cereal had landed on the bed—a bed long devoid of sheets or even a mattress cover.

Stuart wailed, as loud as he could from a prone position. "Mum, you going to kill me? I'll be good, don't kill me . . ." His eyes were red, and his long brown hair was greasy again even after the shower Frank had supervised the day before. He yawned uncontrollably as he yelled, as if he had an odd Tourette's symptom. How could he have lapsed back? Frank had thought the worst was over and so had gone for his overdue dim sum break at Triple Eight; he'd wanted to try the duck web he'd overheard a fellow foodie talking about at the bank.

"No," I said, joining Janet at the edge of the mattress. "It's Rachel, and Janet. We're right here—Rachel, Janet, Frank. We're your friends. You're in New York? You hear me? It's the withdrawal again. You're okay? Stuart, raise your hand if you understand me—"

This is not so bad, I tried to tell myself, but my nerves told me otherwise. I cannot feel sorry for myself. Stuart will live. Janet and I will teach him how to read. My parents are alive and love me. I could get a decent job if I tried. I'll meet someone one day. Maybe I'll write a screenplay. I was jealous of what I imagined Janet was unselfishly thinking: Poor Stuart, he's never had an honest chance. Or, Rachel is having such a hard time.

The conversation about Sy never resumed. Stuart didn't raise his hand, but instead he lapsed into a temperate hell, rocking and moaning at a level I thought I could handle alone for a short while until Frank returned. Janet went home again for her nap.

Meanwhile my parents were on the first leg of their France trip—in a cab on their way to the airport in Miami. The radio station in New York played "Gnome." Mom heard a DJ say this new hot Australian band was touring America. In the right weather conditions, as the chief engineer that first day of my radio internship had bragged, you can pick up a strong-signaled blue-chip New York station many states south. Mom and Dad were supposed to switch to Air France at Kennedy Airport. At the Miami International, Mom changed the stopover in New York to eight hours instead of two. Then they could get a cab back to the apartment and make sure I wasn't going to be embroiled once more by the mishegoss, the craziness, of the Tall Poppies' universe.

When they got to the family apartment, the afternoon of Janet's and my conversation on Sy Cooper, there was no one there because I was over at my brother's loft. Mom left a note on the kitchen table that I was not to hook up with the band and what I should and shouldn't do in an emergency. Then, because Frank's phone was busy (it was accidentally off the hook), they concluded he was home. They got a cab to the loft and rang the buzzer.

I ran down the five flights of stairs in a state of shock. I had counted on withdrawal surprises. In my head they fused with the plagues God foisted upon the Egyptians: need for the Man, frogs, shakes, vermin, vomit, loss of bowels, slaying of the first born. But my parents! I argued with my mother in front of Bowery Bulbs, the store on the first floor of Frank's building.

"We've come from the airport to check on you," Mom said. "We haven't physically seen you for two years, and you act like we're an imposition. What is going on, Rachel? I smell a rat. You two are 'hanging out' a hell of a lot. I heard on the radio that the Tall Poppies are hitting town—Frank's not housing the band, is he?"

"I heard that, too, but no, I haven't told anyone. And I wasn't planning on seeing them."

"I want you to swear to me that you won't see them."

"I won't see them for me, not for you."

She stared me down like she didn't buy this. "As long as you stay away. Let's go upstairs and talk about this more. Can you help us with the suitcases?"

"This is not my place. Frank should be the one inviting you over."

Dad was losing his patience. "You're not making sense! This is farcical. We're your parents. Why can't we go upstairs?"

"Frank isn't around," I said. "I'm thrilled to see you. You guys look so tanned! Why don't we go to the Vietnamese place across the street?—they have great French coffee—"

"I'm having trouble with my bladder," Mom insisted. "I'll have to make number one on the street if you don't let me upstairs."

"You can pee in the Vietnamese place."

Dad rolled his eyes. "Rachel, stop this piffling—we're going up." He pushed past me.

"Sh'ma Yisroel, Adenoi Elohanu Adenoi Echad," I whispered to myself. "Hail Mary, full of grace," I added, hedging my bets.

Frank was a half-hour late. Just me and my folks, and oh yeah, Stuart, the corkscrew of pain on the bare mattress. The coverless addict had glazed eyes and a full erection. Since bumping into Stuart at Eisenberg's, I'd seen his penis a bit too frequently.

"And who's that?" Mom breathed heavily, after a quick now-I've-seen-it-all turnaround.

"A friend of Frank's. He's asleep really. I think this is related to sleepwalking."

"You're watching a naked friend of Frank's?"

"Is Frank homosexual?" Dad said, trying to mask his alarm. "Is that what this is about? I mean it would be okay, but is Frank going to—how do you say that Sylvia—come outward? Is that why he broke up with Ingrid? Jesus Christ, Sylvia—I wasn't prepared for this now—"

"Come out," I said with enunciated disgust. "No he's not a h-oh-moh-sexual, Dad. You're such fucking worrywarts! You always expand everything. Frank and I were planning a thirtieth anniversary party, if you want to know the truth, with Aunt Virginia. Frank's always had people he's met traveling crashing over. This one's from England, I think—Frank's been sleeping on the floor. And I'm here for a few minutes, leaving Frank stamps—we were going to surprise you. But Mom, you're too fucking nosy, huh?"

I did a great job browbeating them—an Academy Award performance. Except for one unforeseen problem: Stuart proceeded to vomit the grains of oatmeal remaining in his stomach a couple of feet from my mother's smallest suitcase.

"Oh, my," Mom said, checking her skirt for vomit.

My father had already inched forward to survey the creature more closely.

"Joe, step back," Mom called. None of us had seen that Stuart was clenching the wooden spiral bedpost Frank had chained him to in our earlier bout of optimism. The carved gargoyle posts were a wedding gift he'd taken from Minnesota after his divorce; his prize because the carver was his friend before Ingrid's. My father tried to take the post from his hand, but Stuart hurled it at him before Dad could get to it.

"Stuart, no!" I cried out. "Oh, God, that's my fucking father!"

Fortunately Stuart's aim was impaired. He hit the sheet instead of Dad's head.

"Dad!" I called out. "Oh, Christ, you okay? Frank said he super-glued that!"

"Frank—Den—Rachel—I need—I need—"

"I told you we should have spanked them as kids," Dad said, having picked up the loose post.

"Now tell the *fucking* truth," Mom said, mimicking our cinematically stylized sewer accents.

"You have to get that boy into the hospital," Mom decided, after a quick rehashing of the Eisenberg Tuna Salad Saga.

"Mom! Don't make this your problem. He doesn't exist. He doesn't have insurance. This isn't your problem."

"Aren't you ashamed of yourself for lying to us?" Dad asked. "You kids are going to kill him with your crazy plans."

I could hear Frank walking up the stairs. He'd bumped into Janet returning after her nap. We could hear them in the stairwell. "He slipped back," Janet said in her trademark clipped tone, "but he's not as bad as the first night—"

"Oh, God," Frank said, when he stepped through the open door.

"Hi, Mr. and Mrs. Ganelli," Janet said. Her cheeks turned a salmon pink. "I guess I'll leave the family alone."

My mother eye-balled her son. "No, Janet—I think you should stay. You should hear what I have to say to my children. We came home to check on Rachel. We heard on the radio that a certain band was in America, and we decided to take a ride over before our plane leaves for France—to insure that Rachel wouldn't do anything misguided. Turns out we were too late, wouldn't you say?"

"I don't know what you are talking about," Frank said. "What band's in town?" A pathetic attempt at a deflection, considering Stuart was naked and moaning five feet away.

"Fools!" Dad hissed. My father has a streamlined head. With his pointy nostrils and angular chin, it looked like his reproach was headed to a vanishing point a foot away from his cleft.

Frank gave me a look much easier to decipher than his old walkie-talkie Morse code messages from our bathroom. *Your band is here? What have you kept from me, you idiot? How did you fuck this up?*

Mom's voice softened a notch to the same tone she uses whenever there's a death. (She's the stoic one who orders the deli platter for the Jewish side's shivahs or lasagna for the Italian wakes.) "Your cousin Benji is a doctor. Joe, can you get the address book out of that suitcase?—in the front zip pocket—"

"Benji's a hand surgeon," Frank said.

"He's family, and not only that, there's something in this world called a Hippocratic Oath."

Stuart looked like a zombie rescued minutes earlier from a cult; he had no idea what the commotion was about. He'd seemed clear-eyed eight hours before, devouring morsels of our childhood.

Why was he back to stage one? I couldn't figure it out. Janet went over to him. My father's and my eyes followed her. "Stuart, don't worry, it's Rachel's parents."

"They're liars! Mum and Pop are dead. Liars. They're going to kill me!"

My father went over to the bed. Two years had passed since I'd hugged Dad good-bye, but he still had a thick head of hair, though his salt-and-pepper strands were now the distinguished silver of a coffee-machine pitchman's hair. I tended to picture him in his pre-retirement suit and tie, yet he was wearing comfy airplane clothes —jeans and the *I Slept Through Haley's Comet* sweatshirt I'd bought him during one of my science conferences.

"I'm Joseph Ganelli, Rachel and Frank's father. That woman is Sylvia, my wife. We are going to get you real help. We are not going to tell the police who you are."

"This is unreal," I whined to Frank. "You said we were over the hump."

"I was helping you out. Don't pin this on me."

No, Frank, I'm the ogre trying to save a desperate man's life. I pleaded with my father to leave Stuart alone, and he crossed past the sheet to a chair near the window, while my mother dialed the hospital.

"Tell him his Aunt Sylvia needs him. He'll pick up the phone if you tell him that—Benji? Hi, honey—no, your Mom is fine—no I need to talk to you. Rachel and Frank need emergency medical attention for a friend and I don't know where else to turn—"

I couldn't listen. Sylvia Levine Ganelli had been in PR before she retired. Even Will, who was in the same profession and a polished speaker, thought my mother unstoppable. She once charmed President Carter into attending a tribute dinner for a client.

"I've booked him in," she said about fifteen minutes later. I pulled my fingers back in fear, hard enough that I almost broke my pinky.

My father addressed us from the window, Moses admonishing the wayward children of Israel: "Your heart was in the right place, but you were misguided. You should have consulted us. We're your parents. We operate out of love. You act like we're coming from someplace else."

When will they stop treating us like infants? Frank offered my Dad water in a struggling artist's spaghetti-sauce-jar glass.

"Benjamin Levine, you're a true mensch," I heard Mom say before she hung up the phone. Then she turned to us. Her naughty children.

"A special fund for young Jewish drug and alcohol addicts without coverage was set up at Beth Israel by a record executive who recovered from a cocaine addiction. Benji plays racquetball with the head of the program. Dr. Mentoff is a very compassionate man. Benji told him it's a dire emergency. He's sending over an ambulance."

"But, Mrs. Ganelli," Janet said, "I don't think Stuart is Jewish."

"He is now, darling. Stuart Lipschitz, of the Melbourne Lipschitzes."

"Isn't that Lipschitzi?" Frank cracked. No one smiled.

"Joe," Mom said, "call Air France and cancel those reservations."

"So you're not going to France?" I said, half slumped against the wall. She didn't hear me. Mom was busy rousing Stuart like he had a 103-degree fever and it was imperative that he take another dosage of St. Joseph's chewable cherry aspirin for children.

"Mom's a professional," Frank said. I nodded.

"You don't play God, kids," Dad said, with the final pulse on the situation.

Mom and I rode with Stuart in the ambulance to Beth Israel's Morris Bernstein Pavilion. The back reeked of Stuart's diarrhea. Frank, Janet, and Dad took a cab. After Stuart was taken away in a wheelchair, I spoke for forty-five minutes with Dr. Mentoff, Benji's racquetball partner.

"He lapsed on you because he never really got over the hump—it takes a full seventy-two hours for that stage to pass. To have him functioning and cognitive when you did is most unusual."

"What are you going to do with him?"

"I know of one doctor who would take his rock-star patients to Jamaica, knock them out with sleeping pills, keep them snoring over the hump, and then apply acupressure massage."

"That's what you're going to do?"

"No, that's what *that* doctor did. I gave him an injection of clonadine—a cotapressin that regulates blood pressure. I'll taper him off for four or five days and keep him in detox for a few days more. For that period of time clonadine's not addictive."

Give him more drugs? This seemed ridiculous, but he's the doctor.

"Miss Ganelli, may I ask you a few more questions?"

"Yes?"

"Who's the patient's nearest kin?" Mentoff's lips extended forward too much—from my angle his mouth looked like a beak.

"He's an orphan."

"How much heroin was Mr. Lipschitz using?"

"I don't know."

"Are you his sexual partner?"

"God no."

"When is the last known time he used heroin?"

Clinton Street. "I don't know. Not for four days at least. He was chained to the bedpost—"

"Chained?"

"A figure of speech."

"Did he snort it, smoke it, inject it?"

"As far as I know, he shoots it up—"

"Intravenously or intramuscularly?"

"What's the difference?"

"Intravenously hits the veins. Intramuscularly he can take it in the buttock, arm, without hitting a vein."

I felt like I was starring in an educational filmstrip for junior high school students. "I guess he was using it intravenously. He used a dinosaur tie to bulge a vein."

"You kids would have killed him," Dad said for the tenth time.

Dr. Mentoff corrected him. "Mr. Ganelli, Stuart would never have died from withdrawal. But he could have physically hurt someone or himself. Punched a hole in the wall. Thrown a glass at your daughter. That's the main danger of cold turkey."

"He couldn't have died?" I asked, wanting to hear those words again.

"He could only die from an overdose. When you're strung out, buying garbage from someone you don't know is the real danger. It can be cut with bad stuff to stretch their profit. Battery acid—will kill you. Roach poison—will kill you."

"My God," Dad said. "They put roach poison in there?"

Dr. Mentoff should have done voice-overs for horror trailers. "Or sometimes, these young kids aren't used to better quality. When there's purer heroin available, the veteran will shoot in smaller doses."

Benji sat in the corner of the room with a bag of microwaved popcorn, and I could hear him clucking. This is what happens when you intermarry and don't discipline your kids, he was no doubt thinking.

The last time I'd seen Benji, three years earlier, we'd had a brutal argument at my Aunt Bea and Uncle Eddie's Passover Seder, over the separation of women and men at the Wailing Wall. My feminism drew from lectures from my rabbi and priest. And especially from Benji, who had met his wife via a proven enthusiasm for Judaism: he'd colead a teen tour to Israel with her in the early eighties. Mom flashed her "Cool it, Rachel" look, but once again the volcano of religious dissent had erupted.

"There's a place for your type," Benji had said. "Leningrad."

Dear Abby would have written, "Acknowledge to yourself that the two of you are at fault, take a breath, politely switch the subject to the hostess's cooking." But fuck Dear Abby, I was in a cantankerous, crab apple of a mood. "How can you pay dues to a synagogue that teaches its daughters that they are dirty because they menstruate? Benji, you went to medical school, for Christ's sake."

"Don't say that at the table," Benji said, disgraced. He covered his eight-year-old daughter's ears. "Such garbage. Aunt Sylvia, you should reel your daughter in."

"She's almost twenty-five," Mom sighed. "She has her own mouth."

"She sure does," Dad said.

Was it *Christ* or *menstruate* that got Benji to head for the coats?

Will had said I should write a letter of apology to them as soon as we got home, but I'd stewed in my arrogant juices.

The next morning in the hospital waiting room, I promised my mother that I wouldn't see the band. Then she wrangled my current work situation out of me.

Mom made me call Temp Solution immediately to cancel my stint with the smut mill. Selena was sick. I didn't have to cop abuse from her about my lack of professionalism in not completing the job.

"What kind of feminist are you?" Mom asked when I finished lying about "my infected sinus" to Harry, the other job placement counselor. "You should report the agency to the Better Business Bureau for sending you there. Sign up with another agency, and in the interim why don't you cash in the bond Virginia bought you at your confirmation? You should have considerable interest by now."

I hadn't thought of that bond. At least five hundred dollars.

"I'm not going to give you money, but you can eat at our apartment."

It was their apartment again.

Janet's vacation was over, and now that Stuart was under medical attention, she'd returned to work.

I called Janet at her cubicle at the Mayor's Office of Film and Television. "I can't thank you enough."

"I'll need you to help spackle the walls for my paint job next month, don't you worry. You should be more frightened that Veemah and Frieda are on to us—they're sure I know what's going on with you. What can I tell them?"

"Tell them I'm in love."

My mother was talking to Stuart, who was pale but cognitive again. Through her old PR sonar, she'd tracked down the name and address of his mother's cousin in Buffalo, who was not to be found when Stuart had arrived after his "murder." Leigh Ann Harmond. Except Leigh Ann had moved from the address some time in the past two months.

"If anyone can find someone, Stuart honey, it's me. I should have worked for the FBI." With this new martyr about, Stuart had reconfessed that he could not read, and Mom had taken a quick cab ride from the hospital to Barnes and Noble's Textbook Annex, where she'd purchased a few adult literacy picture books to work on with Stuart. I flipped through one of the books on the table-tray. "**B** is for **B**ank teller, **C** is for **C**onstruction site." They sent me deeper into my trough. I excused myself to the waiting area and thumbed through an old issue of *Time*. Staring at the lithograph of mollusks and sea horses above the corner couch, I couldn't pair the two Colins I now knew, the unpretentious teddy bear and the callous Machiavelli. I needed him to be there with me. No one else could calm me down. I started talking to myself: I was Colin calling me self-absorbed with a big unthreatening grin. I missed my Colin, who now I saw was an idealized cutout. The Colin who could take the wind out of any crisis by offering me his arms to hide in.

By his fifth day in the hospital, Stuart looked somewhat better. My parents were talking to the nurses down the hall, making plans to take him back to our apartment. Now that his head was clear, I led him through the details of how we'd checked him into a private hospital without insurance.

"How do you say that? Lupschutz?"

"Lip-shits."

"Thanks for doing this, Rachel." My whole family was in the room. "You're all so nice." My mother and Frank had bought him two pairs of Levis, socks, and three different black T-shirts at Canal Jeans. They even bought him a pair of hip-again suede Pumas from Athlete's Foot. Stuart was seated in one combination on the edge of the bed: Pumas, prefaded jeans, black socks, black T-shirt with pocket.

Frank admired his prodigy. "Flawless, if I may say so myself."

"How do you feel?" I asked.

"Not so good," Stuart said. "My knees hurt."

"His knees?" Frank said out loud.

"Obviously not a withdrawal symptom in *Super Fly*," I said, half to myself.

"That movie was about coke, not junk," Stuart said, with a Ganelli-siblings informational lilt.

"Hear that, bitch?" Frank laughed just as Dr. Mentoff entered the room. He looked over at Frank, obviously annoyed. "So are you ready for some more info, Stuart?"

"Yeah, I guess," Stuart said uncomfortably.

"That's my man. Now listen hard. There are two of you inside there. The innocent little boy and the addict. We're going to kill the addict."

My parents seemed pleased by this tough stance, but personally I found the word *kill* distasteful. So did Frank, by the look on his face.

"Going cold turkey without knowledgeable assistance is useless. If you can't make it we'll have to put you on long-term methadone. Seventy-five percent of methadonians use secondary drugs like pot, or it's back to the powders—heroin or crack. There's no easy way out, Stuart. You'll need at least a month of supervised aftercare. After that, I suggest being an outpatient for six months to two years."

"I don't know how I'll pay for that," Stuart said, like he'd broken a car window with a baseball.

"I'm processing you for Medicare with your passport. We can do that occasionally. There's no need to keep up the Stuart Lipschitz charade. We used your given name on your passport, Ian MacKenzie. Stuart's your middle name?"

I winked at him so he'd say yes. "Yeah," Stuart said.

"We'll have you eligible for the aftercare program in about ten days. Rest up at home. Aftercare can be strenuous. It's a daily supervised program."

"What do I have to do?" Stuart asked.

"The methadone maintenance treatment program is like having an elaborate system of foghorns and buoys to guide the way. It's a twenty-eight-day structured rehabilitation. You won't have any free time. You'll attend *one hundred and sixty-eight* lectures, workshops, and twelve-step meetings."

"Worse than law school, eh, Stuart?" Dad smiled, flashing his first smile since he'd met his newest charge. Dad's teeth are superwhite, he had them capped for his sixtieth birthday.

"Wouldn't know," Stuart smiled back with a mouthful of decayed teeth.

"Ninety-nine out of a hundred go back to using junk if they don't have aftercare. If you miss group therapy," Dr. Mentoff continued, "you'll be asked to leave the program. And you can't leave the room unless you have a note from me that you have a bladder problem, which I'm not going to give you."

"A sensitive caring program for the addict in your life," Frank said under his breath.

"Son, we've won awards for our program," Dr. Mentoff said.

Frank smirked. When he hates someone he smirks. "A touch of irony to lighten up the day, sir."

"Frank, I think I need to hear this," Stuart said. "I deserve this."

"Don't buy into this shit, you need the program, sure, but you don't *deserve* anything," Frank said.

"You want me to speak in plain English, Mr. Ganelli?" Mentoff said to Frank. "You better keep your smart mouth clamped shut. This *shit* is the only thing that's going to save Stuart's life. If he doesn't buy into this *shit*, I wouldn't put a nickel on his life."

"I'm sorry," Frank said, visibly humbled.

"So, where were we?" Mentoff continued. "Everyone in the family will have to be there for support. You can't check in with a dirty sample. Dirty Urines won't be admitted."

"Here's the rule, Stuart," Dad said. "You screw up, you get sent to your room and no ice cream." He extended his hand. "The Ganellis will not let you screw up. We're going to be there for you." Dad put his arm around Stuart. Stuart rubbed his hand on his jeans, a nervous habit he displayed at any nice word directed toward him, even when I'd complimented his doodles in Melbourne.

"Watch the medicine cabinet," I overheard Mentoff say to my dad, as I helped pack Stuart's belongings into a weekend suitcase Mom had brought from home.

"I don't get you," I heard Dad respond. I had a sudden revelation. The cough syrup, by Frank's toilet. Maybe that's why he didn't get over the hump.

"The Robutussin. Heroin addicts are obsessive-compulsive people. You have to think ahead."

"I can do that," Dad said. "I play chess." I felt the sharpest twinge of shame just then that my never-bounced-a-check chess-playing father was caught up in all this.

After my parents signed the final release papers, the Ganellis and one Gibbs-Mackenzie-Lipschitz entered the elevator. In the corner an administrator was talking to a nurse. "My son is in finance—he put off jury duty seven times. They had bailiffs come to his office building and arrest him. There's a new push to up the quality of jurors."

The jury-duty notice I'd left to rot on the kitchen table! I'd received a deferral from my last one because of an editorial conference, and then my parents had notified officials that I was abroad three times. When we got home I took another look at the slip. My jury duty was to start the next day.

9

Colin: SALT CITY AND THE BIG APPLE

Phillip threw his green silk shirt off into the sea of faces. A girl sausaged into a glittery seventies-style tube top caught it and proceeded to suck his sweat out of it. Above us, on the enormous screen, the camera zoomed in on her mouth. "Look up," Mick-O motioned with a drum stick. I craned my head back. In the past week and a half, the girls of Buffalo and Syracuse had done crazy things when it came out that we were sleeping a few doors down from Michael Hutchence. But this attention-seeking girl took the fucking cake. I laughed my head off in front of 90,000 hysterical people. The camera caught me doing that, which caused a second eruption of laughter from the Carrier Dome. It was the end of our set, and I was sweaty myself.

"Thank you, Syracuse!" Phillip hollered after a not-quite-thundering applause, like he'd done this for a thousand years. For the not-so-unexpected reprise, we played a cover of "House of the Rising Sun" we'd rehearsed in Buffalo; Angus thought Phillip's ballad we'd always played last in Australia, "My Heart," didn't have enough punch. On our final exit we heard an impatient roar: "INXS! INXS! INXS!" A Carrier Dome official with a harelip escorted us back to our dressing room.

"Bugger me sideways," I said. Mick-O laughed in obvious agreement. Memorial Auditorium was huge, but the Carrier Dome was the most terrifying place we'd ever been in.

"How were we?" Mick-O asked Angus after we'd reentered the dressing room.

"Overall pretty good, though everyone should've been more animated. Phillip was the best, the way he took command of the whole stage. We'll have to work on things before you get to Madison Square Garden. That's the show that matters, right? Colin, you can't stand with the bass in one spot, Americans love action, show business, mate. The best moment came when you laughed at the girl eating Phillip's top, that was excellent."

"How was I?" Mick-O said, plopping himself on the sofa.

"Fine," Angus said, like Mick-O didn't even register. Two pretty girls were calling out to Phillip from the door; he leaped over to sign their autographs.

"How did you girls slip in here?" Phillip asked, sickly sweet.

"We work on the concert board," the leggy black girl said. She had blue eyes I could see from where I was standing. I didn't thinks blacks could have blue eyes.

"The promoters give the concert board backstage passes if we help with the clean up," the other girl, blond with major mascara, added.

"Which one do you think he's gonna fuck?" Mick-O said half asleep, wiping the sweat off his face with his sleeve.

"Neither," Kerri said from the corner, and Phillip spun over and put his arms around her. She shot Mick-O a bloodcurdling look; he was fucking lucky his eyes were closed when it came his way.

I poked my head out the door to see if we could get ice for the Cokes. A small black-haired girl sat on a stool to the right of our dressing-room door. She had a clip-on yellow security pass and her head in a book. A little chunky, but cute. Amazing white skin, like a China doll.

"What are you reading?"

"Poems by Baudelaire," she said, unfazed. I walked towards her to see if she was really reading Baudelaire, like a mini-Rachel. She was. She looked almost smug when I did that.

"Can you get us ice, Miss Baudelaire?"

"That's Ms. Baudelaire to you."

"I stand corrected," I said.

She called to Harelip and asked him to arrange for ice.

"Did you like our show?"

"Didn't see it. I had to stand guard outside your room."

"But you couldn't stop a flea. How much do you make standing guard over me and my sweaty mob?"

"Five dollars an hour. We have work-study grants to help pay for our tuition, and Dressing Room Guard sounded more interesting than last year's position. I do the basketball games, too, you know."

"What was last year's job?"

"I was the mimeographer in the philosophy department."

I laughed, but there wasn't the slightest curl to her lips. Andrew Farris from INXS walked out of the band's top-billing dress-

ing room to go to the toilet. The security girl pointed to him. "I recognize him from the poster. What do you play in the band?"

"I'm not in INXS," I said, "I'm in the opening band. Tall Poppies?"

"Tall Poppies? That's a dumb name."

"Tell me about it. What's your name?" I asked.

"Nadine."

"That's pretty. What are you studying, Nadine?" I felt like a
fucking pedophile or something—I was at least a dozen years
older then her—but she had me pretty intrigued.

"TV," she said, "I'm a sophomore. I don't have to choose a
minor yet, but I think it's going to be philosophy."

"A friend of mine named Rachel once studied TeeVee here," I
said, parroting Nadine's twang, "and physics—yeah—in this uni,
I think."

"What's a *yoo-nee*?"

"University, sorry."

"Rachel your girlfriend?"

"No, a friend. Which do you like best—TV, or philosophy?"

"TeeVee. But I like Wittgenstein a lot."

I had no idea who the fuck she was talking about. "Right, he's
one of my favorites, too," I said, and she seemed pleased.

"Where are you from in Australia? Sydney?"

"No, Melbourne."

"What's that like?"

"Pretty stuffy. Lots of old houses. Where I live is good though,
St. Kilda. Good music and food."

"Are there Australian saints?"

"Pardon?"

"Saint Kilda?"

I laughed. "Yeah. Saint Kilda, Saint Mel, Saint Vegemite."

"I don't think it was an unreasonable question."

Her lack of humor made her even cuter. "Why don't you come in here?" I asked, pointing back towards the dressing room.

"I can't, I'm supposed to stand guard."

"But I'll give you twenty dollars an hour to talk to me."

She came inside with her book. Mick-O now had his clothes off and was splayed arse up on the sofa.

I threw him a towel. "Mate, think you can keep it on for a minute?" I saw the way the room was looking at me. Thank God Hannah thought Kerri was too crass to be friends with, or Hannah would've been in for a telltale report. They looked shocked at the lapse of Mr. Morality. Too bad only Phillip knew I was the diabolical mastermind of their whole fucking trip to the States in the first fucking place.

"This is Nadine," I said, trying to look like I hang out with American teens on a daily basis. "She's our security guard."

"Hi, Nadine," Angus said, a perverted Uncle Ernie. "I'm Angus, Colin's manager."

"Are you from Aus-trail-ya, too?" Nadine asked.

"No," he said, "I'm not from Aus-trail-ya, I'm from Australia."

"Stop making fun of me," Nadine said, wrinkling her little nose. It was divided at the tip, like a backside.

"Got a live one," Angus whispered in my ear.

"Give us a break, mate," I replied.

I got Nadine a pizza section from the food table.

"What do you want to drink?"

"Are there any Welchs?"

"What the hell is that?"

"Grape soda. Catering always throws in a few Welchs."

I took a sample sip when she got one off the table. Foul.

"You know a place where we can go to talk privately?" I asked.

Angus was closely monitoring our conversation. "It's good for you boys to go out with INXS when they're through. You three have got to become friends with them—you'll get more gigs that way."

"Not tonight," I said, and my security guard led the way to a beat-up red Volkswagen.

"I might lose my work-study for this," Nadine said, inserting her key in the ignition. She drove me to the car park near her dormitory. "Freshmen and sophomores aren't supposed to have cars," she said matter-of-factly. "But my Dad gives a shitload of money to the school."

"That's good, I guess," I said. "I thought you had that job to pay for your tuition."

"Well he told the chancellor I needed to develop a work ethic, so they let me take a school job."

Nadine signed me in at the front door of Dellplain Residence Hall. Upstairs on the sixth floor, her roommate was stretched out on Nadine's bed, reading a book.

"Shit! Nadine! You were at the concert."

"Find anything interesting in my journal, Dawn?" Nadine said, expressionless.

Her roommate left the journal on the pillow case and darted out of the room in shame. Nadine closed the door and pulled closed the curtain that separated the two sides of their dorm room.

"Nice girl," I said.

"I hate this school. It's so bourgeois." Her room had no decorations except for an enormous movie poster of *A Clockwork Orange* over her pillow, with a knife towards the viewer—pretty scary face to face.

I was going to ask her more about the movie, I'd been meaning to hire it. But within a few seconds she had her shirt off and leaned towards me with parted lips.

"Hey," I said, "can't we chat first?"

"You want to talk?"

"Yeah."

She opened her tiny refrigerator and pulled out a tangerine. "You want some?"

"Sure."

She started to peel. "Am I too fat?"

"You're not too fat, you're a button. But I like to ease into things." She fed me a segment.

Nadine studied my face; she looked so disappointed that I gave her a kiss.

"What's on your mind, Nadine?"

She ran her middle finger along my groin. "Can I give you a hand job? That's not too intimate. I'm good at that."

I was afraid saying no would scar her sexual confidence for a real boyfriend. I unzipped myself, and she pulled my cock out. She spat a globule into her palm, rubbing her hands together for a second, and then squeezed every inch until I was hard and my head was swimming. Here's the rub, as my Aunty Grace would say: even after her adorably "expert" hand job, I couldn't come.

"It's only a dick," Nadine said awhile later, defeated.

"Listen. That was terrific. You were so gorgeous there. I'm the old man, exhausted from the concert."

"If you say so," she said, looking away from my eyes. I pulled her near me to massage her shoulders. She had a strawberry mark right under her neck, which I quite liked and kissed.

"I'm getting that removed this summer. It's *so* ugly."

We fell asleep on her tiny dorm-room bed.

The limo dropped us off in front of the Hotel Roger Alexander. I was in awe. There was an actual buzzing sound to New York City. I had a list of places I was chomping at the bit to see: the Dakota, where John Lennon was shot; the Empire State Building (if I could view the drop from an enclosed spot); Central Park; and Café Wha?, where Hendrix had first played—even though Rachel had said it was a humiliating tourist trap now. And Rachel! I was going to see Rachel. First thing I did was ring her. I was revved up for a great conversation, but I was nervous that Hannah would come up. I didn't know how Rachel would take that.

"Hello. None of the Ganellis can get to the phone right now, leave a message at the tone," an older man's voice said. I was sure she had said in her one postcard that her parents were now pensioners in Florida.

"Rachel! It's Colin. I'm staying at the Hotel Roger Alexander on Lexington Avenue and I would love to meet you as soon as you get a chance. I haven't heard back from you, Bitchface. Ring me immediately, or I'll say your middle name on stage, 'cause we're opening for INXS at Madison Square Garden in a week, can you *fucking* believe it? Phillip and I are doing interviews this week, and we'd love to see you and hang out with you. You're gonna be my guide, right? We have a *fucking* limousine! I can get you front row tickets for my show. Ring me at 555-1870—I'm in room 1204. I ran to Safeway before I left, brought you Iced Vo-Vos and coffee-in-a-tube, for old times sake. I've missed you."

I felt pretty bad afterwards for saying "fucking" because on second thought maybe her parents were there after all. I was just organically ranting like we did back in St. Kilda.

"Did you ring Rachel yet?" Phillip asked, after checking out our room.

"Yeah."

"Great, I'd love to see her, I kind of miss her, you know?"

"Me, too."

"Are you going to tell her about Hannah?"

"Not right away. Anyhow, she's no doubt going out with an intellectual jerk and she's too humiliated to tell me."

Three days later, I still hadn't heard from Rachel, and I took a taxi down to her flat. A man with a hound held the door open for me like I lived in the building.

"Vinnie, you didn't get the terrier?" another passing neighbor with a frizz hairdo asked.

"I should have. This one keeps sniffing up syringes. I'm returning him Monday before he gives my whole family AIDS."

I got out on the sixth floor. There was no answer when I pressed Rachel's doorbell. I pressed a neighbor's bell. She cracked open her door, and I spoke through the chain. "I'm looking for Rachel Ganelli? I'm a friend of hers from Australia. You wouldn't know her, would you?"

"Cookie," the wrinkled woman in a tracksuit said, "there's no one in the building I don't know. I haven't seen Rachel the past week or so. I heard her come in once though—would you like a pencil and paper for a note?"

"That would be great." She gave me some tape and I left the folded message on the door.

RACHEL, IT'S COLIN! DIDN'T YOU GET MY MESSAGES?? THE POPPIES ARE PLAY-
ING MADISON SQUARE GARDEN IN 3 DAYS. I'M AT THE HOTEL ROGER
ALEXANDER UNDER MY NAME. I WANT TO SEE YOU!!!

I left her the pair of tickets Angus had given me for her. I took a taxi back to the hotel.

A reporter from *Rolling Stone*—the real one, the American edition—was in Phillip and Angus's room finishing up an interview with Phillip for the magazine's Random Notes section. Then Phillip had to ride over to a radio station with Angus. I intended to go, too, but Angus said they only wanted the lead singer.

I was disappointed. "I guess Mick-O and I will have a look around the city."

Around midday, Mick-O and I walked over to the Citicorp Building, a place I'd heard a woman in the hotel lift raving about that morning. "The public atrium's *marvelous*," she'd said.

We were staring at the people in the atrium, eating pizza

from this shop called Alfredo's-To-Go. Everyone walking by looked drop-dead amazing. I was sure every other woman was a movie star.

I was getting worried about Rachel. What could I have done to offend her? Had she wanted me to write her more often?

Mick-O and I continued over to Bloomingdale's, and I bought a bottle of Smoke, the Ivan Stanbury fragrance that Mum had asked for.

"It's modeled on a turn-of-the-century French salon fragrance," the salesgirl said.

"I'm buying it for my mum," I said.

The salesgirl sprayed some on my palm so Mick-O could have a sniff. "Don't you agree that his mother will *just* adore it?" she asked Mick-O.

"It smells like Mortein," Mick-O said. Mortein is Australian fly-spray.

"Is that an Australian fragrance?"

"Yeah," said Mick-O. I had to smile.

I made sure to get the perfume wrapped in a box with a Bloomingdale's label on it; then Mum could show her American gift to her neighbor Caroline. Mick-O laced up a ninety-five dollar pair of Air Jordans in Men's Shoes (it would have been three times as expensive in a Melbourne shop).

Then Mick-O bought a hot dog on the street and twisted his face up after one bite.

We went back to the hotel once more, and Mick-O put on the TV. I finally understood what "cable television" meant, because there were an unfuckinbelievable number of channels to choose from. Angus had bragged to INXS's manager that he had ordered sex channels for *his boys*, the perv; but I have to admit it was pretty interesting to see these low-budget commercials with naked girls. The weirdest one was "Dial 970-PEEE—the extra *e* is for the extra pee"—a golden shower phone line. Mick-O almost had a convulsion laughing at that. I took the channel changer from him and put on the New York City news. Wild crimes were reported one after the other: a prostitute shot in Brooklyn, a trial for a grandmother who shot her fourteen-year-old grandson's drug dealer; a retarded girl raped in a deserted McDonald's.

Phillip and Angus knocked on the door when they got back from the radio station. Phillip wanted to bum a clean pair of socks; the two of them were getting ready to go to a dinner party with the EMI executives. Angus didn't want me to go. He felt that they needed to develop Phillip's identity more with the suits.

"Angus seems to know what he's doing, mate," Phillip said. He took my socks with him out the door, leaving me with the looming prospect of an another dull evening with Mick-O. Still no word from Rachel. I decided to take a cab by myself to Café Wha?, which I found out was on MacDougal Street. I should have listened to Rachel.

There were a million celebrities in the Madison Square Garden audience, friends and fans of INXS. Angus had a list of most of them from the Garden management. Kylie Minogue, in her standard Madonna-rip-off outfit, was in the plum seat, front row center, courtesy of Michael Hutchence. There were supermodels seated there, too. Mick-O was rapt, he had a collection of *Sports Illustrated* swimsuit issues. The first few rows were cordoned off from the rest of the crowd by black twine. According to Angus, there were four security guards on the ground level checking VIP names. He knew for sure that the President of MTV and the head of EMI Records, and their respective entourages, took up most of the second row.

I tried not to process Angus's "helpful information" until after the show. I tried to keep cool and thereby sexy, swirling a glass of Coke in my hand, focusing on calming scenes from back home. I thought about more old neighbors, the Crawleys, who kept scores of crazy pets in their yard in Seaford. They had six cats, five dogs, a cockatoo, and a pony. And those dozen frill-necked and blue-tongued lizards that their kids had caught in central Australia— lizards, which Mum had said, were illegal to keep, like kangaroos and koalas. But the Crawleys kept them anyway in a wired pen and fed them mashed bananas, and eventually they escaped. Two weeks later Dad saw one of the lizards at the local milk bar out front, sitting on the handlebar of one of the parked bicycles.

I was safe in this stupid lizard world, with a half hour to get on stage, when Mick-O came over to me with an equally dumb grin. "There's an old bag outside who says she needs to meet you."

By the door there was a tall woman—about sixty with obviously dyed-black hair—in jeans and a bright pink top. She wasn't bad looking, but I wasn't going to say that in front of Mick-O. "I don't know who that woman is, how did she get past security?"

"I spoke to her," Mick-O said, "she seemed harmless. She said someone at one of the radio stations gave her a press pass because she had an important message for you."

I walked over.

"Can I help you?"

"Are you Colin Dunforton?"

"Yeah, I believe so—"

"I have a message for you, Colin. An urgent message from Rachel Ganelli."

"Rachel? You have a message from Rachel? I've been trying to reach her for a week—"

"Well, she couldn't make it to the concert—she's otherwise engaged—but she wanted me to give you this note."

I took an envelope from her.

"That's it, I guess," she said. "She made me promise to give it to you and leave—what are mothers for but to order around, right?"

"Wait," I protested, but Mrs. Ganelli was already out the door. I was about to follow her, when Phillip introduced me to a fat wanker he seemed to know from the dinner party. The head of EMI Records.

10

Rachel: STORIES FOR GRANDCHILDREN

"No more get-out-of-jail passes," the clerk had said. "Tell it to the judge." A hundred jurors were called down from the main jury room. They expected most of us to be dismissed. Word spread like wildfire; this was the media-saturated De Meglio murder trial: an Italian grandmother who shot her grandson's dealer with a hunting rifle.

A woman climbing the stairs next to me whispered, "He's going to let me out. I have three degrees, and they want malleable immigrants and blacks for trials."

Judge Berliner welcomed us to the voir dire process. "*Voir dire* is from old French: 'To speak the truth.' You are obligated under New York state law to speak and say the truth. Many people in this room think they have indispensable jobs. I assure you that an important job is not enough for me. How many of you have not heard of this case?"

One hand went up. "He'll be on the trial," whispered my new hallway "friend."

The judge dismissed him. A murmur went through the seats.

"This is a pragmatic court. Nothing's wrong with watching a bit of TV. If you've been living in New York City and you haven't heard of this case, I don't want you in my courtroom. The lawyers can dismiss you, but the judge can, too. The one excuse I'll accept straightaway is if you are a woman with a child under six without daycare. If you are in this category please raise your hands now." About twenty hands went up. "Bailiff O'Reilly is going to take names and numbers of these women, and we'll be imposing a serious fine if we catch anyone lying." About a dozen hands went down. The remaining women went over to the clerk single file and were dismissed. "Are there others who believe they cannot sit on this case?" Practically the whole room raised their hands.

"I see," Judge Berliner said. "Someone's going to have to sit on it."

We went up one at a time with our creative predicaments. In the silent courtroom it was easy to hear his consistent reply: "I see. But you'll have to take your seat."

My turn. I went toward the bench and handed him my jury card. "I don't think I could be impartial. My cousin's a recovering heroin addict—I'm his caretaker. Also, I have no money to spare. I'm temping and jury wage is not going to take care of my rent."

"Thank you, Ms. Ganelli, you may take your seat."

"How can you do this?"

"I don't believe you."

"My cousin went through the program! You can call Beth Israel! Stuart Lipschitz—"

"Please sit down, Ms. Ganelli. I've been in this courtroom for thirty years and I know someone inconvenienced by jury duty is not the same as someone who can't serve."

"I'm telling—"

"Sit down, Ms. Ganelli."

I sat there seething. Through the afternoon, Manhattanites unsuccessfully argued their right to rake in more than fifteen dollars a day. A sweet woman I had chatted with a bit in the women's room provided Berliner with her son's Yale graduation ceremony invitation. She was sent back to her seat with teary mascara.

She leaned over to a bunch of sympathetic jurors. "He said a smart son will respect me more if I went through the process."

"Bastard!" the guy to my right said.

Berliner called him up to the stand. "I could fine you in contempt of court, but you're not worth my time." And he was dismissed. Why didn't I think of that?

The clerk rolled the jury slips in a metal barrel that looked like the ones game shows use to pick out "this week's lucky viewer." Sixteen of the eighty-five left in the courtroom were asked to take their seats in the sturdy, wooden jury chairs and four fold-out chairs. The rumpled court-appointed public defender's fly was at half-mast. "Ms. Rachel Ganelli? Ms. Ganelli, you wrote in Ms.?"

"Yes."

"Briefly, what is your line of work?"

"I'm in between jobs, but I have worked as an acquisitions editor for a book firm."

"Are you married?"

"No."

"Do you live at home?"

"What do you mean by that—am I an unmarried woman living with my parents?" Plan B: let the lawyers think I'm a livewire.

He scratched himself on the head and nodded.

"Let the record show that Mr. Presticastro nodded his head in the affirmative," Judge Berliner said.

"I'm subletting from my parents."

"Ms. Ganelli, do you have relatives in the law profession?"

"I have a cousin who's a police officer. I really respect him." How were they going to check on cousins? Safe lie.

"Tell me about your hobbies."

"I like reading trial books."

"Do you think you understand the law?"

"Absolutely. I think I'd make an excellent lawyer." I peripherally caught Judge Berliner's face. He was on to me.

"You have heard of this case?

"Yes."

"How did you first hear about it?

"Where? On TV—I followed it closely, a horrible case!"

"What station did you follow it on? Which anchor person do you like to watch?" He had asked this question before, and when the person in the front row said Fox he seemed pretty happy. But what if he asked me about Fox—I didn't know their anchors. Shit, shit. What do I say? Defense, they hate public TV . . .

"I was in Australia at the time, and I saw it on their public broadcasting station. The ABC. Excellent foreign coverage."

"So, in actuality, you were out of the country when the incident took place?"

Fuck! "Yes." The defense attorney smiled at me. "Thank you, Ms. Ganelli."

"Mr. Lanier, is it? What do you do in your spare time?"
"I'm into UFOs—"

The assistant district attorney, Ms. Gorsham, spoke to us in a robotic manner. Before questioning me, she took a long pause to check her notes.

"Hangs her clothes on Shaker pegs," the high school history teacher on my right whispered.

Ms. Gorsham sat on the edge of her lawyer's table to get the skinny on me. How down-to-earth and confident, I knew I was supposed to think.

"Did you attend a university, Ms. Ganelli?"

"Yes."

"Which one?"

"Syracuse."

"What did you major in?"

"TV, I loved my major, and, uh, science." I looked her up and down. About fifty and rougeless. Barnard or Radcliffe. Jesus, she's prosecuting, she wants me to be smart. Please don't ask me which one.

"Science? How interesting, Ms. Ganelli. What branch?"

Hey what about the TV? Don't you want to hear about my junior-year demographic analysis of Saturday morning cartoons? "Physics." She raised her eyebrow to her young male assistant, who was downright hunky, even in my nausea I noted that. He made a mark on his pad next to a diagram of the juror seats.

After lunch the judge called us back from trial.

"When the clerk calls your name you are free to go."

The clerk read from his book. "Ms. Pfister—Mr. Lanier—Mrs. Chu—Mr. Liss (the history teacher)—Mr. Rodriquez." My name was not being called. "Mr. Molinari." They're dismissing the Italians. *Manga!* "Mr. Stein." Name after not-my-name was called.

"Ms. Ganelli and Mr. De Jesus, after the clerk swears you in, you can join the two others sworn jurors in the jury room. We have eight other jurors and four alternates to secure."

The clerk approached me. "Do you swear to tell the truth and nothing but the truth so help you God?"

Wait a fucking second.

Nine jurors had been picked. Three more jurors and four alternates to go. The bailiff opened the door to our jury room. He looked like Rusty Staub, Frank's favorite Met from the 1973 pennant race: big build, ruddy complexion, and tawny hair. He asked us to write down our requests for sandwiches.

"Who ordered the cappy ham?"

"I did," Mr. De Jesus said.

"What's cappy ham?"

"Kind of ham."

"If we don't have cappy, can I get you a normal ham?"

"I guess."

"Okay then," the bailiff said, "first crisis down. This trial will last about a month, is my guess, but don't quote me on it. Better get used to each other."

A pushing-elderly man in a yarmulke inquired, "Can you ask the judge if we get Monday off for *Lag b'Omer*?"

"Lag what?" Bailiff O'Reilly said.

The juror wrote it down for him to take back out to the court-room.

"What's that holiday for?" asked a forty-ish children's book ed-itor, an oversize, overhealthy blonde straight out of Edna Ferber's *So Big*. During the voir dire, she had said she was of Swedish de-scent.

"It's the day the manna started raining down from the heavens to sustain the Jews in the desert," I said.

"You're Jewish?" the Orthodox juror smiled.

"Half," I said.

"That's one interpretation. It's the thirty-third day of the seven-week period of mourning from the start of the seder—mourning for the Jews who died at the hands of the Pharaoh. Lag b'Omer is the thirty-third day, and *Shuvvuos* is the fiftieth day. That's the counting of the Omer. It's a harvest preparation reprise from the mourning. You can be merry, plant wheat, and have hair-cuts."

"Such knowledge!" the blond editor said.

"I'm a librarian at Yeshiva University," he admitted.

"The counting sounds like the days leading up to Lent," said Mr. De Jesus, the naturalized Dominican bartender from Washing-ton Heights—the other juror selected from my batch.

"The Christians lifted many of their customs from the Jews; some of them I'm sure priests wouldn't want you to know about," the Orthodox juror said.

And the Jews borrowed heavily from the Phoenicians, I wanted to say, but I'd learned my lesson from the last nasty quarrel with Benji at Passover. The bartender was of finer moral fiber than me. A bit later, as the two of us leafed through a stack of old *Reader's Digests*, he told me to call him Louis. Louis said that he realized right off that the Orthodox juror was not used to talking to Catholic bartenders on a daily basis. He knew the man was merely trying to dispense information and not make a judgment, and had therefore forced a smile.

Five more jurors came in: a young woman who also looked Dominican or Puerto Rican, a black woman who later said she was a legal secretary, a young black man with dreds who worked for the post office, the three-degreed white woman from the hall, and the hot Indian or Pakistani guy I'd spotted in the far corner of the jury check-in room earlier that morning, reading Nietzsche. He had light brown skin, a chin-length bob, and a kissable mouth. He introduced himself as Raj.

The bailiff reentered our holding pen. "You will have Monday off for the holiday Lag b'Omer." The big blond woman turned to the Orthodox juror and said, "Thanks! Let's try Swedish Pancake Day." The ones in on the joke laughed, except me, sourpuss with a recovering heroin addict back home.

"A few more items of information I need to pass on. We have a refrigerator," the bailiff said, "but it's pretty gross. There's an inexpensive cafeteria in the building, and there is a decent Korean deli on the corner. I also recommend the vegetable dumplings at Excellent Dumpling House a few blocks down for a good quick lunch."

"How about a microwave?" the legal secretary asked.

"What is this, *Fantasy Island*?" he responded with perfect timing. "This is the New York State legal system. You're lucky the fan is working." Once again everyone except me laughed.

"Don't look so glum," the rasta post-office worker said to me. "How bad can this be?"

A few minutes later the bailiff, known to us now as Kevin, instructed us to join the final four selected jurors in the courtroom.

"Thank you for being patient," Judge Berliner said. "We will begin the trial on Tuesday—one of our jurors celebrates the Jewish holiday of Lag b'Omer. I will not sequester you for now, but you may not talk about this case outside of the courtroom. We can expect media attention on the trial, and I will warn you that if it gets out of hand and the hoopla interferes with justice, I have the legal obligation to sequester you. Please report to the juror room at eight forty-five A.M. Bailiff O'Reilly will give you a pass so you can leapfrog the lines outside the courtroom. Have a nice weekend. You are dismissed."

"You're on the De Meglio trial?" Frank gasped. He'd biked over to the apartment to bring my father's minimum items for living: the *Times*, good virgin olive oil, sun-dried tomatoes, and fresh mozzarella, the latter three from the Italian Food Center on Grand Street. "What about Stuart? You're going to leave it to Mom and Dad now, aren't you? You're from New York City. You don't know how to get off a trial? What the fuck, Rachel? Didn't you say your uncle is a cop?"

"I said my cousin was a heroin addict! And another cousin was a cop. What more could I do?"

"And another cousin was a gun-toting grandmother? You have to appear sincere."

"Look, know-it-all, there's a woman on the trial with morning sickness. The judge wouldn't let her use pregnancy as an excuse —we might have to wait an hour every morning while she throws up."

"I think it's kind of a funny story," Stuart said from the hallway. "Your mum's going to help me get work this week. Don't worry about me."

Was Stuart to be trusted yet? The silverware, the computer, and the two expensive vases could be sold for cash. My parents had delayed their trip for another two weeks. God knows how long this trial would last. Frank was right: I should have been crazier during voir dire. I should have started quoting doctrine or taken my bra off and swung it like a flag. Wouldn't I have done that if I wanted to take control again?

My father had been teaching Stuart how to play chess. Stuart was setting up the board for when my parents got back from their movie. He put the bishops where the rooks should be, and the black king on a white square, but I figured, Let Dad correct him. Next, I made an unconnected decision, like a decision to apply to a certain college while lacing up a new pair of boots. I was going to see Colin. That's what I was going to do.

From my parents' room, I called up the Garden box office. The INXS concert was sold out.

"Are you adding dates?"

"We'd love to, but it's the end of their tour."

How could I get backstage? I could track down the hotel he

was in. I called my old house in Australia to see if they had sublet the place. No one answered. I called EMI and asked for their publicity department. They couldn't release information on the Poppies' personal schedule. Shit, if I only knew an assistant or intern there. My five-star secretarial contacts were in radio and quantum mechanics, not record labels. Richard! I could call Richard.

Thank God for family apartments that are forts of time. On the refrigerator, next to an adopt-a-manatee sticker we had tried to soak off for years, was the unpublished studio number my parents insisted on having when I worked at the station.

A young female intern answered. "Studio."

"Slick Rick, please." That was Richard's brilliant "secret password" to screen out fans who might have gotten ahold of the number.

"You'll have to wait a few seconds, he's still on the air," the perky intern said. Had I sounded this chipper when I'd answered the studio phone?"

"Rick McDonald," a familiar baritone voice said.

"Hi, Richard, it's Rachel."

"Rachel?"

"Ganelli. Your long lost intern? I'm despondent that my name hasn't stayed on the tip of your tongue."

"That Rachel?"

"That."

"How the hell are you?"

I was determined to keep this short. "Great. I'm doing great. Yourself?"

"Wonderful. I got married. Two beautiful kids. I signed another three-year contract—can you hold a sec, Rachel, the promo's about to end."

I stared at my ceiling, waiting for the optical-illusion perception change. Eventually, the ceiling was the floor, and my furniture was hanging from the ceiling. "Hi again. Rachel, would you like to come visit at the station? I'd love to see you."

"I'd love to see you, too, but I'm a juror on a trial starting Monday, and the hour I get off is when you go to sleep."

"A trial? What kind of trial are you on?"

"The grandmother shot her grandson's—"

"You're on the De Meglio trial? I've been reading updates on jury selection!"

"I'm not even supposed to be saying anything. Richard, let me cut to the chase. I have to ask for a one-time-only favor from you."

"From me? What can I do you?"

"I need INXS tickets and backstage passes, if you could swing that. I have a twelve-year-old cousin coming in from Michigan who cried when I told her they were sold out."

"It's always tickets when you're in the radio business," Richard joked. "I'll help you out if I can. What's your phone number?"

"Oh, you're great! 555-2348."

"Isn't that your old number? You're still there?"

"Still there."

"I'll speak to the programming director, Tony."

"Tony's still there?"

"Yes, we're the dinosaurs of the station. That's right—Tony always liked you. I think he would've hit on you if you weren't a baby—unlike me, huh?"

That was a pretty good joke. He seemed brighter than he had seven summers earlier.

An hour later the phone rang. I raced to answer it, a silly thing to do since Stuart was unlikely to pick it up.

"Rachel Ganelli? It's Tony Fedele, remember me?"

"Tony!" I said, with false cheer.

"Rachel, I got the tickets you asked Ricky for. You could've come straight to me, doll—our interns since you have been morons. You were the best, doll."

"Thanks, Tony, I can't believe you got the tickets! Fantastic."

"Now listen, Rachel, I got you a limited backstage pass that everyone at the radio station has, you and your cousin won't be able to get into INXS's dressing rooms—but pretty close. You can try. Flash those legs of yours to the guard is my advice, if I don't sound like too much of a sexist pig. But hell, you know, this is the industry. It's not me, you know? It's the way everyone in the industry is—"

"The passes will be fine. You're the best, Tony."

"How old are you now, Rachel?"

"Twenty-seven."

"Funny thing, I broke up with my girl last month. Perfect timing, don't you think? Can I take you to dinner? You still have that great smile? You were so funny, I still tell people how funny you were. After you get out of the trial, doll, let me take you to dinner—Ricky says you're on the De Meglio trial—you're going to let that lady free, right? Poor old woman. I say shoot all pushers. String 'em by the balls. She's a heroine—disgraceful that she's locked in a cold cell. Good thing a smart girl like you got on the trial—the Italians got to stick together, right?"

Tony had the tickets messengered to me.

On Tuesday, we had a four-hour delay. The morning-sickness woman had the head of gynecology from her hospital come in to get her off the trial, and for once Judge Berliner was impelled to back off from his hard-boiled approach to the American judicial system. I pondered if I could risk getting a note from Beth Israel. Now that the case had started, reporters raced to look into everything. No, it would be safer to ride this out, was my unhappy conclusion. One of the four alternates took the expectant woman's chair: a Rockette at Radio City Music Hall who had protested at the stand that she was part of a dance formation and couldn't possibly serve. Then the assistant district attorney began the outline of her case.

"Good morning—or should I say, good afternoon? Over the next several weeks, I will attempt to prove to you that the defendant, Maria De Meglio, purposely took a man's life. The defense will no doubt want you to sympathize with her story, but you are legally bound to examine whether or not a crime was committed. I will present irrefutable evidence that Mrs. De Meglio is guilty beyond the benefit of a doubt. Despite how we feel about drugs, vigilantism is not legal, and as jurors that is what you are bound by law to do—that is, determine if an action was illegal. I will show that Mrs. De Meglio understood what she did, even if she did it in the name of love . . ."

After her statement we were allowed to go to lunch. I wandered over to Chinatown, two blocks north on Canal, and bought a red satin notebook at Pearl River, a Chinese department store. I wolfed down an egg roll from a street cart and raced back to the courtroom. I could have taken my time. A reporter had spotted a rival journalist slipping a hundred-dollar bill to the Norwegian-descent book editor.

Judge Berliner decreed that since it was the beginning of the trial he was going to dismiss the juror, and we would now be sequestered at a motel. So much for Colin and my tickets. All jurors were going to be accompanied to their homes by court officers to pick up clothes. We were given instructions for conjugal visits.

My mother and father and Stuart were watching TV when I got home. Stuart fled for the bathroom when he saw the officer's uniform.

"We heard," Dad said. "You're going to be sequestered."

"Can you believe this? Mom, can you come into your bedroom? I need your help packing."

Dad offered a soda to the officer. Mom followed me into her bedroom and put on the light. "What a mess. You'll have to survive this. Good thing we came, huh? We've been looking after Stuart. Daddy and I took him to see the new Harold Pinter play. Stuart was great—he stood on the half-price tickets line while we parked our tuchases in a pizza parlor. He said he had never seen a play before, can you imagine? I'm not sure he got the references, but he seemed to love the atmosphere."

"You're great, what can I say? But listen—I need an even bigger favor. I need to give you these tickets for the Tall Poppies and INXS concert later this week. I want to talk to Colin. Please don't judge me. Please go to the concert and give him a note for me. You can take Frank or Dad. But you have to go backstage, and you have to get a note to Colin. The pass should get you to in front of their door. I know you could talk your way back. I got them from the station I used to work for. I need to talk to him. I'm falling apart. I have to know why he didn't tell me. He has to know what's happened to me. I can't believe he wouldn't care." I was squeaking again.

"I don't want my baby to get hurt."

"Colin's not going to hurt me. He'll be mortified when he finds out, but he's not going to hurt me. I want him to visit me at the motel. I think I can get him permission. It'll make me feel better."

"What does he look like?"

"He has a rough, chiseled face," I sniffed. "He looks like he's from the Outback, except he hates horses. He's as venturous as a stuffed bear." I smiled inside for a second, remembering when we went to Phillip's uncle's cattle station together in the movie-famous Snowy Mountains, and Phillip, Kerri, and I were trotting ahead before we realized that Colin had refused to get on a horse, more of a city sissy than me. He later made up some ridiculous excuse about a hammertoe.

"What color hair?"

"Bottle blond, nice and tall, and amazing light blue eyes, ethereal almost—"

"Not Jewish."

"Neither is Daddy."

"That's why I'm going easy on you. I'm a sucker for a great goyisha face. I'll pack your bag. You write that note. Let me give you something that Colin slipped under our door today with these tickets."

"Colin was here? Mom!"

"He left messages on the machine a few times this week. I erased them. I'm sorry, Rachel, but I thought you needed him like a hole in the head."

"MOM!"

"I wasn't going to tell you about it. I was protecting my little girl. Mrs. Frino said she spoke to an Aussie friend of yours today through her chain, that's undoubtedly your Colin. She said she didn't know we were in town, and she told him she hadn't seen you."

I couldn't even yell. Mom believed she had done the right thing, and I had a court officer waiting in my living room.

I grabbed the note and read it. In his boxy capitals Colin told me all about how life is wonderful. I wanted to be near him so badly, but it made me furious that he would casually seek me out like this without admitting his slimy actions. How dare he. How dare he screw my life up like this.

Here's where things get really debauched: my eyebrows knitted like Wile E. Coyote's, I grabbed a pen and a manila pad off the desk.

Colin,
I've been out of town, sorry I didn't get your note in time to meet with you. Congrats on your concert. I'm proud of you.

You may be wondering why I am sending this with my mother. I'm a juror on a crazy trial. This crazy old grandmother shot her grandson's dealer. You can read about this in the paper or watch the news. I'm not kidding! I have to stay at a hotel room for the duration of the trial. I'm not supposed to be talking to anyone about this trial. I'm breaking the law right now! We can only have conjugal visits, i.e., sex visits (!!!) from our fiancés and husbands. When you get this note, I'm afraid I will have already missed the concert. But I do want to see you. Please contact the bailiff at New York State Supreme Court, Courtroom 12, 100 Centre Street. You must tell them that you are my fiancé and that you have arrived from visiting your sick mother in Australia. And they will make arrangements for you to be bussed to my secret location in New Jersey. We're both famous this week, in a strange way. But you're more famous, or will be! I want to catch up on everything. Congrats again on the big news. OOOXXX, Rachel

Mom didn't ask to read it, she'd packed my clothes for me as I wrote out the note. She handed me an envelope, and I made her promise him she'd leave as soon as she got it in his hands.

"Kiss?" she asked with a guilty lilt. She knew full well how angry she'd made me. At the elevator, my mother yelled, "Wait, Rachel!" and the court officer pressed the open button. She handed me a red velvet pouch.

When I'd been almost four, my parents had taken Frank and

me by subway to a nursing home in a far-off land called Brooklyn—to visit my Grandpa Ganelli, who Mom had said was not
going to be able to be visited anymore. I didn't remember ever
meeting him in the first place, and this greatly upset Dad. "Sure
you have, Rachel, he has that big funny beard, like Santa Claus?
We brought him turkey and stuffing at Thanksgiving?" When Dad
gave up on jogging my memory, I heard him say to Mom, "At least
he's going with all his marbles." When the subway emerged from
the tunnel for elevated track, it was snowing. The car twisted and
bent like a snake, and then there was this magnificent white vista
of the Manhattan skyline in front of us, perfect, like in a picture
book.

Later, in Grandpa Ganelli's room, Frank gave him a Polaroid
that my father had taken of Frank and me on the subway car. The
coughing old man got misty-eyed at the gesture. Grandma Rosa
was there; her presence confused me since Frank had told me
that because Grandpa Ganelli refused to go to church, he and
Grandma Rosa were *annoyed*, which meant they didn't live together. Aunt Virginia was there, too, holding my father's hand and
praying, and these people called *relatives* were in a room down the
hall. "I'll have something to remember you by when I'm far away,"
Grandpa Ganelli said. He was hard to hear, so I went right near his
mouth.

"Can I have your marbles?" I asked. "Daddy says you still have
your marbles, and when you go away, I'll remember you, too."

My parents were shocked by this statement, and later on I understood why, but my Grandpa Ganelli laughed, albeit with diffi-

culty. "Joe! Make sure you give her my marbles. Children, I want to tell you a story. See the pretty snow outside, isn't it pretty?"

"Yes," I agreed.

"When I first came to America, it snowed like that. I was the same age as Frank."

"You were?" Frank asked, forgetting about his G. I. Joe for once.

"Come here, too." Frank went closer to the bed. "Yes. It snowed like that except it was even bigger, greater. We were on a boat headed for Castle Clinton, the place where little boys from Italy got to first step in America."

"You were in a castle?" I gasped.

"Yes. I stared out a window: the famous new Statue of Liberty had snow piled high on her open palm."

"Really?" Frank asked.

"The greatest blizzard in New York ever, and they still talk about it today in the history books. I never saw a day with so much snow in Italy. The most perfect snow in the world. My first snow in America and it was the most famous snowstorm of the century! What do you think of that? Do you like that story, children?"

Frank wasn't convinced. "How can the Statue of Liberty have snow on her palm?—she's holding a book in one hand and has a torch in the other! I know, Grandpa, 'cause I went there with my class. And how can you go on a boat in the middle of a blizzard?"

"I like the story," I said, a sentiment echoed years later by Stuart from our hallway, the day I was forced on to the infamous De Meglio murder trial. "It's funny."

"You mustn't forget that story, children. I've waited my entire life to tell it to you."

A few weeks later, after my grandfather died, my father bought me a bag of colored marbles in a red velvet pouch. It had traveled with me to Syracuse, to Australia, and now to an under-wraps motel in Elizabeth, New Jersey.

11

Colin: CENTER STAGE

The top suit of EMI wanted to wish us luck. "I have to tell you," he said with a disposable smile, "I have a good feeling about you guys. Phillip is a quirky good-looking fellow. We're going to pump the violet eyes on the cover. If you kick ass out there tonight, I think we're going to sell some records, boys." He and Angus were two peas in a pod with that "boys" crap. The guy was about four years older than Phillip.

"Thank you," I said.

Michael Hutchence came over to shake our hands. I was off the executive's radar again, if I had ever been on it. I took the extra few minutes before stage call to read the note Mrs. Ganelli had given me. I had to read it twice. Rachel has God-awful handwriting—she wouldn't have made it a week around the nuns in my school. She was holed up on that weird grandmother trial Mick-O and I had seen on TV back in the hotel; she wanted me to come see her under the guise of an authorized sex visit. That made me laugh, as much as you can laugh when you have to perform in front of twenty thousand New Yorkers in twenty minutes. Was she serious?

Phillip pulled me at the elbow. "You should've talked to him more, he's the one who calls the shots."

"What didja do, suck him off? He wasn't interested in anything *I* had to say."

"Oh c'mon, Colin, you're overreacting."

"Yeah, easy for you to say, you're so *good-looking*."

"Jealous, mate?" Phillip asked.

I raised my fists like I wanted the discussion to come to blows. "Yeah, Pretty Boy. See that woman I was talking to before you came over?"

He smiled. "Yeah, that was nutty—what happened there?"

"Rachel's mum."

"Her mum? Where the hell's Rachel?"

"She didn't talk much—she handed me an envelope from Rachel and ran like I had the black death. Rachel says she's stuck as a juror on this crazy trial I heard about a few days ago. She's not allowed to leave her motel room except to go to the courtroom."

"Give us a squizz!" He grabbed the note from me and gave it a read. He kept squinting at her indecipherable words. I translated them: congrats, conjugal, famous. "This is odd," Phillip said. "She could've phoned the hotel before. She had to send her mum?"

"Rachel likes to put on a show, Phillip. You know what she's like."

"Least she's not mad at you."

"Yeah." I figured I'd track down the court first thing in the morning. We had another two weeks to spare in New York after the wrap-up party, for post-publicity.

"Poppies get ready," the pretty Asian backstage coordinator named Beth announced. During soundcheck, Mick-O had chatted her up. He said he was after "a bit of wonton love." Mick-O was from a working-class family, not as rough around the edges as Stuart's, but compared to him my family were regular intellectuals. At least we were brought up without prejudices, and one Saturday a month my grandmum used to take me and Liam on "cultural outings," as she put it, to places like the Museum of Victoria, where there were dinosaurs—or to the Old Melbourne Gaol to see the death masks of the convicts who couldn't mend their ways. Mick-O's use of wonton was in no fucking way clever wordplay on wanton. I long ago came to terms with his existence—he was good for a beer at the pub and he liked people.

Beth escorted us past electrical pipes, a Coke machine, pointed out the New York Knicks' dressing room with the nine-foot doorways, and led us to the edge of the stage. Waiting behind the curtain, I wasn't even thinking about Rachel anymore. This was it. A gig in New York City. Madison Square Garden. Talk about a change in fortune. The audience took their seats to Tina Turner's "What's Love Got to Do with It?" And then Michael Jackson's "Thriller." I plucked a nervous note on my fret. During soundcheck, when we'd had problems with the speakers, the supercilious arse of a production manager had assured us that everything would be working when we got on stage. My bass did sound good.

"Sounds good, huh?" Mick-O asked, testing his babies, his tom-toms, and his snare.

"This is the big time, I guess. On this level even arseholes do things right."

Then, like in a dream: "LADIES AND GENTLEMEN. MADI-
SON SQUARE GARDEN AND FOSTER'S WELCOMES YOU TO
THE DOWN UNDER TOUR WITH INXS. PLEASE WELCOME
THEIR SPECIAL GUESTS, FROM MELBOURNE, AUSTRALIA—
THE TALL POPPIES."

I had a stiffie from my nerves. And the eye tic was at it again.
For our first song, "Red Rope Principle," I crossed the stage a few
times the way I'd been shown by the choreographer. Angus had
hired her the day after we'd arrived in Manhattan. She'd gone over
a few steps in her studio, and for an hour in the empty Garden.
Phillip ate the charm-school stuff up, and I went along with him
even though we were supposed to be a fucking rock and roll
band: half the fun is standing around like a wooden board and
looking like you hate the world. But Angus, without consulting
us, had paid a cool thousand of our performance fee for this
happy woman who'd made me walk across the rehearsal room
eleven times until I was passable. "Colin! You're not strutting,"
she'd smiled. "Look like you want to rape each little girl in the
audience."

"You put up the velvet rope," Phillip now sang—"Wouldn't let
me inside—And like all your men, I'm waiting in line—So obvious, girl—But it works every time."

"It works every time," I sang in harmony with Mick-O.

After crossing the stage once more from left to right, I tried to
focus on a woman in the first row of the audience. There was a
video crew because it was the final show of INXS's four-month
tour. We'd been told that an edited version of the night was going
to be released on video cassette. I wondered how the members of

Yothu Yindi would feel. They did a grueling eighty percent of the tour, and one of our four shows got to be immortalized. Between the cameras and the lighting system, I couldn't see a bloody thing.

When our set was through, Beth whisked us back past the pipes to our dressing room.

"That was great, just great," Kerri said, slipping her hand rather directly on Phillip's arse.

I collapsed on an armchair. I sure wasn't twenty-one anymore.

Phillip slapped me on the back. "A night for you to remember, mate," he said.

"And you, too," I said.

"Yeah," he said, kind of somber.

It would have been rude to leave until INXS was through. Their manager had arranged an hour-long piss-up after the show, after which they would go their way with models and charge cards.

"Take a seat, boys," Angus said. "And Colin, I have a surprise for you. You have a visitor in the audience! She'll come back stage after INXS is done."

Rachel's mother. Yeah. I knew about her already. Maybe she'd give me more information about going to the motel.

"Maybe Rachel talked her judge into letting her see the show," Phillip offered.

On that slight chance I took a quick shower. Brushed my teeth. Toweled my hair.

"Colin!" Mick-O called. "Come out of the toilet!"

I opened the door.

"Surprised to see me?"

"Yeah," I said, shocked.

"Yes," Hannah corrected. She was wearing a teal blue dress that looked insanely great with her red hair. "You haven't picked up a new American girlfriend, have you?"

"Not when I've been mesmerized by Hannah Leser," I said. I kissed her on the lips. She tasted like she'd eaten olives before coming backstage. "I thought you had a ceramics conference."

"The event planner had a heart attack on the second day, so it got canceled. You said you wanted me in the front row of Madison Square Garden."

"Did you know her?'

"No. Just from the phone."

"Oh, well, it's too bad, I guess. What did you think of the show?"

"Good. I couldn't figure out why you were running around the stage so much, but you sang on key throughout."

"Thanks," I said, taking what I could get.

"INXS was driving them crazy out there."

"Yeah," I said. "How's Hector?"

"My cats are full vegans now, and they were getting tempted by those tins of tuna and chicken you left for Hector. I thought it best if I separated them. So I hope you don't mind, I brought Hector over to your mother's. I left Marjoram and Smudgeface with a friend of mine from the food co-op."

"You met my mother?"

"You left her number for an emergency, remember?"

"I guess that's okay."

"Miss Hannah," Phillip said loudly from the couch. "How's the press coverage for us back in Australia?"

"Haven't paid much notice to tell the truth. I heard something on the radio once."

"See," Phillip said to Mick-O, "this is big news."

One of INXS's roadies knocked on our door. "They have some beer for you, but you better come right away. They have to go to a nightclub later."

I thought I saw Hannah smirk.

We went into the other dressing room as casually as possible. We got a round of "Good jobs." Everyone eyed Hannah; she shrewdly kept her somewhat whiny voice silent, so she'd seem more mysterious. Kerri had no such insight. Phillip squirmed while she held his hand tightly, as if he was on a leash.

I couldn't get an accurate reading on Hannah. She'd spent her own money to come out, and yet she kept wavering from being my devoted girlfriend to someone I needed to pick up all over again. One of the record executives wanted to know if we wanted to sniff some heroin, and she said, "No, no, Colin doesn't do that."

"It's a test," she whispered seconds later. "They want to see if you're a serious musician."

I wasn't so sure he wasn't simply a drug abuser, but I didn't mind that Hannah declined for me. Stuart's sorry life was enough to keep anyone clean.

"Who are you sharing a room with?" Hannah said.

"Mick-O."

She squeezed my wrist suggestively. "Think he's going back to the hotel right now?"

"I'll find out."

He was making his own suggestive comments to Beth in the corner. "Mick-O," I interrupted, "Can you stay out tonight?"

"No problem," Mick-O smiled. "Beth, would you deny Colin a surprise reunion with his girlfriend?"

"I guess not," Beth giggled.

We hailed a taxi back to the hotel.

"I'm on the pill now," Hannah whispered. "And my AIDS test came back negative." Hannah had once told me that she'd had a test every six months since she heard about AIDS. She'd been slipped a mickey once by a surfer from Geelong, and was never sure what happened.

"Well, if you're game, I am," I said. "I had an AIDS test two months ago when Phillip panicked over a heroin-abusing bedmate he'd boffed after too many beers. He wanted a mate to go through the test with him." The taxi driver was too preoccupied with a baseball game on the radio to hear us.

I whistled as Hannah came out in a new satin teddy. She did look unbelievable. She peeled back the bottom of the sheet and caressed my legs. "I've missed your exquisite toes, darling."

The sex was good for a change, a state punctured only by Hannah immediately leaping out of bed to remove her smeared mascara.

"Condomless sex—one of the benefits of a real relationship. You could have come in me," Hannah chided.

I almost drifted off to sleep when I remembered I had to go to Rachel's hotel the next day, or forever piss her off.

"This is so nice," Hannah said, gripping my elbow.

Angus knocked on the door. The alarm clock said one A.M.

"Come next door. I got some raw footage from the video tape crew. I have to give it back tomorrow morning before INXS's people find out about it."

"I'm busy, Angus," I said.

"That's okay," Hannah said. "Let's go watch."

It was just the three of us in Angus and Phillip's room. Angus handed me a beer. Hannah passed. "I only drink champagne or mineral water," she said. I glanced at the mirror over the sideboard and caught Angus mocking her words as he rewound the video. About ten minutes into the tape, we could see that I'd mistakenly thrown a sexy stare at a big puffy man with a mustache in the front row.

"I couldn't see much with those lights," I tried to protest, but Angus and Hannah were too busy laughing. I felt very small.

"Oh, Colin," Hannah said. "Have a sense of humor."

12

Rachel: THE HALFIES

The assistant DA's hunky junior associate was going to play the first cassette tape for us, one of three conversations recorded by the FBI after Mrs. De Meglio's arrest. He handed out fourteen headsets to the jurors and two remaining alternates. I hadn't legally made up my mind yet, but you'd have to be a dolt to think Grandma Vigilante hadn't shot her grandson's dealer dead. Her fingerprints covered the gun. As far as I was concerned, the only thing that could get her off at this point was if it turned out that there had been a police violation, like Miranda rights not being read. But in that case, how the hell would the case have gotten past the indictment stage? No, granny was guilty.

A year or so back, I'd bought a week-old copy of *The New York Times* at an Australian newsstand. The dead drug dealer was fourteen years old, from a broken home.

While the prosecution had my sympathy, they were now losing it a bit by "testing" the audio levels for the upcoming confession tape with a convenient snippet of Pavarotti; was that a coincidence, considering Grandma Maria was Italian? I imagined that the jury pro in the DA's office had instructed them to get it subliminally in our minds that the murderer is Italian, like ice cubes that read *sex* in a liquor ad. Hunky Assistant then took the even more obvious opportunity to connect with his jurors, as his senior partner studied her notes for the next round of questioning. One by one he asked us if we could hear okay, a time to repeat our names and make legal eye contact. "Mr. Kaluzny can you hear?" Fred nodded. "Mr. De Jesus can you hear?" Louis nodded. "Rachel, oh pardon me, Ms. Ganelli, can you hear okay?"

Now *that* was going to keep me in his camp, saying my first name like that. Was he thinking I was adorable, too? This was like *Bonfire of the Vanities*, when the schmucky Bronx assistant district attorney fumbles every time he sees a classy fox of a juror from upscale Riverdale. Except this lawyer was a catch; he was polite and *très* cute. And while I wasn't social register or soap opera–siren material, he could think I was spunky and attractive, crazier things had happened, it was possible. And he worked in the same office as John F. Kennedy Jr., how pop-culture cool was that? What a trip it would be to grab a beer with JFK Jr. when Legal Boy and I finished up on the trial. We could double date with Darryl Hannah, or whoever the Prince of Camelot was screwing at the moment.

"Are you paying attention, Ms. Ganelli?" Judge Berliner asked. He looked asinine with remote headphones dangling around his neck.

"Of course, Your Honor," I said. Did I say the words *Your Honor* in a courtroom? Do we learn etiquette for life's oddest moments from our parents, or TV? I tried to make eye contact with Assistant Hunk. "Yes, I can hear it perfectly."

"Mr. Cohen," the judge said, "I don't think you need to go down the line. Is there anyone on the jury who cannot not hear the tape clearly?" No one raised their hand. "Proceed with the case then, Mr. Cohen."

The senior ADA asked for extra minutes to move the evidence from her cart onto the prosecution table in an orderly fashion. Young Mr. Cohen still looked a bit shaken up by the judge's admonition, and busied himself with a notepad, checking off each confession tape as it went on the table. Cute indeed. And Jewish. Mom's side of the family would love him. *My niece met her mensch while she was on the De Meglio murder trial.*

The jurors and the courtroom took the opportunity to chat, not a legal worry if we kept it to meaningless banter, like asking around for a hard candy to soothe a sore throat. "I think the junior district attorney likes you," Louis whispered. He sat directly to my left.

"Oh please, stop," I said. "He made a mistake. You think so?"

"Unless he said your name in a calculated move to get you to convict, like their playing opera music on the tape levels."

"Can you believe that?"

"What do they think, we're idiots? By the way, I'll take him if you don't want him." Louis licked his lips.

"You're gay?" I formed a mock-shock letter O with my mouth. "Half."

"Bi and Catholic?"

"The Pope would have a heart attack, but I still believe in God."

A little sniff of laughter came out of my nose. "The halfies—the Italian Jew and the bisexual bartender jurors from hell," I said. "Outsmarting all of them."

"They might want us to have this conversation—then they're smarter than the two of us."

"Okay. Jurors we are going to resume. Mr. De Jesus and Ms. Ganelli, I trust you weren't discussing the trial."

Eagle-eye Berliner.

"No, Judge, I was admiring her unusual brooch." Louis's reply struck the entire courtroom as a particularly odd response, and there was a collective snicker. Berliner let out an unguarded grin, which made him seem more human.

"Your Honor, I'm afraid we are still waiting for the one last essential tape from the DA's office," said Ms. Gorsham after we quieted down. "Can we take a short break?"

"Please come forward to the bench to discuss this matter." The lawyers approached the judge.

"I won't object," I heard the schlumpy defense attorney agree.

"Very well, we'll take a half hour break." He addressed the full courtroom. "I want to remind the lawyers, and the jury for that matter, the more breaks, the longer the trial." We were escorted back to the jury room.

"Is it Wednesday?" I asked, grabbing my favorite seat.

"Thursday," Louis said, reaching for the two-pound bag of M&M's Bailiff Kevin had brought us. "Hey, did you hear that Berliner is sixty-four?"

"Please," I rolled my eyes. "Try again. He's about forty-five."

"Nope, sixty-four. Kevin told me when I was out by the water fountain."

"The legal system is probably what keeps him young. If he left his dictatorship, he'd probably shrink up like the heroine in *Lost Horizon*."

"It's hot in here," Mrs. Ricasio protested. She went over and opened the window, getting soot on her yellow sundress. "Nobody gives a damn in here except me."

Leslie, the Rockette who had replaced the pregnant woman in seat one, was now our foreperson. She leaned over to me and Louis. "Do you think Mrs. Ricasio is okay? Should I ask the judge to send us back to the hotel?"

"Mr. Nessenbaum doesn't look so well either," I said. Mr. Nessenbaum's face was flushed, and he was resting his head on a copy of the *Times* with trial references cut out of it.

"I need a shower," Louis said. "That fan's a joke."

"The woman's seventy-five," Mrs. Ricasio said. "How come we only have the choice of murder in the first degree?"

"We're not supposed to be discussing the trial yet," Raj, the cute Nietzsche reader reminded us. He'd had a conjugal visit the previous evening from his pretty Columbia journalism school grad-student wife, at which time I reluctantly gave up on him as a distraction from my boredom and woe.

Fred Kaluzny sipped his canned iced tea. "Isn't it cruel," Fred asked, to no one in particular, "how cats and dogs only live such short lives and then turtles get to live to a hundred and forty? Rats live for three years but they kind of deserve it."

Our foreperson Rockette knocked on the inside of the door, and Kevin answered with his usual cheery whine: "Is this a demanding jury or what?"

"Our exhausted crew needs to go home," Leslie said.

"You have to write out your request," Kevin said.

Leslie asked for a reprieve in a tight one-room-schoolhouse handwriting that lacked modern curves and flourishes; she was a synchronized kicker in more ways than one. At least my writing worried people a little.

A few minutes later the judge summoned us in and officially called it a day. We were escorted to Forlini's on Baxter Street, one of the less touristy standby Little Italy restaurants I knew from childhood; Dad had his old reliables in Manhattan if our family was too tired to trek to Arthur Avenue in the Bronx for the real thing. The sixteen of us law-abiding jurors were given three huge platters of cold antipasto to share, a choice between pasta and a side salad, broiled sole, or veal parmigiana. Then, coffee and spumoni. After the lousy deli sandwiches and overcooked vegetables we'd stuffed down that week from the court cafeteria, we were most enthused. When everyone was through with the restrooms, for the third day in a row, we were escorted via minibus back to our motel rooms.

13

Colin: LURE

With her day-old arrival and our new condom-free commitment, Hannah would never put up with an overnight visit to Rachel. But I'd resolved to see her. I opened the steaming door.

"I'll be back in a tick, I'm getting some fags down in the lobby."

"Say 'cigarettes,' Colin. If you don't speak proper English no one's ever going to respect you."

"Cigarettes."

I planned on ringing Phillip from the lobby phone to recruit him in my lie. This was getting to be as natural as shaving. I saw Kerri wearing her black vinyl cap. She was on the couch, eyes glued to the front door.

I pulled the brim of her cap so she'd look up. "Kerri, is Phillip up in the room? I have to ring him."

"Phillip? He didn't come home last night. They lost me yesterday at the Palladium."

"What? Who's they?"

"He phoned me this morning from an after-hours club. A pathetic excuse about Angus and him wandering around with too much vodka. He's on his sorry way back now. How could he lose me? Is that the craziest thing you've ever heard? Is he rooting around on me again?"

I answered her with my silence. Fucking clueless. I had always pitied her, but it wasn't my place to give her the scoop on Phillip, an only slightly more discreet sex maniac than bloody Mick-O. Why did she put up with his bullshit? It was obvious that he didn't give a toss. Kerri once told me that she grew up in Coober Pedy, the mining town in South Australia where to beat the heat everyone lives in deserted opal shafts. Now it's a tourist trap; there's a new hotel constructed around the abandoned shafts. Even before the tourist dollars though, residents learned how to compromise: blistering sun, but a steady wage. Perhaps bubblehead Kerri was a legend back home in the Outback, a brave girl who cut loose to Melbourne, and now the States. Maybe Phillip was another Coober Pedy–style compromise for her.

"I'm going to give him a little slack for the tour. But, Colin, you tell me if anyone gets serious. I want to be the one to marry him. I put in my time all these years. I've earned the payoff. Will you promise to tell me?"

I nodded and coughed. I couldn't believe she still wanted him. "What did you think of our final gig?" I asked, to change subjects. Shit. I had to hurry this along. Hannah would be suspicious.

"It wasn't a gig, Colin—it was a stadium concert. You were on display to the major music journos and execs in the States, but you were prancing on stage like a kid to a record. I'm your friend, so I'm going to tell you this: during the concert, I overheard Marty, one of the A&R reps, complaining to the head of EMI about you as unnecessary overhead. And your good friend Angus was saying

'I told him not to strut across stage like an idiot, but he wouldn't listen.' Angus said how great it was that Phillip held court center stage."

If this wasn't spongecake Kerri I was talking to, I would have been devastated. She had it wrong. "Angus and Phillip *want* me to strut," I explained.

"Rubbish. Fucking Angus's setting you up. Marty's his partner in crime. Truth is, since Buffalo, Angus's been hinting to Phillip that he thinks he'd be better off solo. Phillip's been knocking the idea back, but his ego might not hold out. If I were a fan of Angus, I wouldn't be telling you this. Phillip needs to be punished, too. He thinks he's such hot shit now. I drove him out to the Bendigo gig when his car was unroadworthy and in the panelbeater. Every week I do his bloody laundry. If he can't keep his peter in his pants, he better know where he came from. Be aware, Colin. You're the nicest guy in the band. You don't deserve the lying shit I get. But please, don't dob me in as the source."

"Of course not," I said, trying not to let my voice crack.

"Marty had Phillip try out for a soap opera role as an Aussie detective. He thinks he can launch his career with tie-in ballads— like his friend did for Rick Springfield years back on *General Hospital*."

What was left of my own ego toppled onto the floor. Between my visit from Hannah the day before I was supposed to see Rachel, and now the news that my risky claim to fame had merely been a launching pad for Phillip's pedestrian career, a wondrous week was tinged blue, like rancid fruit. Which fat-arsed cunt was Marty, and why did he have it in for me? The A&R reps were difficult to distinguish by either name or importance, like Greenland and Ice-land.

"Why don't you go back up?" I asked with tremendously false composure. "Take a bath before Phillip comes back, so you can be calm and have the upper hand."

"I'll sharpen my knife. When he walks through that door, I'm going to take him to the forest and chop his head off."

"Before you do that, can you get my new shirt back from him? I don't want it to be bloodied."

"Talk to you later, Colin. Watch your back."

I took her seat on the couch, waiting for Phillip. What could I say to Hannah? A bellboy asked me if I wanted anything from the bar. I gave him a dollar to go away. "Thanks for asking," I said.

Only two minutes had gone by when I saw Phillip walk into the lobby without Angus.

"Hey, mate," he said, when he'd reached my square of lobby carpet. His eyes were red, and his pupils giant black circles. "You missed a real scene last night."

"They'll be a real scene for you, upstairs. I rang for the hearse and arranged the plot. Kerri's mentioned something about a knife and the forest and your head."

"I wish she'd get off my back. I didn't invite her to America."

"But she came. Look, I'll leave that to you lovebirds to work out. I have my own problems. I have to spend a night at Rachel's motel, and Hannah would never let that happen."

Phillip grinned. He was not alone in Kingdom Slimedom. "How should I cover?"

"I told her I was getting a packet of fags. Can you knock on my door in fifteen minutes and say I need to do a sleep-over TV interview in New Jersey? Tell her you have to do a bigger one for *Musician.*"

"That's ridiculous. She can check it out with Kerri."

"Kerri hates Hannah, you know that. She once told me that she wants to pull the rod from her bum. After you calm her down, she'll be into it."

"You are one evil bastard, Colin. All these years I thought you were an angel. But that's silly. Who sleeps over in New Jersey for an interview? It's half-baked."

"Make it Boston then. I'll get some facts about Boston from Rachel."

"Hannah might want to go along on your trip."

"I'll cover that."

"So you're not going to tell Rachel about Hannah?"

"I'm not sure about that yet." I wanted to ask him about the back-stabbing nonsense Kerri was on about, but it was easier to keep to one mess at a time. "See you soon," I said, heading for the lift.

"That was a long five minutes," Hannah said.

"Sorry, I had to take a crap in the lobby."

She cringed her nose. "Disgusting."

"I'm going to take a shower now."

"I certainly hope so," Hannah said.

I had a head full of suds when I realized that I'd left the note Rachel's mum brought me in my jeans. I should have given the court address to Phillip and binned the note in the lobby along with my cigarette stubs. Hannah might see a corner of the letter peeking out of the back pocket. But nothing seemed strange when I got out of the shower.

About twenty minutes later, Phillip and Kerri knocked on the door. He had his arm around her. They had patched things up. Poor Kerri.

"*Bass Player* magazine rang," Phillip said. "You're going to have to do that interview in Boston for this afternoon. The car's coming in an hour."

"What interview is that?" Hannah said.

"It was supposed to be in two days. It's my only solo interview. I have to do it."

"So what am I supposed to do?"

"I thought you might like to spend the day with us," Kerri said. I was right. She was going along with us; she hated Hannah that much. "An EMI executive's taking us in a helicopter to the Hamptons. He told us that's where New York's beautiful people go for the summer. They don't have to work during the week. Phillip has his interview at seven tonight, and then maybe we can go see a show on Broadway."

"Actually, that sounds fun. I got a new bikini." Mentioning the upper classes to Hannah is like putting out sugar water for a fly. She was happy. But although they were carrying out our lie perfectly, I was a tad miffed that I hadn't heard about this helicopter earlier. Did this support Kerri's conspiracy theory? And I was nervous about Hannah in a bikini surrounded by rich New York men. When she left with Kerri and Phillip a half hour later, I grabbed a cab to the court address where Rachel had promised transportation to her motel would be waiting.

Walking down the blue carpeted halls of Rachel's New Jersey motel, I had a gratifying shock. Even if INXS's entourage didn't treat me like a first-class citizen, and there were rumblings of a rocky path ahead orchestrated by Marty and Angus, I was—at that precise moment—a successful rock musician. And while I wasn't sure what lay ahead sexwise, I was about to spend the night with the woman I most wanted to be proud of me. My mum would accept me no matter what I did. Even Hannah would be pleased if I read enough and tried my hardest to be genteel. But not Rachel; she expected perfection of everyone around her, even though she admitted she in no way held taut reins on her own life. That is Rachel's ultimate charm. You can spend your life with people who will let you relax in mediocrity, like Mick-O and even Hannah. You'd have a pleasant, stress-free existence, and maybe that's the way to go—die among the salt of the earth. Or you can surround yourself with exasperating friends and lovers who respect your intellect and demand that you use it. Rachel could see through an idle bastard quicker than anyone, having dabbled a bit too much with lack of direction herself. But as I neared the end of the corridor, I knew she had to respect me more than when I'd last seen her. Having performed in front of a sold-out Madison Square Garden was pretty bloody close to perfection.

"Wendell," the guard at the door told another blue-clothed guard, "let Rachel Ganelli know her fiancé's back from Australia."

"She the pretty one?"

"Yeah."

She'd eat up that compliment if I repeated it. Rachel never thought of herself as pretty. She wasn't conceited in that way, which is what made her pretty. She was conceited about her brain, which is what made her, if you weren't in the mood for her, annoying.

"Rachel!" I called. The guard let me through to a lobby. I spotted her black hair. Was it combed out for me? She always wore it in a ponytail, and I used to tell her in Melbourne she should wear it down. "Rachel!" I called.

"Sweetheart, you're dripping!" She kissed me with closed lips. Outside, it poured relentlessly and the wind whistled, amplifying my Heathcliff-arrival effect. My mother used to joke over rainy breakfasts that she was waiting for Heathcliff to ride up our driveway in hot pursuit of his destined Cathy so Dad would have to fight for her affections. I could tell the others in the lounge were dying to be introduced, but Rachel used the thunderstorm to rush me down the hall into her room.

"Let me get you towels, honey!" she said, as we were leaving the lobby. It felt great to be near a real friend. I liked our little engagement play. In her room I plopped down on the hideous bedspread with my jeaned legs spread open. "Come on, Sheila," I continued the game, "I came here for me conjugal visit. Woman, you ready for your root?"

"Sorry, Bruce," she said, in equally put-on lower-class Australian. "I haven't seen you in so long, I've gone lesso with the other bird jurors."

"Right, there's my sarcastic wench," I laughed. "Pretty good. You're not emphasizing the first syllable anymore. Been practicing?"

"I had an Australian houseguest before I got sequestered."

"Yeah? One of your friends from Dog's Bar?"

"No—"

"Wait, before I forget," I said, unzipping my duffel and handing her a Safeway shopping bag. "Australian goodies. As promised, bikkies and coffee-in-a-tube. And I got you a snowglobe from guess where?"

She picked up the Niagara Falls snowglobe, shook it, and put it down again on the night table. "Thanks. I don't have this one."

"So who's your guest?"

"Someone you probably don't remember. So, Mr. Rock Star, how was Madison Square Garden?"

"Amazing. It's crazy that we got these opportunities after Stuart's death." How easy it was to lie now. But this wasn't hurting anyone. "I wish there was another way, but I'm not taking this trip to mourn too much. We might be back in the States in a few months if the record sells here. It was intense to be on stage, Rachel, to feel accomplishment. We went to a pub near the Garden afterwards, and a girl asked *me* for *my* autograph, can you imagine?"

"That's great."

"I'll shut up for a bit. I'm sure you have heaps to tell me. Like how the hell you got on this trial?"

"I've been trying to figure that out."

"Bet you have a mega-job you're on leave from."

"In a way you can say that."

"Tell me about it then."

"A little later," she said.

"I heard on one of your news programs that there was a grandmother involved."

"Yeah, Grandma Rambo blasted a fourteen-year-old's head open."

"Keeping an open mind?" I teased. "Wasn't he a dealer?"

"I haven't discussed it with anyone in detail, but I don't need to fuck up six weeks of my life to know she's guilty as hell."

"Poor Grandma. If I know you, you're the jury ringleader, and she doesn't have a chance."

"You're off. I'm the outcast. They think I'm an oddball."

"It's like calling Kojak bald."

She did this weird fake giggle.

"Hey, another thing I almost forgot—we were in Buffalo and Syracuse—I saw your old uni, we played the Carrier Dome. I talked a bit with the current work-student security—"

"Work-study."

"Work-study girl—"

"Person."

"Rachel, she's a girl, she's nineteen." I threw a pillow at her. She didn't throw it back.

"What have you done in New York City?"

"Mick-O and I went to Bloomingdale's," I said.

"Together? That's somewhat a gay male stomping ground in the city."

"Now you tell me. I could've scored."

It looked like Rachel's mouth was stuck.

"The trial's giving you the shits, isn't it? Talking to you today is like getting ink from a dried-up well."

"Colin!" she said suddenly. "How could you?"

"What? I was kidding—"

"Colin—I know—I know about the murder you concocted with Phillip."

I could have slit my wrist that second, but I said nothing.

"I ran into Stuart in a luncheonette on Fifth Avenue—he was eating a tuna fish sandwich. A dead man in a coffee shop eating a tuna fish sandwich!—what's the matter, Stone Fucking Face, aren't you going to scream 'Mercy me, Stuart's alive'? Or is it not such a surprise after all?"

My face must have been stiff and white. (I've blotted out those first few seconds.)

"Not like I ever loved the guy, but by your standards I'm his new patron saint. My brother and I took him in, and he's pretty much off the kick, for now at least. Right now he's at my folks' place reaping the rewards of overprotective parents. He had no more money and no home—he was going to sleep on a fucking park bench! While the two of you concocted that horrible plan to get yourselves into fucking Madison Square Garden! You were my best friend. How could you of all people lie to me? Why would you lie to me?" Rachel's hands were shaking.

When she told me that she knew about the murder scheme, I think maybe I thought she was kidding, that she would say, "I know you got him shot, didn't you," the way I'd say "C'mon! You bribed the examiner!" if a brilliant mate came in dux of the class when final exams were posted. But then I saw her lower lip quivering and realized she was furious and, more than anything, disillusioned—that she did know. I had failed her, a fact that felt worse than lying to my parents and sixteen million Australians,

minus the handful of others in on the scam. Rachel had me terrified. I didn't know what to say or do. I do remember eventually
lashing out at her.

"Are you any better than Phillip and me luring me in here?
Torturing me? Why didn't you ring me and get the whole story?
You had to lure me in here like a madwoman?"

"You arrogant bastard. How can you turn this around like
that?"

"Do you want to hear the whole story? Or have you already
convicted me, too? Pretty bloody fucking hard, Rachel, when
you're handed moral grandstanding on a platter." I glared at her.
"What are you going to do?"

"I don't know. That's what I wanted you to tell me."

I sat listlessly on my chair for a few minutes. I could hear her
breathing out of sync. Finally, I spoke: "Rachel, listen—I was
dying in Melbourne. You've had a top-rate education. All your life
you've been told you that you are capable of enormous achieve-
ment. My parents are great, but they had no expectations for me.
They wanted me to be a good bloke, like one of their friends. My
school had the barest essentials: maths, English, history, science,
and religion. I would've killed to switch places with you. You
talked about being editor of your primary school newsletter. You
were only ten! Acting out those radio plays. Fencing. Jesus, we had
a field and were told to kick a football around. You have no idea
what kind of chances you were given. What can I do if my music
fails? You used to say it yourself—I'd rot in the print shop."

"Go to my house."

"Your house?"

"Go and help my family take care of Stuart until I get out. I won't do anything to you—I'm not about to turn you in to the cops."

"I have to go home. I have to tour Australia again in three weeks. That's when I'll be able to help you out. Believe it or not, this tour is costing us more than we'll make. In Australia we'll start raking in the cash. I can fly back in a few weeks. I can give Stuart money to get him going."

"He doesn't want your goddamn cash," she said. (I suspected if he was anything like his former self, Stuart would more than love my dirty cash.) "You can't leave me with this. Quit the band and help me fix this mess."

"How am I going to do that? Give me a month and I'll come back and help you. How can I break up the band now? Mick-O has nothing to do with this. Our manager has nothing to do with this. I have a special visa for the tour. What am I supposed to live off of? Oh, God, I'm sorry. I don't know how, but I'll make this better."

Rachel lay across the bedspread. She looked up when she realized that I was crying, too, something she'd never seen me do in the two years she'd known me. Whether I was sobbing in shame or terror, even I wasn't sure. An officer from the court knocked on the door.

"Okay in there?"

"Yes, sorry," Rachel said, through the crack, "we were catching up, if you know what I mean." Rachel forced a grin. She closed the door.

I came up behind her and touched her on the shoulder. "I'll marry you if that's what you want me to do!"

We were both startled by my sudden solution. Jesus, is that what I wanted?

"What?"

I had opened my mouth, and it seemed indecent to back off now. "I can get working papers then, and help you."

"That's not such a bad idea," she said. "You can sleep in my bed now, and when my parents leave, Stuart can take over their room, and you can move to the sofa bed."

"I'll quit the band tomorrow morning and face my hell."

"Is that what you think—that marriage to me would be hell?"

"Are you toying with me? I'm saying I love you, that I'd destroy an EMI contract to make it up to you. Isn't there a moment in your life you can let the last word slide?"

"I've missed you, Colin."

I didn't answer for a while. She pushed the hairs on the back of my neck up, then smoothed them down again. "Rachel, I've missed you like hell, too. This is the one horrible thing I've ever done. You have to believe me! Listen. You're scaring me with your mood swings."

"I'm scaring *me* with my mood swings."

"Rachel, I've been seeing this girl Hannah since you left. I was besotted with her at first, but now I'm pretty sure I can't stand her anymore. She just arrived in New York to surprise me."

"You're dating someone?" she said, suddenly sharply attentive.

"Where is she now?" It was a comic site, like seeing a baby stop crying when she sees a ring of keys. I couldn't tell her that, of course, so I kissed her on her crown. Jesus, Rachel, I almost said, what have I done?

"At the beach with Phillip and Kerri. I'll ring her right now to break it off if you want me to."

"You can do that tomorrow," she said. "I can't imagine you with anyone. Is she pretty?"

"Yeah."

"Brunette?"

"Redhead, like Fergie."

"Oh."

"You'd hate her. She loves Rilke and Verlaine."

"She reads?"

"What, I'm supposed to be with a beautician?"

"I didn't mean it like that."

"You meant, she's smart like you, right? Believe me, she's bright, but she's no Rachel Ganelli." Her anger over Stuart pushed to the back for the moment while she contemplated this new information.

"Shit. I didn't think you had a girlfriend."

"You didn't write back."

"I was going to eventually. I was flat from everything: leaving you, Stuart's death. But then I found out what a scummy thing you did."

"I didn't set about destroying your peace. You have to understand that. If anything I wanted to impress you."

"By staging a murder?"

"By getting a better contract. You *are* my best friend. I tried to keep you out of it. You went away before we could get anything going. I really wanted to have you as my legitimate girlfriend."

"You did?" She twisted a strand of hair.

"And furthermore, what were the chances of you ever bumping into Stuart eating a tuna fish sandwich?"

Unexpectedly then, Rachel started to laugh.

I reached for her hand. "Rachel, what do you want me to do?"

"I want to order room service. I have a twenty-dollar court allowance for snacks." She sat down by the phone, recovering from laughter- and cry-induced sniffles. I handed her the box of tissues from the bedside table. She lifted up her mouth to meet my lips, and we had a sad passionate kiss.

I admit it. Even with our kiss, Rachel had me spooked. Back in Australia, she'd boasted that she was exactly the wrong person to cross, that she'd often inflicted comeuppance in unexpected ways, like her sweet note about paying her a visit her in sequestration. She'd once admitted that her boyfriend before Will, her college boyfriend, had dumped her in total bastard mode, and she'd ingratiated herself among his friends until he suffocated in his own support system. Rachel never needed a long list of reasons to justify her decisions; and it was obvious I gave her more than enough she deemed valid. At that moment, I wanted to be a rock star, and I sure as hell didn't want to be thrown in jail. I was scared shitless: Rachel had me fenced in.

True, it was not an entirely horrible circumstance. My marriage offer could be reneged at some later time, when she was calmed down. I rather liked the idea of marriage to Rachel, even if it was only a temporary fantasy that she'd bought into. I needed Rachel on some level in my life. But at this point my heart wasn't jumping through hoops of relief and love. What about Hannah? I couldn't just drop her like that, could I? Plain and simple, I was saving my hide. We all have our tactics.

14

Rachel: HAILSTONES

After our kiss, we stripped to our underwear, tacitly agreeing not to take it further. Colin spooned me with his downy knees. His scent—a natural musk, a few too many cigarettes, and the papaya conditioner he used to keep life in his many-years-peroxided hair—startled me with soothing memories of watching late-night Australian TV under the living room doona, the Australian word for comforter. Before I fell asleep, I looked at the palm he had swung around mine in his sleep. For a second I was sure that I could see our hands stripped of their layers of skin, like in the illustrations for "X-ray specs" in the old Johnson Smith novelty catalogue.

Colin had salvaged his life. No one in the end got hurt. What the hell did I have to show for my advanced test scores? Fuck-all. What would I do if I was still driftwood in hyperachievement circles in a few years? Since graduation, God was it six years now?, living my life felt like eating white chocolate: everything good was there, but it never truly satisfied.

Around two A.M., large pellets of hail started hitting the window pane. I sat in my red bra and panties mesmerized by their random rhythms and sizes. I had once commissioned a journal article on hail from a meteorologist. The earth sciences acquisitions editor at Bell Press had been fired for hauling publicity copies of new Bell titles to the Strand and other used bookstores for cash. Gordon made me meet the fired editor's appointments at a conference in Atlanta. Earth sciences never clicked with me the way physics did. I had to give myself a crash course on hail in the hotel room— with xeroxed pages from our firm's tiny library. Hailstones form in spring or early summer mostly between latitudes of thirty and sixty degrees, slices of the earth that include New Jersey. They are associated with thunderstorms; the stone's nuclei need to be carried by turbulent winds to ever germinate. Super-cooled water, still liquid at a freezing temperature, hits the icy atmosphere and the nuclei freeze over, melt and freeze again, thaw and ice over once more. A hailstone grows with each pass through the atmosphere. At a certain weight, the updraft can no longer support the stones.

I had goosebumps from the air-conditioning; I shut it off. I tried to imagine this redhead reading poetry to Colin during sex. From the curtains, I stared over at him and tried to imagine marriage.

A relationship is so much like a hailstone. If you could carve through either one, a cross section would be layered like an onion or a tree trunk.

15

Colin: C'MON YOU LITTLE FIGHTER

The motel room smelled of perfume and summer morning sweat. Rachel lay diagonally over me—not a good thing, as I'd woken up with a morning tent and above all I needed to take a horse piss. Answering nature's call at six A.M., I wrestled free from the sheet and her legs. The shock of the previous evening came back to me as I returned to bed. I lay there with harsh-angled light on my eyes, panicking. Rachel, sound asleep, stretched an arm over her pillow. With this new view of her armpit, I saw that she had bothered to shave—even though she had baited me to her motel room to chew me out. And of course!—the perfume—in the Siberia of jury sequestration, she had bothered to scent herself. These revelations hit me like blocked-sinus spray, and I instantly felt a notch or two better. She hadn't lied. She honestly had sought an explanation, not blood. Had she brought perfume or borrowed it from one of her fellow hostages? I grazed the bumpy texture of the not-quite-surfaced hair growth under her arm. My finger must have tickled, because she smiled in her sleep. Safe, on another plane: the old Rachel who relished life. Hannah never smiled in her sleep.

My offer to marry Rachel had been a rash one, but even more

disturbing, she'd gobbled it right up. To take back the proposal hours later would be insulting and foolish. Hannah's reaction worried me, too: Would she rage or beg when I cut the cord? Another solution was needed, one where I wouldn't risk losing Rachel's friendship. After all, Rachel was still in the driver's seat, and Phillip and I *had* committed fraud. She could flatten us. The alarmed reactions of the others if I left the band—Phillip, Mick-O, Angus (who would no doubt breathe a sigh of relief as well), the boiled suits at EMI—was stomach-churning to think about. It was easier to shut down again than to face my uncertain future.

Two and a half hours later, I woke up once more with a spanking headache. As per my usual cure, I reached for my fags. Rachel stared at me from a chair as she towel-dried her hair. She was dressed in her high-tops (were those bloody things a part of her body?), her cut-offs, and a tit-revealing pink T-shirt. Everyone loved Rachel's tits, most of all Rachel. She called them her "grandmother's gift." Stuart had once declared that they were the size of two big juicy oranges, while Phillip had thought they might even be as large as grapefruits.

"Gross," Rachel said, making a very Hannah-like face. "A Marlboro's the first thing you grab for when you wake up? I was going to leave you a note—I have to get on the minibus in twenty minutes. The guard down the hall's arranged for you to get back to the city in about an hour. No one else had a conjugal visit yesterday."

"Good morning to you, too. And Jesus, that's quite the court outfit."

"Don't start on what I wear again, you're not my husb—" Her voice softened. "I called my mom while you were sleeping. A guard monitored me—half my sentences didn't make sense. I told her that you had come back from visiting your mother in Melbourne for a conjugal visit—that we talked it over, and you want to make amends to Stuart while I'm on the jury—and that you were going to be a financial help toward getting him a new life."

"How'd she take that?"

"She was confused and insisted that she was in control—'I don't need his money.' I also told her to forewarn 'Cousin Stuart' that my 'fiancé' is moving into my room, and that it's still a secret. It's hard to talk cryptically—the guard gave me suspicious looks. I left it that you'd come over around noon, and the two of you could work it out. She agreed to at least talk to you this afternoon at the apartment—my dad has a date with his old work cronies, and you don't want him calling the shots—he's too righteous. Mom's a bit much, but she won't bite."

"Did you tell her about the rest of the conversation?" I asked cagily.

"No. Are you kidding? With the guard listening? We're already supposed to be engaged. Besides, she was freaked out enough on the other end, and I don't think she's going to understand the marriage part of our solution."

Mayday, oxygen needed! I hadn't imagined it; she'd taken my offer to heart. I wasn't going to change her mind in twenty minutes.

"Please don't tell her we're getting hitched," she added. "I'll ask Judge Berliner about getting permission for tomorrow—I'll need an escort to the marriage license office during lunch. I'll tell the judge we want to speed the date up for your working papers, and that we'll have a blow-out ceremony in a few months. He thinks we're engaged, so it's a plausible story. Hopefully it won't leak into the news, but the reporters can't print my name even if it did. Why don't you come back tonight and tell me how the talk with your manager went? And with that woman you're seeing."

I fidgeted with a filter inside the ciggie packet. "Rachel, I'd thought I'd wait a bit on that until everything is sorted out with the band."

"But, we agreed last night—"

"I'm going to do it," I said, calming her down but at the same time practically sealing my escape hatch.

She kissed my neck. "I hated having you as an enemy. You're doing the right thing now. We might even like being married. I can't go this alone."

"Rachel—"

"Rachel Ganelli, into the minibus please!" one of the guards called.

"Bye!" she said, running down the hall. "Come back tonight."

"You're from Australia, right?" the guard asked. "Out of town this week, I heard. Marrying that tall girl that got on the bus, right? You two must've been at it all night!" My nuts burned as he spoke. To keep them from sweating in the unreal heat, I'd sprinkled them with quite a bit of the powder Rachel had in the bathroom. I'd thought it was baby powder, but it was some kind of medicinal powder for heat rash. Like putting hot sauce on your balls. "Always wanted to go to Australia," the guard said as we headed for the highway.

The guard dropped me off in the front of the hotel. I heard a creaking noise and thought the maid had plugged in the vacuum. I turned my key and Beth, the backstage Garden manager, was, in *Penthouse* letter terms, "banging her shapely Oriental rump against the up-thrusting rod of my grateful bandmate." Got himself "wonton love" after all, the bastard. The room reeked of weed.

"God, I'm so embarrassed," Beth cried, as she ran straight into the bathroom, bare arse and all. I didn't get a look at the front.

"Oh shit, mate," Mick-O said with a sheepish grin, "back so soon? How's Rachel?" He leaned over to the floor. "By the way you two-timing bastard, Kerri clued me in on your lie to Hannah. Mum's the word."

"Ta."

"Fancy a choof?" he asked, offering me a bong hit from an enormous blue contraption. Mick-O liked to push the pot-impunity clause in the Poppies' no-drugs agreement to its absolute limit.

"Where the hell did you get that monstrosity?"

He lowered his voice to a whisper. "At a shop on Eighth Street. With another girl who I'm going to ring tonight when Beth's back at the Garden. I met her at a pub the other day when you went to Café Wha? A Puerto Rican bird with a tight arse. But first you got to leave. I have to finish up—" He gestured towards the bathroom. "She's a wild fuck."

To Mick-O, America was the great provider, a country abundant in wheat and naked ethnic girls. "Yeah, uh, mate," I said, too self-pitying to be disgusted. "I think I'll go down to the lobby pub.

"Where's Hannah?"

"She left a message that she stayed overnight in the Hamptons. She made some friends and will be back tomorrow."

What to make of that? "Come get me when you're, uh, through, and I'll tell you what went down with Rachel."

"Great!" He tilted an imaginary slouch hat towards me, the kind tourists think Aussie men wear to brush our teeth. "Remind me to shout you a beer when I'm down there for being such a cobber."

Down in the empty lobby pub, I sat on a leather stool. The bartender was reading a paper and playing Supertramp's "It's Raining Again." He looked peeved that I had interrupted his easy day.

You're old enough some people say / To read the signs and walk away. / It's only time that heals the pain / and makes the sun come out again. / It's raining again . . . C'mon you little fighter / No need to get uptighter / C'mon you little fighter / And get back up again. / Oh get back up again. / Fill your heart again. . . .

Soppy pop songs like that make millions. Supertramp was an embarrassing seventies band, like the Alan Parsons Project, or even worse, Kansas. Shameless pop music, however, can be life-affirming in certain situations. It's amazing how many epiphanies can come out of such a restricted format. Even Paul McCartney had inspiration to offer through pop music, although he's such a disappointing person. I would never sit down and play a McCartney tune for anyone. I'd be afraid they would think I was a wuss. But there's a post-Beatles song Paul McCartney wrote, "Single Pigeon," that has one of the best melodies I've ever heard—even if the chorus almost ruins the whole thing. Unlike Rachel, though,

I've never dwelled on perfection. If there's good in the offering, why look the gift horse in the mouth?

Mick-O, still slightly high, emerged from the lift, ordered himself a Heineken, and grabbed a stool next to me.

"You done fucking your brains out?" I asked.

"Hot and spicy Chinese platter, mate."

"You're a case and a half, Mick-O."

"How's Rachel? Hard to imagine her sitting for weeks, not making a peep. Does she still think I'm a waste of space?"

"I don't know Mick-O, she didn't mention you. But I asked her to marry me."

He almost choked on his beer. "Aw, bullshit, Colin!" he laughed.

"Mick-O," I said, "where can I start? I saw Rachel."

"How is she?" Mick-O never liked her much. Then again, she hardly ever took anything he said seriously.

"We had a lot to talk about."

"Oh shit, I smell a messy situation. I knew you missed her, but you seem rapt with Hannah, I mean what a body Hann—"

"Stuart's not dead."

"C'mon, Colin. Seriously."

"Seriously. He's living in Rachel's apartment with her parents while she's on jury duty. Phillip and I gave him $2000 to pretend to get shot and up himself to Buffalo, a place we idiotically thought was in Canada. There was no mob. Rachel found out about it a month or so back when she bumped into him on Fifth Avenue. I didn't know she knew until yesterday. She's kept it quiet, except to her family, who have taken it upon themselves to help Stuart kick the habit."

Mick-O looked pale. "I'll bare my bum if you're not totally shitting me," he said.

"You're gonna have a cold arse, mate. Stuart's okay for now, but if I don't marry Rachel and calm her down, she could get us all into jail. She wants me to get working papers, stay in the country, and help the Ganellis jumpstart Stuart's life. The only others filled in are my friend Peter, who got him doctored papers, and a handful of Phillip's mates from the Ambulance Corps and morgue."

"Ambos? They pretended he was dead?"

"A grand hoax that's greatly improved your love life."

"What's next? You fucked my mother? Jesus Christ, Colin. How could you and Phillip keep this from me? Who's going to believe me that I had nothing to do with this if the shit hits the fan?"

"Rachel couldn't understand why I'd keep it from her either. Phillip and I didn't want to get you involved."

"We are involved. Bloody cunt of a Christ. What were you thinking!? Not only did you put my arse out there without me knowing, now the best Chrissie pressies are being taken away before I can open them. If no one's talking, let's keep going and make our money. You can knock sense into Rachel."

"Mick-O. It's not going to matter—a source of mine told me that EMI is getting ready to give Phillip a solo contract. We're ants to be squashed, you and me. I don't know where to turn. I haven't told Phillip yet that Stuart's resurfaced. I'm sorry, Mick-O. Christ, I'm sorry."

"Sounds like we need another beer."

In Australia, a mate is a mate is a mate. I had often tried to convince Rachel that Mick-O is not a bad lot. I gave him the rest of the details and asked him what he thought I should or could do next.

"While Hannah's still out in the Hamptons, he said "Go talk to Rachel's mum. See that Stuart doesn't get mad. Or we're going to end up in the slammer. We'll work out the Phillip crisis tonight."

You don't smell the urine in the movies. Holding my nose down the subway stairwell, I looked for the platform Rachel had told me to find. The F train.

I took an orange seat. A pretty girl in a hot miniskirt outfit complete with white go-go boots smiled at me. Her big, necky grin revealed an Adam's apple; she was a cross-dresser. I kept a straight face and stared above her at an odd advertisement for "torn ear-lobe" repair. What the hell was I going to say to Stuart? A man with terrible BO squeezed in next to me on my left. And what about Rachel's mum?

Once out of the subway, I wandered around the neighborhood in procrastination. There were a few benches on the corner of Bleecker Street and Avenue of the Americas. Sixth Avenue to the natives, Beth had said. I sat down: a breather before the unpleasant encounter that lay ahead. A chance to reflect.

"Jesus loves you," the woman on the next bench said to me. "You look like you need Jesus."

"I just have indigestion, ta," I said so she'd leave me alone, but really I wanted to think through my worries without purple Marys and turquoise Jesuses in stained glass above me, reminding me that rock and roll and a long, hard kiss are sins.

I had despised Catholic school. My parents weren't particularly religious—Dad wasn't anything—but Aunty Grace and Mum had wanted Liam and me to go for Nanna. Rachel had three-hour doses of Sunday school; I got the full-week war scars. During Rachel's first Christmas in Melbourne, we agreed: the best part of religion was the stories.

I was getting myself riled up, and I didn't need that with my task ahead. I took a breath and sat back and listened for a while to the rolling Rs of conversing passersby.

My thoughts drifted to Seaford again, to Liam and Aunty Grace.

Liam and I were inseparable for years. We even co-owned two cats we found; during a cold weather snap, they'd crawled into an empty box my mum put out. "Colin! Look in your box—it's moving!" Liam had called. When I poked my favorite stick into the box, out came a stereo meow. Four eyes blinked, and a tabby and a pearl-white kitty emerged. We named them Sylvester and Casper; they were more like puppies or ducks than cats, the way they followed us around.

Liam and I would go poking around with our sticks near Aunty Grace's Niagara Falls, that open drain a few blocks from our houses. We were careful. Nearby there were heaps of dandelions, which were magnets for bees. Liam would hold our triangular sippies, glugs we called them, as I would lift up the rock slabs. We would find snakes and mammoth centipedes and earthworms. Our teacher once told us that a few hours west there were worms we could be proud of, for they were the biggest in the world. "In Gippsland," she'd said, "the worms are so big that you can hear them under the street. The residents even have a special giant-worm day when they wrap worms around themselves. In Gippsland, they are proud of their worms."

We were after frogs though, and different kinds of toads. We were frog and toad obsessed. Brown tree frogs were common, but still a treat. I found a warty black toad with three red stripes down its back. Roo lived in Liam's house, in a pot under his bed, until Aunty Grace was changing linen and heard him croak.

Less than a decade later every household had a lawn, and there was middle-class development stretching even further down the peninsula, towards Mount Elisa and Mornington. When I lifted up the slabs for old times' sake, I couldn't find the frogs—only sugar ants, and their big ugly cousin the bull ant, a hilarious creature who doesn't fear man and looks like a brawling pub drunk: C'mon, I'll have you. By now, however, Liam and I were more interested in the beach than the dirt. We would grab two towels and kick around a Champion Nerf ball in front of the Seaford girls, who had taken on a scary significance. From puberty, we attended the same all-boys Catholic school.

In 1977, during a total solar eclipse, I remembered telling Rachel, we got our first kisses. Glenda, the girl Liam liked, had a beachside house and invited us in to watch the eclipse on telly. Outside the window, and on the screen, the sky turned pitch black. The Indian myners, chocolate brown with bright yellow beaks, thought it was twilight and started to sing. So did the starlings. Why could we could hear the singing birds that on a normal sunny day were quiet? Because of the eclipse, Glenda guessed. She had a cardboard viewer from her school, which we took turns looking through. You'd go blind otherwise.

Glenda turned the dimmer switch to a brighter setting. She slid up next to Liam on the couch and tugged the gray streak he'd had in one section near his temple since he was a kid. Shortly thereafter her friend Jane stroked my pants' leg. Magically, we now had girlfriends. We had no idea what to do, except suck face like on soap operas. But the girls seemed pleased with our inexperienced kisses. Ten minutes later, the eclipse cleared and the four of us went for a stroll on the sand.

"What became of Liam?" Rachel had asked, after we'd fooled around in the shower. We'd dressed and gone to the Galleon for a coffee. No one else ever thought much of my family's stories—like the rise and fall of Ace O'Malley, Mum's dad, who I never met and who'd been the defending bantam-weight boxer in Victoria before World War II. Or my father's days as a jazz singer in the fifties, trying to learn the black American sound from a record, before he threw in the towel at the lack of money in the local industry, and learned how to fold and sell chemises and boatneck jumpers.

"Liam's a brickie," I'd said.

"A what?"

"A bricklayer."

"Oh," Rachel said, raising an eyebrow like she was embarrassed for me.

She offended me every now and then, with replies like that. Liam wasn't a surgeon or a psychiatrist like her cousins, but he did okay. He still lived out near his mum in Seaford, because Uncle Patrick had died, his sister Anna had moved to Sydney, and my parents had moved back to the city when I started my courses at uni. Liam loves brickwork, I wanted to tell her. He supervised a staff of ten and could call out the different masonry styles like top-forty hits—Flemish, American, and English, where on every other row the bricks are mortared with the smaller sides exposed. Liam worked hard. Harder than Rachel. His wife, Dolly, bought him a wooden-bead massage seat cover for his sore shoulders, the kind the taxi drivers use in Melbourne. His hands were big and muscled from manual labor. Mine remained small. I'd only managed the card factory and then the print shop. The closest I came to putting in a hard day's work, Liam liked to rib me, was carrying my amp and guitar (or bass) to my gigs. In his crowd, big hands were a badge.

It wasn't worth getting defensive about. We had our own situation to work through. I was afraid of naming our current state, so I'd bided more time by sharing the animals I, too, took for granted. I told her about the bull ants and the missing frogs. "Frogs are the first to go; their skins are porous," Rachel had rattled off in explanation at the Galleon, picking at her shepherd's pie. "They're sponges for impurities in water and mud," she said. "Maybe humans will have more time to adapt."

Rachel's mind always amused me, the way she knew that Pluto was discovered in 1930 and that whole frog species were preserved only in formaldehyde, while, in a much sillier mind sector, were stored the phone numbers of TV sitcom families. Even among the amazing Yanks I met over the past weeks—fast talkers who threw names and concepts around like Frisbees—Rachel still stood out as a true original. But, like I tried to tell her back in the New Jersey motel room, she was judgmental and at times, spoiled. I got up from the bench. How did I get here in front of her family's white, American-brick building, attempting to untangle the stickiest wicket of my life? With all her intellect, and even after what I'd done, Rachel wanted to marry me, a flattering and confusing scenario.

In a shop across the street from Rachel's building, I further stalled, buying Kudos, a chocolate bar I had never seen in Australia. Kudos was one of Rachel's favorite Scrabble words. She was never content to win by a million points. Getting creamed got boring after a while; after the first year she lived with us, Phillip and I would call her on American spellings, which weren't in the *Macquarie Australian Dictionary*. That put us in stitches. She fumed if she racked up a seven-letter word like *colored* without a *u*. At game's end, Phillip and I would have a smoke, or click on the footy. If the losing side was St. Kilda, the team we barracked for, we would call the winners cunts, a word that disgusted Rachel: "You're worse than NFL moron fans." Apparently no one used the word cunt in America, except in porno movies.

"It doesn't have the same weight in Australia," I'd say. "Housewives use it." She'd roll her eyes and clean up the Scrabble board, making sentences with the words we had used and calling out the best ones.

I rang the Ganellis' downstairs buzzer.

"Who is it?"

"Colin. Rachel's friend." Her mum buzzed me in. I nervously headed for the lift, thinking of Rachel's favorite Scrabble sentence—*What silly dooms await us as we vie for zippy lives?*

"Hello, Colin, we've been expecting you," said the same tall woman who'd visited me backstage. Mrs. Ganelli was still more than okay-looking for a woman her age. She looked like Rachel except that her eyes were a light, not dark brown, and her forehead was a bit higher. "I'll get you an iced coffee, Colin. You are going to need it. You can sit over on the couch." Standing near the couch was a tall and slickly dressed bloke with a funky haircut. Her brother, I guessed to myself. Rachel had always skited about how *cool* he was.

"Mate, been a long time," the groovester said. Stuart? His greaseball hair was gone; he'd always used bargain-shop hand cream or Vaseline in his hair to keep it stiff, or sometimes it was simply dirty. There was color in his skin. On closer look, he was still a bag of bones, but healthier. His eyes weren't glazed over—he kept my gaze.

"And we thought you'd stay dead," I said, sitting down, my knees ready to give out anyway.

"I was an addict then," he said. Mrs. Ganelli froze in her tracks with my coffee, to hear his next words, but they didn't come.

"Yeah," I said.

"You see Rachel?"

"Yeah, last night. She wants me to help you get your life back in order."

"We're doing fine," Mrs. Ganelli said.

"Rachel wants me to stay," I said to Stuart.

"No kidding," he said ironically.

Mrs. Ganelli sat down on the rocker and breathed out. "*Ffufff.*" Rachel had imitated her parents all the time, and it was strange to see her mum really do that. I wondered if her dad really said "pif-fling," but I didn't want to wait around and find out.

"She's headed for another disaster. Don't you agree, *ffufff*, it's best you leave, Colin?"

I didn't want to grovel or go into the whole "who did what and why" bullshit. I'd made my own bed. I'd had enough of guessing my fate. "Whatever I can to make things okay again. I was a real shit—oh, sorry, Mrs. Ganelli—"

"Shit?" she smiled, a toothy smile like Rachel's. "That's nothing. You should hear the vile crap that comes out of my kids' mouths. Frank says it's because how they didn't get enough zinc." She laughed at that. I didn't quite get the humor.

"Frank is so wry," Stuart agreed. Wry? When did he start using that word? Stuart was like Rachel's cousin.

"Colin, honey, is something wrong with your eye?"

"It's a tic," Stuart said. "He get's it when he's nervous."

"You don't have to be nervous of me. It's my husband you want to avoid."

"Joseph's quite a square bloke if you ask me," Stuart said. In an earlier time he would've immediately asked for a twenty after those greasy words.

"Isn't he a sweetie?" Mrs. Ganelli asked, blowing him a kiss. "Anyway, before we digress, dear, I think you should leave the mess alone, but I guess it all depends on what Stuart wants."

"Are you thinking of returning to Australia?" I leaned over nervously. "My panel van's in good nick. I guess I could give over the papers—"

"You want me to go back?" Stuart asked.

"I don't know. I'm scared what they'll do to me. To us. I don't know what would happen. There's a lot of people involved—"

"I imagine there'd be quite a brouhaha," Mrs. Ganelli said. "It's certainly a sad situation. You should've thought this through, darling." I couldn't imagine Mum saying "brouhaha." She'd say "mess" or "uproar."

"There's nothing there for me," Stuart said, running his fingers through his hair. His nails were clean, probably the first time I'd seen them clean since he met Melissa. He was a good-looking bloke now, clean and sharp.

"What about Melissa?" I said. Should I mention my run-in with her?

"Who's Melissa?" Mrs. Ganelli asked.

Stuart said nothing. "Nah," he finally repeated, "there's nothing there for me. I'm not gonna say a word. What does Phillip think?"

"Phillip doesn't know."

"Then let's keep it that way."

"Who's Melissa?" Mrs. Ganelli tried again.

"No one, Sylvia."

I held out a hesitant hand to him. He took it. "Rachel says you don't want any of the money off the record deal to make things better."

"Why would she say a stupid thing like that?" Stuart smiled. "This is an expensive town and I don't reckon I'm any angel."

We laughed at that, which punctured the tension. Mrs. Ganelli went to answer the phone. Stuart leaned over and said, "I think you should stay for Rachel—she and you make a good team."

"I heard that!" Mrs. Ganelli said before picking up the receiver. "Please, Stuart, don't be a cupid."

"I'm going to see Rachel again tonight. I'll tell her you said so."

"Oi," Mrs. Ganelli said, like a footie player. Stuart guessed my thought and knew better: "That's a Yiddish *oy*, not a footie *oi*," he explained. "How can you see her anyway?"

"They're pretending they're engaged," Mrs. Ganelli answered. I wasn't ready to tell her it wasn't pretend anymore. "Wrong number," she said to the phone. Then she handed me a piece of paper with her account number on it so I could transfer funds for Stuart to use, to get going again.

16

Rachel: THE BLOOD-BRAIN BARRIER

"How come we didn't hear about your fiancé?" Louis said, as I climbed on to the minibus.

I wanted to reflect on my emotional night with Colin. Fat chance: everyone on the bus was waiting for my answer—including Fred Kaluzny, Mr. Stray Quote.

"A month after Colin proposed to me back in Melbourne, his uncle developed a tumor. He's very close to his uncle—I never thought he was going to go through with the move to New York. I didn't want to talk about the engagement in case it fell through." I was disengaged from my anti-probing lie. I could lie all morning if I had to.

"Too bad, Rachel," Mrs. Ricasio said. "I was going to set you up with my handsome young gynecologist after the trial. He prefers women with dark hair."

Raj and Greg snickered at her inadvertent vaudeville joke.

"You two are awful," Mrs. Ricasio said, "I didn't mean it that way."

"I think the ADA's assistant will be disappointed if he gets word of your engagement," teased one of the quieter alternate jurors whose name I still hadn't processed—Lisa, or Paula?

I held up my palms in theatrical protest. "Enough, guys, enough."

"Something's not adding up," Louis said. He pushed *start* on his Walkman. "I'm going to pump it out of you."

"Louis, there's nothing there."

"What?" he asked loudly, from a more rhythmic universe.

Humid, still air trapped and amplified that *singular* fragrance of industrial New Jersey. Even though the air-conditioning was broken, Fred asked the driver to hit the automatic window button to close out the smell. "Lefties," he then said, "die on average nine years earlier than everyone else."

"I'm a lefty," our Rockette said from the seat next to the driver. "My longevity line goes from my joint to my wrist."

When the bus talk shifted to lefty death, my psychic weight lifted some. The Statue of Liberty's hand loomed in the horizon. I thought of Grandpa Ganelli's arrival-in-America story, and how he had exaggerated it for his grandkids' entertainment. I fished in my knapsack for the bag of marbles and rolled two on my knee.

Grandma Rosa rarely acknowledged her dead, annulled, turned-atheist-on-his-seventieth-birthday husband. Once, baby-sitting us, she caught us throwing frozen frankfurters out of our bedroom window (for what reason I haven't the vaguest idea). We were seven and nine, old enough to know better, and therefore banned to the kitchen, where Grandma Rosa was knitting a blanket for my father.

"Just like your grandpa. Always with the pranks. Eat your Froot Loops." Had Grandpa Ganelli's humor skipped a generation, like twins? Would a child by Colin be as science-serious as Dad?

Would it have my Italian-Jewish-brown eyes or Colin's Irish-English blue? This marriage was supposed to be a finger in the dike. I had to stop thinking like this.

The jury van let us off on Centre Street. A media zoo had formed outside the courts.

Safe in our guarded quarters, Kevin played Omniscient Bailiff but wouldn't fill us in. "Finish your muffins—we're starting on the dot."

In our regular kindergarten-style single file, we entered the packed courtroom. Ms. Gorsham, the ADA, was heavily made up; she'd never been before. I couldn't wait for halftime analysis back in the jury room.

"Mr. Presticastro, call your next witness please," Berliner said.

"Maria De Meglio," Presticastro said.

That explained the cameras. Maria De Meglio had been rumored too devastated by her arrest to testify. The courtroom hushed. Louis and I were jurors numbers eight and nine; we were front row flush left, right near the witness chair. Mrs. De Meglio was fat yet tiny; the court clerk secured phonebooks for her to sit on. Mrs. De Meglio's mouth seemed two sizes too small for her soft, fleshy jowls, like it would hurt her to eat a big bite of hamburger. This was our nefarious defendant?

"Please state your name."

She looked straight at the jury. "Maria De Meglio."

"Your address for the record?"

"196 Sullivan Street, Manhattan."

"Good morning, Mrs. De Meglio."

"Good morning." Mrs. De Meglio was wearing a red and white

shift that could have been bought off a Woolworth's rack. I'd caught her tan orthopedic shoes as she walked to the stand. Her fashion sense reminded me of Grandma Rosa's.

"For the record, why do you think you've been asked to testify today?"

She looked straight ahead. "On July first, 1991, my grandson checked into the hospital and almost overdosed. I was, how you say, not myself. How could a nice boy like Bruno who never did anyone wrong end up at Saint Peter's mercy?"

"Relevance!" Gorsham protested.

"Your Honor, state of mind!" Presticastro said.

"I'll allow you to proceed, but Mr. Presticastro, please keep this kosher."

"I went home and cried. My daughter has no husband. He was killed in a car accident. My husband, may he rest in peace, died before Bruno was ever born." Her accent was raspy and old-worldly.

"Relevance!" Gorsham protested.

Berliner stole a quick look at the reporters. They were on the edge of their seat. I could tell that he didn't quite mind the media attention.

"She may proceed." He glanced over to Presticastro. "But move this along!"

"She works two jobs to support Bruno. There is no man for him, no, how you say, role model. So I took him fishing and bought a gun so I could take him hunting, like Poppa did with my brothers back in Italy. The gun was loaded because we shot rabbits a week earlier."

"There is a big difference between a rabbit and—"

"Leading!"

"Sustained."

"Mrs. De Meglio. Did you shoot Derrick Johnson with your hunting rifle?"

"I don't remember."

Louis poked the side of my leg twice. Our cryptic code for "what a load of shit." But I'm listening to you, Mrs. De Meglio. Heroin pushers deserve it. What about our kids, Grandma? What about Stuart? It amazed me how right-wing the courtroom setting was making me.

"Mr. Presticastro tells me I was wild with anger that day. I don't remember. They say I shot him, I must have shot him." Mrs. De Meglio paused to sniffle. "I am a decent, church-going woman. I never done anything bad. After he was in the hospital they wouldn't let me see him. My daughter brought a Polaroid camera and took a photo of him, because they wouldn't let me see my grandson. Imagine, my grandson might die, and all I could see was that photo."

"Mrs. De Meglio, I would like you to look at exhibit forty-nine."

Presticastro passed Mrs. De Meglio the photo her daughter had identified the previous day. We had not been allowed to look at it then.

"Is this the Polaroid of your grandson?"

"Yes."

"How do you know that?"

"I remember it. And the district attorney—"

"Ms. Gorsham?"

"Yes. She showed it to me after I was arrested. I think she showed it to me. I was so upset."

"Are those your initials?"

"Yes. So I think she showed it to me—"

"Have you seen it since?"

Mrs. De Meglio burst into tears. Jesus, no one can give her a tissue? I reached in my pocket for a tissue and held it up for the court to see.

Berliner glared at me. "Can someone please give Mrs. De Meglio a tissue? No one from the jury is to give her a tissue. A neutral tissue, please. Mrs. De Meglio, please try to answer the question."

"No," she said through her sobs. The clerk handed her a tissue box.

"Your Honor," Presticastro said, "I would like to pass the photo of Bruno De Meglio to the jury."

"May I look at it first?" Assistant Hunk asked. "There were two photos her daughter took. I just want to make sure it is the one corresponding with our evidence sheet."

"I have no problems with that," Presticastro said.

Cohen showed it to Gorsham. She nodded. "Oh, yes," Cohen said, "This is the right one. I'll just pass it over to the jury for you," he said, headed straight for me, even though Louis's seat would have been the logical starting point. He pressed his thumb into my hand during the baton pass-off.

"I'll do that next time, Mr. Cohen," Presticastro said, his annoyance seeping through. For Presticastro to say Cohen was making personal contact with the jury would sound cynical. He'd only handed the photo to me. Cohen liked me, *for sure*. I looked at his finger. No ring.

"Ms. Ganelli, when you are done looking at the Polaroid, please pass it around," Presticastro said.

In the photo, Bruno De Meglio looked worse than Stuart. He was so young for a heroin addict. Where did he get the money? What did he steal or did he hustle like Jim Carroll? Fourteen was young when you look at it under a microscope. Would I kill for a grandson? You bet I would, I determined. Shit, was the court artist sketching me? I tried to keep expressionless.

"Thank you, Mrs. De Meglio," Presticastro said when Fred Kaluzny passed him back the photo. "Your Honor, I have no more questions." As Presticastro hovered in front of me, I could see his cranberry corduroy slacks had bare patches where his thighs had rubbed together. A court-appointed slob.

"Let's take a twenty-minute break, and then, Ms. Gorsham, you can start your cross-examination."

"Good Morning, Ms. De Meglio," Gorsham began.

"Mrs. De Meglio," she replied.

"*Mrs.* De Meglio, forgive me. I only have a very few questions for you, Mrs. De Meglio. Four, to be exact."

Mrs. De Meglio nodded nervously.

"The first one is, did you know Derrick Johnson before you shot him?"

"I do not know such trash!"

"But did you hear of his name before?"

"Bruno once talked of Derrick, his friend."

"Thank you. The second question is, when did you know that Derrick was your son's dealer?"

"I called all his friends. I needed to know who put my grand-son at Saint Peter's mercy."

"When was this? The day of the shooting?"

"No, two days before."

"So you had time to think about this terrible predicament your grandson was in?"

Mrs. De Meglio looked over at Presticastro. I was getting furi-ous on her behalf. Even I could have protected her better from these questions. Our feisty rosary-bead vigilante was screwing her-self. Couldn't he have rehearsed this obvious line of questioning with her?

"Mrs. De Meglio, you must answer the question," Berliner said.

"Yes. But I was not myself. I was in a stew."

"You were in a stew for forty-eight hours though, correct?"

"Yes."

Presticastro was staring at his nails. He'd obviously gone into the trial a defeated man.

"Thirdly," Gorsham said, "I am going to give you my own pho-tograph. Can you identify who is in this photo?" A poster-size blowup was brought forward to the witness stand. The jury didn't get a look at it.

"Do you recognize this photo?"

Mrs. De Meglio's face dropped.

"Objection!" Presticastro said. "This was not the size I ap-proved earlier."

"We have simply blown it up for easier viewing," Gorsham said.

"Overruled," Berliner said. His face was hard to read. What was this photo?

"Your Honor," Gorsham said, I would like to enter this photo as exhibit fifty-three."

The clerk recorded the evidence.

"Mrs. De Meglio, can you tell the court what the photo is of?"

"Derrick Johnson," she said, very low to the ground.

"Finally, Mrs. De Meglio, did your grandson, who according to our earlier witnesses has now recovered—"

"Objection!"

"Sustained. Ms. Gorsham, please watch your relevance."

"Mrs. De Meglio, did your grandson ever tell you how old Derrick was?"

"Fourteen," she said softly.

"I'm sorry. I didn't hear that."

"Fourteen."

"The same age as your grandson Bruno?"

Mrs. De Meglio nodded. I really wanted a look at the blowup now.

Cohen brought out an easel, and Gorsham put the photo on it so we could see. It was Derrick Johnson; his brains splattered over the room.

Several jurors gasped. "*Ayyyyeee!*" Derrick's mother screamed. "He was only a boy!"

Even though I have twenty-twenty vision, I pretended to fiddle with a contact lens. In the few seconds I squirmed, I spotted a reporter I hadn't seen before, leaning in to catch every last jury reaction. I knew her from where? And then it came—Jennifer, my brother's girlfriend his senior year at the High School for Art and Design. About five years back she wrote an article for one of those women's magazines on penises she had known. One penis she called Dr. Hook. Ingrid was in the living room with my folks, showing them photos of the happy couple's funky home in Minnesota. I showed Frank the article in the kitchen, where he was cooking pasta. Frank laughed at my audacity, but he wouldn't tell me if he was the proud owner of Dr. Hook. He whistled a high C through a dry ziti until I left him alone. Think of anything, Rachel, anything, to keep from processing that picture. I wanted to run out of the room, but, abruptly, I let out an extended shrill sound, an animal being slaughtered.

Louis grasped my hand. "Are you okay? Rachel?"

The court artist turned a page on her pad.

"Jurors, Ladies and Gentlemen visiting the courtroom," Berliner said. "This is a rough part of the trial, but I will have to ask you to try and keep from reacting. You must keep an open mind. We will take a fifteen-minute break so Mrs. Johnson and Ms. Ganelli can pull themselves together."

I grabbed the closest chair to the door when we returned to jury quarters. My hand was trembling. Everyone was embarrassed for me.

"Rachel," Louis said, "tell us what's in your head. Why aren't you talking?"

I wasn't talking? I felt like I was talking. My brain was on overdrive.

The De Meglio trial was the proverbial straw on the camel's back. The infected blood of disaffection, seeping through all these months, had finally blitzed my brain. Colin. Jesus, Colin, my fiancé of sorts. My *second* one. How could I have humiliated Will, the nicest guy in this or any universe, when the invitations for our wedding had already gone out? (Boom!) I'd let a stranger on a plane pinch my nipples when I couldn't even go beyond a kiss and that shower with Colin. (Zing!) My remoteness from my mother. (Wham!) How could my selfish mind drift into dried macaroni when before me were families who had endured personal holocausts? Derrick Johnson's mother's words echoed with me again. He was only a boy. My emotions, like Derrick's brains, were all over the room.

"Wham!" I said.

"Rachel—do you want a Lifesaver?" Greg asked. "Rachel?"

"Let her be," someone said. "She looks ill."

"Shh, Rachel. You're incoherent. It was a ghastly photo. Don't try to talk. Take a breather."

Until the trial, my proxy for religion had been the fine tuning of knowledge. Where am I on the map of the world? Where are we all on the plane of infinite planes? Pop culture and place as secular reference points.

Why suffer unanswerable questions when there's the option of folly? Spending forty minutes pinning down that Ethel Maye Potter was Ethel Murtz's maiden name on *I Love Lucy* soothed me. And if I could get five others to remember a precise moment that drew blank faces from my elders and younger cousins—like the week in the early 1980s that the ass-hugging Sasson jeans changed their pronunciation because of a hair salon owner's lawsuit—I had proof of my exact seconds on Earth. If you don't accept the juggernauts of a Messiah and past lives, how else but through common popular ground can you tell yourself we're in the morass together?

Fred poured several inches of his Perrier into a paper cup for me.

And that map, I thought, the one Jorge at the public library had gotten a facsimile of for me. The great old map from the 1800s in the Library of Congress which shows the second expedition of the vessel Pinta returning from a voyage around the island of matrimony. There are many rough waters to cross—Gulf of Flirtation, Whirlpool of Reflection, Undercurrent Bay—but then the journey leads to calmer waters of comfort, delight. The ship's final path led to Land's End, one hundred feet from Port Hymen. Inland from Port Hymen looms the holy church.

It hit me in new dimensions, like I'd just purchased a relief map of my life: cold facts weren't enough. I wanted Colin near me so that love could fill the doubting gap. But did we really love each other? And by obsessing on Stuart, I was trying to do good without someone of the cloth patting my head. I was pounding square pegs into round holes. I had to let Colin and Stuart be. They were square pegs. Oh how *shameful*, another part of me said suddenly, all you are thinking of is Rachel, Rachel, Rachel.

"Shameful," I said.

"Yes, shameful," Greg said, snagging a pretzel from the table, "she *knew* what she was doing."

"Rachel, don't worry. We're not buying the saintly grandmother act. She'll get life." Fourteen jurors nodded.

"Not if I have anything to do with it," Raj said.

"But you know she's guilty," someone behind me said.

"I believe in fucking up the American jury system," Raj said. Raj sing-songed every word, even his personal manifesto. Raj, our most unanticipated anarchist.

"Bullshit, College Boy. I work hard every day," Greg said from the other side of the room. "My brother dealt crack so he landed in jail. I love him, but he should be there. If we don't punish those who take God's name in vain, how can the system work?"

Fifteen minutes of bickering turned into forty-five. What was keeping Berliner?

Kevin knocked on our door and led us back to our seats. Rougeless Battle-ax and her hunky assistant were smiling. They smelled victory. Presticastro looked over at me, too. And Judge Berliner. Then I noticed that Maria De Meglio was gone.

Over the bench: IN GOD WE TRUST. "Jurors—during the break, a plea bargain was entered. The District Attorney's office has accepted it, as it will save New York State thousands of dollars. The clerk will come into the jury room in a few minutes to arrange a time for a court officer to deliver your personal items. Ladies and Gentlemen—I thank you for your time. You are dismissed."

Berliner and the attorneys from each side came over to shake our hands. I noticed Assistant Hunk had a ring on now. He had played my singleness like a book. What were the targeted weak spots of the other jurors? The lawyers had done their jobs. Their scientific tactics had broken through New York cynicism, the tire-thick coating over our rawest fear.

17

Rachel: OF FLUKES AND FLOUNDERS

It wasn't noon yet and I was out on the street. Three weeks in a hellhole and I couldn't even deliver a verdict.

About now, Colin would be telling my parents that I wanted him to move in with Stuart and me when they finally left for Paris. Should I race home and stop him? *Oh, by the way, Colin, I had an epiphany on the courtroom floor; I'm going to let you go, you lucky lab rat.* Maybe I could begin to deal with my unexpected reentry into everyday living in a few hours, but not now. I started walking toward the Bowery and Grand where Frank's loft was. I needed to cool my head, let Frank joke about my courtroom crack-up.

It was only a few blocks from the Centre Street courthouse to the Bowery. Tar droplets were scattered over the asphalt from the searing sun. If it was this hot mid-June, God save us from August.

Frank didn't answer the doorbell. I still had a set of his keys from our time with Stuart. I figured I'd help myself to ice cubes to rub on my neck and wrists. I climbed the five flights of the former flophouse-turned-artists'-lofts, panting from lack of exercise. The Elizabeth Motor Lodge didn't exactly have a four-star nautilus room. And there was that delightful extra poundage from three weeks of waist-slimming treats like meatball heroes and the un-limited supply of Entenmann's boxed cakes. In sequestration, as on a long plane ride, each course of food is high entertainment.

Puffing, I opened the door, raced for the freezer, and plopped a cube in my mouth to suck on. The shower was at full blast; an ancient plumbing structure in the middle of the kitchen area. Frank was home. Good. The shower curtain—black vinyl with the international male and female symbols you see at bus terminals—was a cheap find from some East Village boutique. I'd bought it with the remnants of my temp check, a thank you for my brother for helping me dedrug Stuart, even if Mom and Dad thought we were well-intentioned simpletons.

"Frank! I let myself in. I'm going make some iced tea, want some?"

"Rachel?" the shower curtain said. "What are you doing here?"

"Haven't you been watching TV? The trial was dismissed. Grandma plea-bargained."

"You couldn't call?"

"I've been in sequestration for three weeks. Aren't you thrilled to hear my whine? I'm in another of my trademark funks, and your place is closer than Mom and Dad's."

"I have company here—"

"Where?"

"In the shower. A friend is here with me." He turned the water off.

For the first time I noticed that there was a tidy pile of pastel clothes on the sofa. As square a package as the bundle of six starched shirts you'd get back from a Chinese hand laundry.

"Janet?!"

"Oh, Frank, how could she know?"

Confirmed. I leaned back into the couch, my mouth slack-jawed. How could they? I'm in the middle of sequestration, and she's having the time of her life porking my brother? After everything we went through?

Janet grabbed a towel off of the peg and emerged, her evenly-tanned legs dripping. Her blond hair was brown with water. "Rachel. This is not about you. We love you. Our relationship is about us."

"We? Since when are you a *we*?"

In the background I saw a hand reach for another towel from the peg. Moments later Frank emerged too, bright red and wet. He'd obviously just gotten some sun with Janet, probably at Jones Beach or Sheep Meadow.

"God—I'm having a nervous breakdown and you two are getting it on? How long has this been going on?"

"Since you started jury duty," Janet said, embarrassed.

The ice cube was melting in my palm.

"Rachel," Frank said, desperately looking for his jeans. "This is not about you."

Janet retrieved the jeans from her pile, and Frank slipped them on under his towel.

"Don't 'Rachel' me. Unreal. All I wanted to tell you is that I've decided not to get married. Jesus Christ, I can't believe you backstabbers."

"Married?" Frank asked, my hateful words hitting Teflon. "Who were you getting married to?"

"I'm out of here. Have a nice relationship, kids. Happy to provide my meaningless existence as a stepping stone for your rapture."

I headed for the door. "Please," Janet called after me. "Stop being selfish. Calm down. This is a good thing. This isn't a bad thing. Don't you want us to be happy?"

I flung the remaining chunk of ice back toward the sink and hit a hook-shot. I raced down the stairs. I hated feeling sorry for myself. In my zero-competition elementary school, students received comments instead of grades. Mine had been virtual clones from year to year. "Sunny and smart." "Laughs at everything." "Always a smile on her face." What had become of the sweet, optimistic child? When had I become such a lemonball? I reached into my knapsack for a tissue—and pulled out the napkin Danny Death had given me with his phone number, back at Coffee Bar. I found a quarter. So I rang him.

"Hello?"

"Danny?"

"Who's this?"

"Rachel Ganelli. I met you in Coffee Bar about two months ago? You bought me the slice of blueberry pie and told me what a selfish person I was?"

"Oh yeah, getting on with your life?"

"I could use another yelling at."

"Where are you?"

Harold is a motherfucker was scraped in the metal on the phone. "On a street corner in Chinatown. I've lost my center again since you bought coffee—"

"You getting ready to off yourself from middle-class self pity?"

"Yeah. Lucky you. You get to be the white knight."

"My armor's at the dry cleaners. But come over to my place. I'll happily shoot bullets through every pile of crap you put before me. Let me give you the address. One hundred Avenue C, between Sixth and Seventh Street. Buzzer seventeen."

That was a block down from where Will and I had rented our studio apartment. Granted, Danny wasn't exactly the Dalai Lama, but beggars can't be choosers at eleven-thirty on a weekday morning. I'd take whatever guru figure I could get my hands on. There'd be a twenty-minute walk to his place. I mapped out the quickest route. Bowery to Sixth Street and across. Past CBGBs, where Danny and his circle had invented a new, angrier generation.

I counted on my crowded head to distract me from my growing litany of affliction. Wasn't there anyone in there who could save the day? I tried hard to muster the four-eyed geek who had served me so well during the SATs. What could be more relaxing than a meander and a think about tomato varieties—beefsteak, and that new crossbred variety that's long and slim and slices like a cucumber? When a gang of New York punks walked by as I passed Third Street, however, it was my third-rate Edith Wharton who took over the internal mic. Twenty years had passed since Danny Death and his intentional hair-botching took the stage. These were the punks guidebooks warned about? "Watch your purse in Alphabet City, an ominous, but colorful district of punks and drug addicts." Ominous types who once played varsity lacrosse or field hockey: what Fodor's never says is that half the black-walled rotting-couched apartments are graduation gifts from Connecticut and Westchester parents. Like Will's parents. Even Danny Death had told me that he was a lawyer's kid from Scarsdale.

At Sixth Street between First Avenue and Avenue A, New York's Little India, restaurant merchants hawked their lunch menus. A man in a turban was brazen enough to shove one into my clenched hand. I lifted a thumb for it out of reflex. The owners knew who they had to please to keep up their customer flow; the flyer had a Shiva above each section. Shiva picture, then the list of curries. Shiva, tandori selection.

Veemah had brought me back a Shiva when she returned from Agra. I'd asked her for a Taj Mahal snowglobe. Life becomes momentarily bearable with such an indulgent frosted–Pop Tart of a request. And people like to be asked to bring back an item from their enviable journeys, I've discovered: I have over two hundred.

"Suri couldn't find one," Veemah had apologized, crunching her toast.

"Who's Suri?" Please don't let this be another servant.

"He's a family servant. I had him search for a snowglobe for two days."

"Veemah! I didn't want you to do that."

"Oh, don't worry, he got paid well for his troubles. Look, you don't give money to the homeless anymore, right? You accept the New York status quo. So don't judge the way things work back home. Anyhow, no more tangential rubbish, open it up, it's a bit tacky, but—"

I had ripped the newspaper wrap open to find a tiny carved figurine with exotic white markings. "It's a Shiva—actually it's a mini-Shiva, a shivling. It represents the god of art and destruction.

Sometimes Shiva is a goddess though. There's a huge Shiva cult in India."

"Thanks, Veemah, it's great."

I crossed First Avenue and thought, *I should have tossed that bastard/bitch of a deity out my window.* My life was a sea of destruction all right. Now Shiva had Frank and Janet under command, too.

"C'mon up," Danny said through the buzzer. "Fifth floor." Was Danny's building the only one in lower Manhattan to escape gentrification? Even my and Will's old building down the block had lights at the top of every stairwell. When I reached the third floor a rat lumbered by en route to its destination, so jaded by rule of its kin over the building that a human ranked as mere scenery. I knocked on 17.

"Hey," Danny said at the door, from behind mirrored sunglasses. Danny's mop of graying black curls was tied back with a girl's elastic hairband, the same Goody brand I used. The railroad flat was as stark as a Zen temple. I'd have expected celebrity punk furniture like bubble-shaped TVs, faux-leopard bath mats, or at least a poster or two from his past. I knew from articles that he'd spent his 1970s money, but wouldn't there be a luxury or two from selling rights? All I could see was a pile of tapes near a foam mattress, a ridiculous number of cigarettes cases, and an old-style boom box from the days of afros and hustle lines.

"Want some iced tea?"

"That would be great."

"Love those shorts by the way." There was a cracked mirror propped up against the door. I took a look at myself as Danny ran the tap over his ice-cube tray. My make-up was smeared. My ass was peeking out of the denim. Colin was right. They were too short; I looked like a slut.

"Enjoying your rights money?"

"Is that what you need, money?"

"No, no—please don't think that. I didn't come here for money. I came, God help me, for your company."

Danny winked. "Good. There isn't any. I prepaid my rent for two years, and bought a few hundred cases of cigarettes." He gestured to the far end of the room toward a hill of Lucky Strikes and Camels. He put down my glass of iced tea. "I was afraid I'd put it all in my arm."

"Didn't you kick the habit a year ago?"

"Twenty thousand to an ex-junkie is like an alcoholic winning a stash of scotch."

Above his head was the apartment's sole decoration: an odd painting on rice paper. A couple floated in midair, needles stuck in their arms. The colors were more intense than watercolors but equally delicate, as if they had been breathed on by a smack-addicted angel.

"Food dye. Nice effect, don't you think? I painted it last year, when I had five dollars to my name. So what's new with you?"

"Two hours ago, I was released from the De Meglio trial. I was a sequestered juror."

"Don't have a TV."

"The killer grandma?"

No response.

"Trust me. It's the biggest trial in the city."

"Means nada to me. What else have you been up to?"

"Remember my roommate that was murdered? It was a scam. He's living with me. I found him alive in a sandwich shop. The semi-boyfriend I had was in on it, and then my boyfriend's band got famous, and they showed up in New York for a Madison Square Garden appearance—and then my parents came home when my semi-boyfriend's song got on the radio—and then my brother and one of my closest friends were fucking while I was in sequestration."

Danny shrugged his shoulders at my rambling words. "So?"

Didn't anything faze Danny Death? "Maybe I wasn't clear about everything that's happened. Let me start again. The dead guy's *alive*—"

Danny wasn't flinching.

"Look, Danny, this is amazing stuff—"

"Is it? You haven't answered my question. "What have you been doing? To get on with your own life?"

"I thought about religion during the trial, and how it's a crutch."

"That's a start—isn't that a bit simplistic though?"

"Don't tell me you go to church?"

"Why are you here, Rachel?"

"I have nowhere else to go."

"Go inward." He offered me a familiar white bag. "Goldfish?"

I took a handful. "Yeah, well, I'm afraid inward is an ugly place."

"I suspect deeper down it isn't. There'll be a garden of Eden if you go inside. And I'm an atheist, in answer to your question. But I believe in humanity."

I sipped my tea, served in one of those horrible "witty" mall mugs from the eighties. *Life's a Bitch, Then You Die.*

"Like my mug? It kind of embarrasses me. My aunt gave it to me."

Here in Danny's house, I loved that mug.

"Do you want to be married to Colin?"

I laughed tensely. "Fuck, how did you know his name?"

"I remembered it from Coffee Bar. I listen."

"Evidently."

"So do you?"

"I want to be grounded. Colin concocted that crazy murder-to-recording-contract plan. A totally fucked thing to do. But even so, the second I saw him, I felt better. He's like a walking cup of chamomile tea for me. But I'm twisting his arm to stay with me. I know that on some level."

"The way you overanalyze, you know that on all levels."

Danny wasn't so scary. He was a sweet puppy dog. I put my finger on his scar, and followed the jagged line with my finger. "What's that scar from?"

"It was after my drummer OD'd on the shit I gave him. I tried to kill myself. Guess I wasn't trying too hard. Hard to die from a cheek wound." He took a lime out of the filthy fridge and squeezed it in his own mug of iced tea.

There were lighter scars along his neck. When I leaned forward to touch them too, my thighs stuck to the vinyl red seat, jiggling like giant gummy bears.

"What are these?"

"Nothing too exotic. Acne loves those lymph nodes. I was an ugly child, and an even uglier James Dean wanna-be."

"And a sex-symbol rock star. The world copied your style. Richard Hell. Sid Vicious. They took your sound, not to mention your hairdo. How did you spike those curls anyhow?"

He took a cigarette pack off the hill and tore off the plastic. "Many worlds away."

I leaned over to kiss him, but he pulled his face away.

"Save it for Colin. You'll feel better about yourself. There's a tape on the mattress. John Coltrane. Pop it in the cassette player."

Nicotine-stained middle-age pudge-fest has-been rejects desperate girl and then orders her around like a domestic. Whose jerky idea was coming here?

I didn't know this tape. A live performance. Coltrane's first notes were hesitant, a worm crawling out into light. A few shrill Cs and Es. Then ordered chaos ensued. Free jazz. No rules or regulations. Coltrane playing from the insides. Eventually the music's gospel hit, a tree falling on a toe.

Danny smiled at me. "You know the difference between a fluke and a flounder?" It was an enviable ferocious smile of gray teeth and kindness.

"I think so."

"Tell me then."

"They're salt-water flatfish, with two eyes on one side of their—"

"Not getting my drift. See, Rachel, you're a kook like me. A fluke's eyes are in a different place than a flounder's. We're like Picasso people. Both eyes on the side of our heads, when most of the world has them staring down the straight and narrow. You know, as a fluke gets older, its eyes start to move closer to the top of its head."

"Really? I've never read that—" Come to think of it, wasn't a fluke a type of flounder?

"Okay. Shh. Listen up—no more floundering, okay? That's the wrong fish. You're going to be a fluke from here on in. Author yourself a crazy benevolent life, and who the fuck cares if there's a God? Call your brother and your friend. What do you want? Confirmation from me that they're assholes? Okay, they're assholes, but all brothers and friends are assholes. I'm an asshole. You're an asshole. Everywhere an asshole. Go easy on people, Rachel, or you'll start to clear rooms."

"Coltrane's in our church, Danny, isn't he?"

"What is this, the 700 Club? What the fuck are you on about, *our church*?"

"Jesus, sorry for asking."

Danny smiled, went over to the old-style boom box, pulled out the Coltrane tape, and handed it to me.

"Here's your wafer, missy. Bite in. Remember, it's a leap year."

18

Colin: THE GOLDEN HANDSHAKE

Hannah was just back from the Hamptons. She had things to tell me, she said, sitting on the hotel bed. I was sure that she was on to me about my overnight with Rachel.

"I met someone."

"You met who?" This I hadn't seen coming.

"At the Hamptons. At the party Kerri and Phillip took me to, I got into a conversation about Australia and one thing—"

"You're kidding."

"No. I want to be up front about this. If we were lovers for a long time, I would feel torn up, but even you would have to admit we hardly know each other. We hardly have sex."

Not for the want of trying.

"And frankly, I never really respected the music industry. It was an exciting few weeks, but I think I need a man of higher surroundings to be my partner."

You social-climbing bitch. "What does he do?" I said, trying to look indifferent.

"Public relations."

"And you respect that?"

"He writes pages and pages a year. He practically writes three novels a year if you add up his press releases."

"So what are you going to do, drag him back to Melbourne?"

"No, actually, I'm going to move in with him. He's an Ivy Leaguer. He has connections. I think he can help me get a spot teaching ceramics in Manhattan."

"That's crazy."

"Please don't make a scene, Colin. Let's be nineties about it. Let's be adult. This is what I want. He's wealthy. He can provide some stability for my art. He fly-fishes and luges."

She started to pack her suitcase.

"Look, I'll help you with that."

"He's downstairs. I just need to take it to the elevator."

"No, why don't I take them down to the lobby. I want to meet the luger."

"That's a little weird, don't you think?"

"This situation is a little weird, don't *you* think?"

Her Hamptons friend was big but not fat, like a swimmer. He had a square head and had on brown shorts and white socks.

"Will, this is Colin."

"Oh. Nice to meet you," he said, raising a confused eyebrow to Hannah.

"Look. No hard feelings. I wanted to talk to you in person."

"I'm so sorry about this situation. I know what it feels like to get the knife put in you. My fiancée left me a month before our wedding. For Australia, as a matter of fact."

I had a bolt of recognition, the Hamptons had sounded familiar: Rachel had told me how Will loved the Hamptons and how she'd sulk in the group van they took out there. What a fluke. I tried to control my smirk.

"That's how I got talking to Hannah. I hate that country with a passion. It represents all that is sad to me. I saw this pretty face and heard her speak and asked her to tell me three wonderful things about Australia."

"The smell of eucalyptus, filigree latticework, and ferns," Hannah repeated for my benefit.

"You were engaged to Rachel Ganelli?"

Will looked at me in horror. *Confirmed*, as Rachel would say. "How would you know that?"

"I know her. She's my friend. I just saw her today in a hotel room. Rachel Ganelli."

"The one who hated Rilke!" Hannah said. "You just saw her today in a hotel room? I knew she was a vile creature."

"She's back in New York?" Will said, his face pained, his voice wavering.

"You seem so different from Rachel."

"How's that?" he managed to pipe out.

"For one thing you're not wearing purple and red."

"She only started going overboard with the colors those last few months before she left."

"Why did you love her?"

"This is so appalling," Hannah said.

"I can answer that." He looked right at me. His eyes were bluer than mine. Rachel had said we had about the same color. "Because every pore of Rachel was alive." He gave me his business card. "Tell her I'd like to hear from her. That I hold no malice, and that I'd love to take her out to lunch. Would you do that? Would you tell her I said hello?"

"Like hell you do," Hannah muttered.

"Sure," I said.

"And what are you going to do today, Colin?" Hannah said, in a sudden recovery.

"Actually, Rachel and I are getting hitched. She's been sequestered on a trial and I got to visit her as her fake fiancé. But we decided under the covers that we really do want to get married."

Will looked like he was going to croak from apoplexy. Supposedly, that happened to my granduncle, who lost his muscle control in a shock.

"You son of a bitch!" Hannah said. She pulled Will's arm before he could respond, and grabbed a cab.

In my room I looked at his card.

William Reynolds
Vice President
Peterson & Smith Corporate Communications

I ripped it up. I didn't know what I wanted from Rachel, but I didn't want Will back on the scene.

Phillip, Angus, and Marty, who turned out to be the executive with the waxy forehead I recognized from backstage at Madison Square Garden, were disemboweling me in the EMI office in one guiltless motion, like a butcher. I was in quicksand, except I could only register that the arsehole firing me looked like Hardy out of Laurel and Hardy. My friends and housemates were on the opposite side. Phillip and Mick-O sat still as a blackboard as Marty fed me his horseshit.

"It's not you, personally," Marty said. "It's hard enough to cross over one artist. But three men over thirty? Impossible. The company wants Phillip. He's tested well with the audience. With the girls, and with young men who don't view him as a teenybopper. I don't have to tell you it's a youth market. We need to put a young thing on bass. Michael here is going to do drums for a few more months, until we find a good young drummer."

"Sorry it didn't work out, mate," Angus said, clenching his thumb with his other hand.

Mick-O couldn't look at me. So I had him all wrong. If he'd been kicked out, I would have quit. He didn't give a shit about playing, like I did. He wanted the money. Even if he knew they were giving him the boot as soon as they found his replacement. Stuart was more loyal than this friend-turned-cunt. Rachel would've gloated, if she was there. She maintained from the first month she met him that Mick-O was as loyal as whoever's buying the next round.

"Here's my bottom offer: a $25,000 check. You walk off with more than most musicians make in a lifetime of gigs. And you get the memories of touring."

"I'm going to check it out with a lawyer." I'd signed a contract. I didn't actually have a lawyer. But Hannah's brother was a lawyer, maybe he could speak to me. I could bring everything down with a few choice words: Phillip and I staged Stuart's murder. I'm telling the cops that's how we got the fame.

Phillip shifted uncomfortably. He couldn't even look at me. Sure, mate, say a little prayer. What's keeping me from mangling your bones with the same knife you bloodied?

I'd said I get back to them the next day. "Mate," Phillip said, as I headed for the door with the gut-wrenching question mark hovering above me. I knew they'd broken my contract. But was I up for suing?

"Mate? You listening? Try to understand . . ." I glared at him. I had other places to go. I was supposed to meet Rachel. Having been kicked out of the most unlikely Australian crossover band ever, I now had to deal with my equally unlikely impending marriage. Just like Hannah, Rachel had called and said that she wanted "to talk" and to meet at a place near her called Coffee Bar.

"Hi," I said, kissing Rachel on the cheek. I wanted to hold on to her for my life. "You order the silver pattern yet?"

"Colin! You look like you're about to cry!"

"Do you have any allergies?" I asked. "That's the kind of thing fiancés are supposed to know, right? I'm allergic to penicillin."

"Let me get this out right away. I think we should call off the marriage. Stuart will be okay somehow. I'm going to temp some more and start looking for a real job. I called around. There aren't many editing jobs going, but I'll even take administrative assistant work if it can get me back in the market."

"What's gotten into you? I've met your mother. I was getting used to the idea. Now suddenly I'm not good enough?"

"Death," she said, sucking salt off a sunflower seed.

"Isn't that a smidge depressing?"

"No. Danny Death."

Here we go. Drama Queen has her crown on. She liked to reveal words sometimes, then you had to ask her questions. "You've been listening to your punk albums again?"

"No, I know him now. I met him when I came back. He sat next to me in this same coffeehouse. He ordered me a blueberry slice."

"You're kidding? I thought he OD'd years ago with the rest of those phonies."

"He thinks I should let you go. And stop obsessing on Stuart."

"You told *Danny Death* about Stuart?"

"Calm down. He's the only one I've told. Except my parents and Frank."

"Jesus."

"And Janet."

"Janet? Who the hell is Janet?"

"She's the woman who helped save Stuart's life for me while you were waltzing around our country. Remember? My family talks loud, but we keep it to ourselves. We're breaking the law, too. And Danny and Janet are cool. Janet's pissed me off royally this week, but she doesn't pop a secret. Danny doesn't even know the band's name. He doesn't care. He's very Zen—"

"Danny Death is very Zen?"

"I'm trying to say everything's okay."

"Fine."

"Fine."

Looking at a picture of the Mona Lisa or listening to "Hey Jude" you think how corny it is because of the over-bombardment of images and associations you already have. So you forget the original power. Rachel's irritating habits clouded her core. When she was in a bad mood, she'd yammer. Even in a peachy mood she'd talk too much until you forget how special she was. Rachel looked pretty standing there, annoyed as shit with me. She seemed to have racked into focus, when I'd gotten even fuzzier.

I didn't want to lose her. "Rachel, really. I'll do my bit for Stuart. I was getting used to the marriage idea. It'll be an adventure."

"No, it's okay. I have myself."

"I've been offered $25,000 to opt out of the band voluntarily. They want Phillip to go solo."

"Phillip? Are they out of their minds?"

"Is it okay to talk to you about this? I'm sure you think this is just punishment."

"I told you, I've moved on. Listen, are you taking it? Why don't you stay around for a few months?"

"How can I do that without getting married? I'm illegal."

"I've never heard of the Immigration Bureau hunting down Australians. They're racist. If you had brown skin they'd give you hell. My friend Veemah immigrated here. Her family has about five trillion dollars from financing Indian movies. She went to a Swiss finishing school. And they still gave her hell because she has an Indian passport. You have enough money to sublet. I'll help you find an apartment."

"Who says I'm taking the money?"

"Take the money! I don't see that you have a choice. A band needs trust to succeed. And it wouldn't do any good turning in Phillip on a scam you cowrote the script for, now would it? Maybe you can waiter or something so you don't use up your money." She sipped her tea.

"Waitering seems like a big fall from Madison Square Garden."

"Then use the money to intern a bit. Try out jingle writing. I think my friend Frieda could help. She knows people. Everyone wants a free manservant."

"I'm a little old for interning."

"I'm a little old for temping. You try that out and I promise I'll hunt for a real job in a few weeks. We'll attack our goals in tandem. I have to temp to get some pocket money."

I frowned at her.

"I might have to send you over to Danny's for a yelling. The worst that would happen is that you'd hate jingle writing—but at least you'll make the decision to avoid penning tunes for potato chips and tire companies based on first-hand experience. The way I look at it, jingle finger sure beats taxi neck. What else can you do? Maybe you can try out for a new band, but you're kind of old for that, too."

She was so fucking blunt. I didn't think she ever intended to hurt anyone. She'd chat chat chat, and go too far. Rachel could be cruel without being mean.

"What are three things you love about Australia?"

"Three things?" Rachel said. "I couldn't answer that."

"Please."

"I like the way it's so big but unpeopled that I can get lost in my mind and work things out slowly without pressure."

"And two?"

"I guess I love Iced Vo-Vos. You can't find strawberry and coconut cookies in New York. They are so good! But you already know that, you brought me a bag."

"And three?

"Well there's the trams, and the pubs on every street corner and the way everyone says 'right' instead of 'okay'—"

"You have to pick a third."

"You. I guess you're the third reason. That's why I see now that we can't get married. You need to live your life, not mine. You have a lot of achieving to do, and I'm just going to ruin it for you."

19

Rachel: THE MEAT OF CHOICE

I was the worm trapped in the jumping bean, hopping around in blind determination to get anywhere. But I took Danny's advice, for the second time. I called it off with Colin, and we were both relieved. I phoned Frank, and Janet answered, which annoyed me to no end, but outwardly I accepted their budding relationship. I needed to repaginate my life, to move on from self-loathing, the most boring neurosis.

On the Stuart front, my mother came through on her hospital promise to him. Stuart's second cousin in Buffalo, Leigh Ann Harmond, was here in New York. Mom found her by placing a Desperately-Seeking-Susan ad in a Buffalo newspaper, and had four calls with the news that Leigh Ann had left Buffalo a week before Stuart's drugged arrival in town. Her husband, a spokesman for the Buffalo bus system, was hired away by the New York Port Authority, headquartered in the World Trade Center. They were living in Independence Plaza near Battery Park.

Mom, Stuart, and I took a cab downtown to see her.

Stuart was squashed between us on the middle hump of the backseat. "What should I say?" He'd been apprehensive ever since Mom broke the good news. He was a fixture on our sofa bed, a second son. Did he secretly hope that the eccentric Ganellis of Greenwich Village were his long lost relatives, instead of Leigh Ann Harmond formerly of Buffalo?

"The truth," Mom said.

"Maybe not quite the truth," I said. I didn't want Colin getting in new trouble. Who knew if this woman was a churchgoer and would feel it was her duty to go to Australian authorities about his scam?

The middle-age woman who answered the door wore a long-sleeved dress with felt trim. Blizzard living habits must be hard to break; it was an odd first impression on a summer's day. I was sweating in my gauze skirt and cotton tank top. "Mrs. Ganelli? I'm Leigh Ann."

"Please—Sylvia. This is my daughter Rachel, Stuart's friend, and this is your cousin Stuart. How kind of you to see us."

"Come in! I have some lemonade waiting."

"That would be great," I said.

"Stuart, this is a pleasure. I never knew you existed until Sylvia called. I understand you missed us by a week in February."

Stuart nodded.

"We knew we had your mother in Australia," Leigh Ann continued "but Margaret never wrote us that she had children. How old are you, darling?"

Margaret Gibbs. Learning his dead mother's name was more intimate than watching him vomit in Frank's bucket during withdrawal. It would be cruel to ask more, but I wanted it. What was her maiden name? How did she get from Buffalo to Australia? Did Stuart's father really die picking up a baby stuffed with a grenade? Or did he die from an alcoholic liver?

"Twenty-eight."

How ridiculous this was. I glared over to Mom. Were we trying to pawn this ex-junkie off on Leigh Ann? She didn't know him from a can of Foster's, and he was an adult.

"You got your grandmother's eyes."

Stuart perked up. "I never met me grandmother."

"She had those big roundeyes eyes and light brown hair."

"Like me," Stuart said.

"Like you."

Mom saw her emotional window of opportunity, earlier than expected, but she knew it was there. That's why she was the New York chapter of Women in Public Relations' Woman of the Year three times in ten years. "Leigh Ann—Stuart has no living relatives, and I thought as his only family link, and as a mother, that you would want to meet him."

"How long are you in town, Stuart?" Leigh Ann asked softly.

"I'm afraid he can't go back to Australia," Mom answered for him.

"Pardon?"

" 'Cause I'm dead," Stuart blurted out.

"Pardon?"

Now it was my turn to cut in. I hoped I could salvage the connection to Leigh Ann. "I think Stuart means that figuratively, right Stuart? He had some hard knocks and he's moving past them—"

"Actually, I was a heroin addict in Australia. But I'm not anymore. I'm in an aftercare program. I was better off dead in some people's eyes, including my own. But now Sylvia and everyone's been teaching me to read, and I reckon I'm not contagious. I passed the AIDS test."

We should have had a rehearsal in the cab. Having Stuart talk was like bringing out the wailing four-eyed baby at an adoption agency.

Leigh Ann picked up a white glazed swan and stroked its grooves. She put it down. And picked it up again. "My son was a crack cocaine addict—he lost his job four years ago in Buffalo— now he's a substance abuse counselor."

"Leigh Ann—my daughter and son have taken care of Stuart since his arrival, and it's time for him to start taking care of himself. He's got a clean bill of health. And he's a lovely boy. I wouldn't bring a rotten egg over to your home. I'm a very conscientious woman, as I can see you are. My husband and I have delayed our trip to France. We were supposed to go four weeks ago, but my daughter and I wanted to make sure Stuart had a family member to fall back on." She leaned in for the final sell. "He needs a home while he finds a job."

Leigh Ann paused. I was sure we were going to be shown the door. "We have an extra bedroom, Stuart. You can do some carpentry for us in exchange, while you find a better job and your own roof over your head. The place is such a mess, but even with Dick's salary—a good one for Buffalo—in Manhattan it's not enough to get all the extras done. You won't believe the condition of the foyer. The last tenants drilled holes the size of carrots in the walls. We want to build a cabinet system right over that. You have a knack for carpentry, darling?"

"A bit," Stuart said hesitatingly.

"Oh, he's being modest," I said. "He was in scaffolding. He's great with all sorts of things, like fixing locks—" Or picking them open at least.

"Perfect. You can move in tomorrow. I had Dick's Vancouver cousins here—a week after we moved to Manhattan." She reached for Stuart's hand. "This is my family now. He'll have to say yes."

If I was a Vermonter instead of a cynical New Yorker, I might say "Leigh Ann Harmond is good people." In any case, it was truly a touching moment.

My mother nudged me, a nudge shielded by her pocketbook. "He mooched a bit," she admitted minutes later, while Leigh Ann took Stuart on a tour of the bathroom's chips and scratches.

"He needed a shove out of the nest," I said. "He got too dependent on us."

"You sure you're not jealous of my babying him?"

"Mom!"

"Don't worry. You did right by him. Even if you don't like him much—and I think he *is* a lovely boy by the way—everyone deserves a second chance."

"You were fantastic, Mom." She was. She'd saved my behind. I'd got in over my head, and this might be the last time Mom and Dad would bail me out. From here on in, I promised myself, I would attempt adulthood. Good-bye, Prolonged Childhood. I kissed her cheek.

Mom turned teary. "God, thank you for that, Rachel. You're my baby girl, you know? You were my morning glory. You always have me there for you, do you know that, honey?"

"Yeah, I know. And vice-versa." Open communication can be embarrassing.

I peeked in the bathroom. Stuart was scrubbing tile grout with a ratty toothbrush. "We'll have to go over the details tomorrow when you move in," Leigh Ann said, "but I wanted you to see first-hand how vile everything is without a handyman around. Gawd! Look at those spiderweb cracks on the ceiling!"

"I have a new job for you," Selena said, as I watched Stuart pack the last of his things. "For the head accountant at Ivan Stanbury. I'll let you in on a secret. He's looking to try out a temp for a few weeks to see if he wants to hire permanently. He asked for a college-educated assistant, full salary, $28,000. If I were you I'd start preparing the résumé."

Eight thousand less than I made as an acquisitions editor two years earlier, but I didn't hear my phone ringing. I prepared my uniform—pantyhose, heel-saving Reeboks, and a thirty-percent-polyester gruesome Crest-toothpaste-blue dress Aunt Virginia had bought me in a hurry when I was seventeen and temped winter break for her priest. "He's in a bind," Aunt Virginia had said on pre-senting me with the ghastly thing, "and I'm running for treasurer. You shouldn't be wearing anything good. His sister works there and you want to make her feel like a well-dressed executive." I pinned the dress under with a safety pin, a makeshift seam. Dress-ing down is good advice for temping in general. There is probably a historical precedent, even from the times when women didn't fill the dredge jobs. Benjamin Franklin wouldn't have wanted his printing apprentice dressing like a dandy.

Marvin Schneider, Ivan Stanbury's comptroller, is a horrible man. I wish some mobster tough would shoot *him* down.

"Mr. Schneider? I'm Rachel, from Temp Solution?"

"Take dictation?" Not even a hello. And it was eight fifty-five, I wanted to get in my customary coffee and pee. I hadn't even looked over the phone system yet, which sometimes requires an engineering masters.

"I do fast longhand. I wasn't told I was supposed to take dictation, but I'll give it a shot."

"What's the matter with the girls today? The agency keeps sending me illiterates. I told them I wanted a permanent girl." He glanced over my attire. Maybe I shouldn't have worn blue polyester to a fashion executive's job. Psychologists would say I tried to sabotage my chances of permanent work. "You'll have to do for today."

I bit my tongue.

"Are you listening? What did they send me, an airhead? I want you to take a memo down. Grab a pad." I raced to the desk and grabbed a legal spiral. "Confidential memo to Ivan Stanbury. Semicolon. As per our meeting in Colorado, I have decided to greenlight the project, though I still stress my gut feeling is that it's nutty—"

"Excuse me, Mr. Schneider, can you go a bit slower?"

"For Christ's sake. As per our—"

"I got that. From stress, please."

". . . my gut feeling is that it's nutty. However, you had such a surplus year in linen that you can afford one or two indulgences. And, the darn population at the ranch has substantially increased, reducing the selling point to point six three per pound, a reduction of at least twenty-five percent. I'll grant you that this is causing less forage for our cattle, and according to Bart, he's had to decrease the herd by approximately one hundred and fifty head. Bart met Thursday morning with Spanky, the exotic game rancher who's had moderate success with camel, alpaca, and llama. Bart told me that Spanky's overview is that 'if you can afford to start it up, it's the product of the future, and is definitely not a fad.'

"New paragraph.

"Of course, money is not a problem; I'm afraid, however, that the media will have a field day if this is a disaster, which would affect confidence in our stock. I've met with Tommy's risk management guy who disagrees with my first reaction to you that product liability exposure could offset any potential gain by this venture. Tommy thinks this man is the genius of the corporation. He feels that a limited mail-order line could be a natural outlet to get more press for the winter clothing and linen. He thinks you might even get on television with a gimmick like this.

"New paragraph.

"In any case, the one sure winner in this scenario is Spanky. I'm told he went public last year and had no buyers. Once they hear that Ivan Stanbury is using his services, he'll have an avalanche of investors in the new meat of choice. Spanky also told Bart that the antlers are rich in testosterone, which reduces blood pressure, relieves arthritis, and improves male sexual performance. I personally love the prospect of the latter."

You're gonna need more than an antler to get a woman in bed, you ugly old Scrooge. And what the hell is this idiotic memo about?

"In any case, Ivan, I will sign off on the project. I've let Deborah know that she'll have to alert media on Wednesday. I say let's not waste a second. The Christmas catalog media will start in about ten days.

"Regards—Got that, Susan? Read it back to me."

"Okay," he said, when I finished. I stumbled on a few words because of my sucky handwriting. "Good enough. When you're done typing, set up the conference room for five, and don't use paper cups! The last girl used paper cups when Stanbury came down. I fired the idiot on the spot. First get my mail from Orlando. I like to have it with my coffee, and he won't make the rounds for another hour."

The baboon didn't deserve my real name. And his goddamn underarms stank. A man who I assumed was Orlando the Mail Slave pointed to the slots. Schneider's mailslot was the biggest. Part of his contract, no doubt, like a corner office and a company Lexus. One o'clock didn't come soon enough.

I rode the Macy's escalators in a trancelike state. Now that my charade of a marriage had been called off, I felt somewhat better, but misery had been replaced by dull acceptance of the uphill road ahead. Life without Colin would be sad. Recovery is sad. The mannequins on each floor were dressed in shirts and skirts of a ghastly tan hue. It felt strange to notice normal things again, like seasonal colors. Welcome back to Earth, Rachel. This is what you missed? I took a stool by the neon-lit yogurt counter, *Self Treat*, staring toward a video monitor of the latest Betsey Johnson dresses.

"Didn't I just see you on the escalator?" a woman asked from the neighboring stool. Talk about Bronx accents. She had too much blue eye shadow on.

"Yeah, I'm temping at Ivan Stanbury this week."

"I'm Sandy. I'm temping, too, for Ivan himself, if you believe that."

"Really? I have his comptroller, Marvin Schneider."

"Do you like him?"

I paused. What the hell? "Nah, he's a pig." Sandy laughed so hard that it was obvious she wasn't a company spy. I ordered a fresh-squeezed apple juice and a chicken salad pita. Sandy ordered a yogurt with carob chips, a substance beyond comprehension to me. "So," I said, resuming our conversation, "how's it working for the big man? Does Ivan wear his own cologne?"

"You know, I peeked at his credit card bills. Someone in his family is addicted to J. Crew. Can you imagine the fashion king ordering $1000 a month from J. Crew? I won't even meet him. He and his assistant are in Venezuela until Monday. They had me come in to answer his phone and fax him in an emergency. No one can see me. I'm surrounded by solid oak paneling. He even has a private bathroom I use, with a shower and floral toilet paper with his monogram."

"Perfect!"

Our food was served, and we toasted our chance meeting with plastic cups of water. Having a lunchmate buddy could make this week bearable. I missed Keisha from Bell Press. Now that I was out of my red-zone funk I should call her. Maybe Mom was right. I could ask her if she'd kept in touch with anyone at Bell, if she knew of any job openings there.

"I went through Stanbury's personal papers from eleven to twelve," Sandy continued. "I was bored. I think he's having an affair with Janine Evans."

"The tie designer?"

"Yup! He keeps a computer diary, and he taped the code word inside the private bathroom cabinet. I guess his regular secretary doesn't use that bathroom."

"Or look in his cabinet."

She smirked.

"Any other dirt?" I asked.

"Nah. Boring stuff. He's selling the excess elk off of h s Colorado ranch as steaks. He sounds like a spoiled schmuck."

That's what that nutty memo had been about. "I've heard of that ranch. It's always in the architectural mags. His o vn casual Ponderosa. Took thirty interior experts two years to get the casual look."

"Outrageous," Sandy said.

"You know they kill excess animals in Australia, too, kangaroos. Since the population explosion after they got protected-animal status, they've let a set amount get killed every year. You can buy sliced pouch steaks now in city supermarkets."

"Get out of here? Pouch? You've been to Australia?"

"I lived there for two years—Australia's a great place," I said coolly, like a proud 1940s buckaroo wife with a dusty, taxing, but gorgeous outback vista out of *A Town Like Alice.* "Maybe selling elk is the Meat of Choice project his dickhead comptroller referred to in a memo I typed for him."

"Stanbury said Marvin Schneider's underarms stink."

"Really? He wrote that? They do, you know."

"He said Schneider had shocking odor at Spanky's Elk Farm, and he was mortified. He wanted to schedule a talk to tell him."

"No way!" I laughed. I bit into my pita; the chicken tasted like Silly Putty. Frank had once made me chew a wad of it when I'd stumbled in the living room and spilled Yoo Hoo on his new comic. "My guy is pure prick. I'll go to the end of the week and no more. My temp counselor said he was looking to hire. No fucking way."

When I returned from lunch the office manager said, "I'm sorry, Susan, but we ordered a shorthand girl." I didn't even have the satisfaction of quitting the cruddy job.

"Can you fill out my timesheet then?"

"Your office will pay you for four hours—your manager told me to tell you. I don't need to fill out your form and you should call her."

Doorslam! Watch your heel. Shit. I'd already counted on this week's money. Before I left, I printed out another copy of the memo and shoved it in my knapsack—to prove I had typed everything correctly in case Selena gave me a hard time.

I called her from the lobby phone.

"What happened?"

"I typed his memo correctly, but he—"

"Well Christ, Rachel, I don't have anything else yet. I don't know what to tell you. Go home, and I'll call you this afternoon if anything comes in."

My parents had left for France, and with Stuart at his second cousin's place I had the family apartment solo again. I put on *The Price Is Right*. Colin called just as Dan from Hawaii was about to putt his way from the first hole for a new car. He was in good position to win; he'd guessed the five higher-marked products. I was surprised that an electrician from Hawaii knew that cereal cost more than roach motels. I would have been putting from way further back.

"Hi," Colin said. "I was going to leave you a message. I thought you were temping. Had the meeting with Angus."

"Have you decided what you're going to do? Was Phillip there, that Benedict Arnold?"

"Yeah. He was there, squirming in his chair. They're giving me a certified check next week if I don't contest them."

"Litigation isn't pretty. Too bad you can't invest it in elk."

"Don't get you."

"Long story. Ivan Stanbury. He's bigger than anyone in the States."

"Huge in Australia, too. My mum asked me to bring back his perfume, and my dad wears his underwear."

"No wonder he has twenty-seven floors," I said, twisting my hair into a spiral. "A real Croesus."

"A what?"

"A very rich man. Croesus was the name of a king of Lydia famous for his riches."

"Ninety-eight percent of humanity doesn't get your drift. Why can't you just say a very rich man?"

"So sue me, I have a decent vocabulary. And it's not that unusual a word. Just because you don't know that term doesn't mean that ninety-eight percent of humanity doesn't."

"God, you're worse than Hannah sometimes."

I went quiet for a few seconds and Colin said, "You okay?"

I was surprised how much that stung. "Yeah, just an exiguous perturbation in my trachea," I said, and we both half-laughed.

"Anyhow, Miss Vocab, I still don't understand what Stanbury has to do with elk."

"From the info me and this other temp who snooped around got, I figured out that he's about to invest in elk as a food source. Kill the excess elk on his ranch and attach his name to the meat like a designer shirt."

"Like boutique kangaroo."

"Yup and two days until the press announcement. His comptroller made me write a memo saying the 'project' will cause stock in Spanky's Game Farm to skyrocket."

"Too bad they know who you are."

"If I was evil I could make a killing. The comptroller thinks my name is Susan. So does everyone else at that firm. They sent me home at twelve without even signing my timesheet because I don't know shorthand. Or it could have been my polyester suit."

"Your what?"

"You have to see it to believe it. It was great for the fire extinguisher company. I blended right in."

"I'll bet."

"Yeah, stop interrupting. I'm losing my thread of—oh yeah, what I was saying was that no one at Ivan Stanbury, Inc. knows my real name. Hah! You and I could be rich in forty-eight hours. Almost as good as the lottery."

I fished in my knapsack for the crumpled memo. I read the whole thing to him.

"They're doing a press announcement on Wednesday?"

"Yeah."

"Rachel! Let's do it. The whole lump sum on the gamble. It's dirty money anyhow, what do I care? I was going for the fame."

"Shut up, Dodo brain! I'm only fantasizing here—your last scam is enough to rock three men's consciences."

"I'm serious. I'll split it with you. You said they don't even know your name. I'll buy the stock, to make it even more removed. It's my money. Let's take control of our lives."

"I'm going to quash this stupid idea right this second. I know you got away scot-free once, but don't tempt fate. It's illegal. *Comprende?* Insider trading."

"Information a temp learns is insider trading? Come on, Rachel, you don't want to temp forever. I'll give you money—you can write screenplays. I'm an eccentric rock musician who traveled across America on tour and fell in love with elk and antelope. Nobody will blink."

"You'll need a stockbroker." I was contemplating this?

"Do you have something like the Yellow Pages here?"

"We invented the Yellow Pages, Colin."

"Can you tone down the sarcasm a bee's dick?"

"Look, Colin, this is a ridiculous idea, I was *kidding*. Let's nip it in the fucking bud."

"So snippy! You're bloody condescending to a man who's

about to make you rich. I'll ring one at random. I'll play eccentric stockman."

"The whole thing stinks. It's morally wrong, like my Dad forcing me to pretend I was still five on museum lines when I was a short nine."

"I can't imagine you were ever short."

Good, he'd moved on. Only our old style banter after all. "I shot up when I was twelve. Before that I was the class shrimp." The woman with a Frida Kahlo unibrow won both *Price Is Right* final showcases; she got the bid right within a hundred dollars. I clicked the mute button off and heard her scream—a scream worthy of the first car on the Cyclone. I was transfixed.

A veteran newspaper editor had once informed my Syracuse Introduction to Mass Communications class that most people clip articles and either pass them on to their friends or look at them at a later date with new perception. "In this way, journalism's the noblest medium," he said. "TV will kill itself."

Not when suburban unibrowed women standing in for the everyman win double showcases. Journalism doesn't have a chance. "Oh shit, Colin, I'm tempted by the elk scam, okay, you satisfied?"

"Really?"

"We have to look into it more. No promises. I'll meet you at Forty-second and Fifth in an hour. How about the stone bench next to the left lion?"

"I don't understand what you mean."

"The main New York library. There's two lions out front. Let's check a few things before we blow the dough. I can't believe I'm saying this."

After I hung up I helped myself to Chunky Monkey ice cream straight out of the container. I figured I'd hop a cab to the library. Mom and Dad had graciously stocked the refrigerator before they left, and guilt, guilt, left me a few hundred dollars. The doorbell rang. I wiped a bit of chocolate off my chin. It was Frank and his darling Janet. I need this now?

"Can we come in?" Janet said.

"Yeah," I smiled, with great effort.

Janet sat in Dad's reclining chair, and Frank wandered about the living room, stopping at the glass bookcase to examine my snowglobe celebrating the fall of the Berlin Wall (like he hadn't seen it a gazillion times before).

I settled in a lotus position on the carpet. Janet was visibly un-nerved by my leg-bending.

"So how's the new couple?" I tried out. Yuck.

"Pretty good so far," Janet said. "I know you called, but, well I just wish we had your blessing."

"What an unusual couple you make," I offered.

"How's that?" Janet said cautiously.

"Well you're all about espadrilles and sundresses, and here's my brother in a thrift-shop shirt, so green and shiny. You look am-phibious, Frank."

"Amphibious?" Frank said. He knew what I was doing. Will used to say that I have the subtlety of a minivan.

"Reptilian." I pulled at a stringy bit in the knee of my jeans.

"Are you calling me a snake?" Frank said.

"Well, yeah." We both laughed, a wavy Ganelli laugh—you get points in my family for a well-thought-out insult. Janet looked relieved that maybe, just maybe, the dastardly duo were truly off the hook.

I uncrossed my legs and reached for my toes. "So guess what? I've been talking to my friend Colin."

"Your *friend* Colin?" Janet said. "*Colin* Colin? From the Tall Poppies?"

"Yeah. We're working it out. Mom even met him, thinks he's a nice guy. I'm taking the subway to meet him in a few minutes."

"Working it out?" Frank said. "He's a lying creep."

"He was misguided, that's all. He's very cute."

"Jesus," Frank said. "Women."

"Are you free tomorrow?" Janet said, touching my shoulder. "That sounds like a story I've got to hear. You name the place. Our treat."

"Lutèce," I said. "Or the Four Seasons."

"Ha, ha," Frank said. "How about Chinatown? The Nice Restaurant on East Broadway?"

"That would be nice," I said.

"How's Stuart?" Janet said.

"He's doing pretty well. Mom's got him applying to Juilliard for percussion, if you can believe that."

Janet snorted.

"I can more than believe that," Frank smiled.

"You know what I think?" Janet said.

"No, what do you think?" Frank asked in a tender voice I hadn't heard since his early days with Ingrid.

"This whole experience reminds me of an enchanted journey, a ride in *Chitty Chitty Bang Bang*, where everything could happen, and everything does."

"That's a great metaphor," Frank said. "I really like that."

"Yeah," I said. Even though I had come up with that very same metaphor in our freshman year screenwriting class. Oh great, Janet, you're even usurping my metaphors.

Let it go, Danny Death said in a new bubble over my head. Doesn't mean shit. Against the gravitational pull of disgust, I forced another grin.

"Oh, God," Janet said, " I feel so much better. I've missed you so much, Rachel." Her eyes were tearing.

"I love you both, too," I said. When I stood up, Frank whacked me on the arm in our standard ceremonious sibling apology.

Colin gave me his own love tap after we'd spotted each other by the lion.

"My Aunt Virginia once told me that these lions are called Patience and Fortitude."

"Which one is which?" He wet his finger and wiped a tiny remaining spot of chocolate off my lip.

"I get them mixed up."

I led the way through the grand Astor Court, up the opulent marble stairs. In the imposing main research room, the size of a football field, I located the microfiche page for the Colorado Yellow Pages. I turned the knob, scanning for elk. No listings.

"Try game," Colin suggested.

I rolled until I got to G. "Found .! Spanky's Wholesale Game."

I copied down the number. We went back down two flights to the phone booth near the men's room. I called the New York Stock Exchange public relations officer.

"Hi, my name is Karen Jones, and I'm a senior at Murray Bergtraum Business High School."

"What can I do for you, Karen?"

"I need to follow a stock for my end-of-year assignment and I got the weirdest one. It's for game. Spanky's Game Farm. I can't find it and I need to turn the paper in on Tuesday! Can you tell me what it's listed under?"

"We normally don't give out that kind of information. I can send you general info about the market, if that would help—"

"Oh, please, I'm really stuck! I'm desperate!"

"I have a daughter who's thirteen. You sound sweet. Hold on, dear, let me see. No, I don't see it. But let me look it up on the database, it may be on the American Stock Exchange—yes, here it is! You have to look under SPKGM in the American Stock Exchange listings. They're not affiliated with the New York Stock Exchange. Be nice to your parents."

"I will! Thank you!"

I flapped my paper in triumph, and Colin gave me a peck on the cheek. "For evil," he said, like a James Bond villain.

"I walk the line," I said, in my best Johnny Cash impersonation. "Now it's your turn."

He dialed the hotel. "Yeah—can I have the room of Angus Wynne?—Angus, it's Colin. Look, mate, I'm still upset about before, but I spoke to my lawyer in Australia and he advised me to take your check. I want it in twenty-four hours though, or the deal is off."

Two days later, the day Ivan Stanbury was scheduled to release information about his personal elk-meat line, Colin and I took the train to Philadelphia for a field trip. We were too antsy to stay in his hotel room, and he hadn't done much touristing yet.

Our first stop on the self-guided walking tour was Christ Church. A dour-faced man clasping a clipboard told us about Jacob Duche, a Tory who chose allegiance to the crown in Canada.

"Duche's sister chose revolution," the guide said. "Her husband Francis wrote Psalm Sixty-five. I had a Canadian on the tour last week who saw this church as the Mason Dixon line. This is the ugly side of the revolution. Many of our most prominent families lost their shires."

"I wonder if the city of Philadelphia knows their emissary is knocking the Founding Fathers?" I whispered.

Colin shrugged and reached for my hand, as casually as back in St. Kilda. It felt right. We'd forgotten a major financial scam was on the day's menu.

Colin and I sat in Benjamin Franklin's pew while the guide spoke to us from the front of the church. Benjamin Franklin invented the stove, first thought of daylight savings time and bifocals, proved that lightning and electricity are the same thing, was a diplomat, a postmaster, wrote an almanac, published the newspaper, and created the lending library.

Philadelphia's not a city to visit if you're in the mood to rest on your laurels.

We continued on to the Hall of Independence, where they signed the Declaration of Independence. Were people so short in the 1700s? The Hall was markedly low to the ground.

"Thomas Jefferson drafted the Constitution at thirty-two," the park ranger said in the orientation room.

"Four years to match his greatness," I said quietly. "Fat chance."

"But did you know that Thomas Jefferson's manuscript went through eighty drafts by his peers?"

"Now that's the kind of info I want to hear," I whispered.

"Who's complaining?" Colin said. "I'm a year past the use-by date. At thirty-two, I did jackshit." We continued on to the Hall's courtroom.

"At thirty-two, you performed in front of thousands of fans. *I've* done jackshit."

"Shh!" said the man sporting a Coast Guard cap to my left.

"You went to Australia on your own."

"Anyone could do it with $2000," I said, as we walked toward the room where the actual signing took place.

"No, Rachel, they couldn't. You're hard on yourself." He paused. "First I've heard of Thomas Jefferson. What else did he do besides write a piece of paper? Did he invent the telephone?"

"You're not serious? That was Alexander Graham Bell—"

"Oh yeah. Stop looking at me like a dumbarse. Didn't Jefferson invent the egg whisk?"

"Let me continue."

He stuck his lip out like a kid pretending to be a dimwit. "Duh—the meat tenderizer?"

"Thomas Jefferson was our—"

"I'm taking the mickey out of you, Rachel Ganelli. I'm beginning to think you were the dag no one wanted to pick for tag."

"—third president. A great man but a hypocrite. He wrote the Declaration of Independence but had plantation slaves."

The guide looked relieved as we exited the tour to have it out.

"Why would I know about Thomas Jefferson? I'm an Australian. Do you know who Gough Whitlam is?"

"Yeah."

"Bullshit. You don't know anything about him do you?"

"Colin, you're baiting me. Don't do this. You're not achieving anything."

"Got you, ha! The great Rachel is stumped. Stalling."

"Gough Whitlam was Prime Minister of Australia from 1972 to 1975. He was the first Labor Party leader to win the premiership in twenty years. He pushed an agenda of women's and Aboriginal rights—and national social security. He was ousted by a little-known rule called by the Queen's representative, Sir John Kerr, The Governor General."

"Okay, you know it. I give—"

"Also of note: Christopher Boyce, a cipher clerk, found out that the CIA had Sir John Kerr as their agent. In essence they overturned Whitlam's socialist policies, like they toppled Allende's Chile in 1973. *The Falcon and the Snowman*, book by Robert Lindsay, film directed by John Schlesinger. Timothy Hutton as Boyce. Sean Penn, not yet married to Madonna, as his blackmailing friend. Soundtrack by Pat Metheny. Title song by David Bowie."

"Oh I see. He's a *movie reference*. You only know him 'cause it was a movie story. That's not real knowledge—"

We walked a few yards and were now standing in front of the Liberty Bell.

A guide addressed a horde of ten-ish kids. "The first time it rang, it cracked and was recast. In 1835, it cracked again. Repairs were made. In 1846, it cracked once more as it rang for Washington's birthday. No one could fix it this time."

"How come they didn't throw it out and get a new bell?" Colin whispered.

"There was love in it," I said. "It was precious. It means more that it has survived."

We sampled the native cuisine: cheese-steak sandwiches. They were cheap, and between us we had ten dollars left. I wanted a Philadelphia snowglobe with the Liberty Bell in it; the closest gift shop, at Betsy Ross's house, only had one with Independence Hall. Colin called his Yellow Pages stockbroker from the pay phone inside of the shop. I had to go outside to pace. Colin could have lost his shirt on whimsy.

He came out with a thumbs-up. "The bloody mother lode!" he screamed from across the street, and my arms went numb. We kept breaking out into sinful laughter, like Bonnie and Clyde. According to our calculations on the New Jersey transit, we had made $200,000 off designer elk. Enough for Colin to buy a small recording studio, and for me to give a go as a screenwriter. We could even give Stuart something to start off his new life. Colin had told his broker to sell, even though if we waited, we could have had truly serious dough.

"There's something I have to tell you," Colin said as we rolled past Newark.

"Shoot."

"I ran into Will the other day."

"Will?"

"Your Will."

"Will Reynolds? What are you talking about?"

"He met Hannah out on Long Island. This is rather unreal, but he's dating her now. She always wanted to move up a notch." He shielded his head, waiting to be hit.

"You *forgot* to tell me?"

"I wasn't going to tell you. I was afraid you'd go back to him."

"Jesus, Will and Hannah? Jesus. You're pulling my leg."

"I suspect she's always thought Australia was too uncouth for her. Except for the fact that he stole my girlfriend, he seemed like a perfectly nice guy. He had nothing except nice things to say about you."

He was serious? Will with Colin's redhead? But then, at this point in my year of mishegoss, the link didn't seem implausible. Weird things were plaguing me that year; happenstance made perfect sense. I stared out the window. We've swapped places, I thought. She's got my goddamn precious upper-middle-class destiny.

"You're right, he is a nice guy," I agreed. Colin gave me a bewildered look, and I gave him an "it's safe" smile. Convinced, he reached for my wrist.

"So this is how it turns out," he smiled.

I pulled him to me and planted a big smackeroo on his lips. "Yeah," I said afterward.

As the train rolled toward the tunnel entrance, the new moon rising over Frank Sinatra's Atlantic City billboard, I remembered the Christ Church guide batting for the Tories, and I thought, morality is in the retelling. Who's presenting the history?

Once, while I was still at Bell, a man perched on top of a discount store across the street from my office had started firing bullets at the western-facing windows of our office building. He'd been fired from a textile company on the third floor, two below Bell Press. Our building's voice, the same one that informed us of fire drills, announced, "Ladies and Gentlemen, please go to the center of your offices, away from the windows."

In the conference room, the vice president continued to dictate a letter to his assistant as forty of us filled the remaining chairs and floor space. The head of publicity asked me if I wanted a stick of cinnamon Trident. Over the loudspeaker we heard "Ladies and Gentlemen, the police have killed the man, there is no more danger," and we resumed work. There were too many tri-state murders that day; the incident barely warranted a mention, even in the tabloids. Since none of my friends read about my midday mayhem, no one ever believed it happened.

Thanks to:

Abigail Thomas

Shannon Ravenel, a thoughtful editor; and Liz Darhansoff, a happening agent

Lynn Pleshette and Catherine Luttinger

The writing circle, especially the caffeinated after-hours Syndicate: Jill Bauerle, Marcelle Harrison, and Kathy O'Donnell; two dear friends and damn sharp readers, Joan Dalin and Corey Powell; and Mark Jessell, Deb Reading, and Warrick Wynne in Melbourne, quick on the E-mail Australiana

My brother, David Shapiro, for, among other things, yelling at me in Chinatown (circa 1990) that under no circumstances should I accept the job offer from Proctor and Gamble

Paul O'Leary—my pillar, my joy, my partner in crime

Credits